PENGU
CLIVE

T.S. Tirumurti is Counsellor at the Embassy of India in
Washington DC. He is the author of a travelogue on Kailash-
Mansarovar. This is his first novel.

Clive Avenue

T.S. Tirumurti

PENGUIN BOOKS

Penguin Books India (P) Ltd., 11 Community Centre, Panchsheel Park,
New Delhi 110 017, India
Penguin Books Ltd., 80 Strand, London WC2R 0RL, UK
Penguin Putnam Inc., 375 Hudson Street, New York, NY 10014, USA
Penguin Books Australia Ltd., 250 Camberwell Road, Camberwell,
Victoria 3124, Australia
Penguin Books Canada Ltd., 10 Alcorn Avenue, Suite 300, Toronto,
Ontario, M4V 3B2, Canada
Penguin Books (NZ) Ltd., Cnr Rosedale and Airborne Roads, Albany,
Auckland, New Zealand
Penguin Books (South Africa) (Pty) Ltd., 24 Sturdee Avenue,
Rosebank 2196, South Africa

First published by Penguin Books India 2002
Copyright © T.S. Tirumurti 2002

10 9 8 7 6 5 4 3 2 1

Typeset in *Adobe Garamond* by SÜRYA, New Delhi
Printed at Chaman Offset Printers, New Delhi

For my mother, Kalpakam, and father, Srinivasamurti

CONTENTS

ACKNOWLEDGEMENTS

A special word of thanks to Gowri, for being a fierce critic and wife, sometimes both at the same time; David Davidar, for giving my manuscript an immediate nod and making this book a reality; Bhavani, my daughter, who didn't understand why I preferred writing a book to spending time with her after coming back late from work; Vishwajit, my son, whose only concern was that the book should be at least half as interesting as his Hardy Boys.

Thanks also to Ravi Singh, for transforming this ugly duckling into a swan; Kamala Ganesh, Gowri's aunt, for letting me use her most original limerick on the Tam-Bram male; Pavan K. Varma, for encouraging me and infusing in me the confidence that 'it was worth taking a shot'; Diya Kar Hazra, for seeing this manuscript through its crucial final stages; S. Muthiah, whose brilliant book *Madras Discovered* gave me an insight into Chennai landmarks; P.S. Sundaram, author of *Tiruvalluvar: The Kural*, for a superb translation from Tamil; Mathangi, my sister, for being a sounding board; and to Avanija, Bhargavi, Shyama, Abhiram and Tribhuvan Ram, my nieces and nephews, for being there.

It is a matter of regret that my grandmother—the real Paati—Sundari Ammal, is not alive to see some of her wisdom reflected in the 'Paati' in this book, and that I lost two of my uncles while the manuscript was in its final stages of completion—C.S. Ramachandran of the Indian Civil Service and R.K. Narayan, the author.

SABARMATI

When Sundaram decided to skip his early morning walk and began dusting the brass and bronze objects in his spacious drawing room instead, it was clear that the day was going to be tense. 'Where does all this dust come from?' he cursed under his breath.

Sundaram coughed.

'Why can't you let Muthu handle the dusting when he comes in?' suggested Lakshmi coming out of the bedroom and heading for the kitchen.

'Muthu is becoming totally useless,' Sundaram cursed again. 'I can't imagine why he can't dust these at least every other day.'

'He put Brasso only last week,' Lakshmi added helpfully sensing that her husband was becoming increasingly irritable.

'That's not the end of it. These have to be regularly dusted and maintained.'

Another puff of dust, this time from the handsome brass Thanjavur standing lamp. Sundaram broke into a coughing fit. The revenge of the Thanjavurians. He was not from Thanjavur but Tirunelveli. He was saved by a whisker from being a Thanjavurian when his mother married a good-looking bachelor from Tirunelveli in preference to the other eligible bachelors from Thanjavur. The horoscope of the Tirunelveliite matched best with her own and her family had no doubt about the match. Thanjavur lost.

Not that Sundaram had anything against Thanjavur.

Other objects in the room were getting a good whipping. A hundred-year-old bronze *yali* with a winged angel seated on top. A strange combination of Hindu tradition and Christianity. In some ways, like Chennai itself. Fascinated, he had bought it cheap, by weight, at Moore Market, adjacent to the Madras Central Railway Station. The shopkeeper didn't know what he was selling. Sundaram saved the Hindu angel from being melted and moulded into a bathroom doorknob or a washbasin tap.

The angel on the *yali* was lucky. A few decades later, Moore Market had been razed to the ground by a fire, wiped away from the face of Chennai. Another symbol of the cold, imperial British colonial legacy vanished. The vendors of old books, costume jewellery, lovebirds and parakeets, old furniture and perfume ran with whatever they could grab while the crackling fire ate away their earnings. Later, they shifted to the pavements in front of the Grand Town Hall and colonized it with their tin and cement structures. The cold, imposing Town Hall—the grand Victoria Public Hall—was swamped with wine shops and hawkers selling plastic wares, pressure cookers and stainless steel tumblers. Rajan Wine Shop. Muthu Wine Shop. Arumugam Plastics. Kali Body Works.

Sundaram had quite a collection of objets d'art. In fact, one must confess, Sundaram had quite a refined taste. The antiques looked exquisite. The rectangular drawing room was full of wooden carvings, brass and pottery. Thank God the room was big enough to accommodate his fancies. There were two large windows to let in light. Sunlight came in through the grill in square patches and formed rectangular patterns on the mosaic floor.

Lakshmi would have liked to throw most of Sundaram's fancies out. The place was becoming a museum.

Whip. Whip.

Sundaram stood like a circus lion trainer taming his lions

and tigers with the long reach of a whip. A large garish Thanjavur painting of a blue Krishna hung on the wall just above where the *yali* with the angel stood. Krishna chewing his right toe. Gold leaf overlay done in the old, traditional style—not like the Thanjavur paintings of today, Sundaram thought to himself. It was a hundred and fifty years old at least. A family heirloom from Sundaram's grandfather whom he had never seen but was grateful to for this garish Thanjavur painting. The gold paint on the wooden frame hid the patches eaten off by white ants.

Not that Sundaram had anything against Thanjavur.

The 'plop' of the newspapers falling softly on the gravel outside could be heard only by the trained ear. Sundaram glanced quickly at the clock. 5.53. At least someone was working efficiently. The newspapers were being delivered on time. He stopped dusting and walked briskly out of the room across the long verandah, down the few steps and onto the driveway. The papers were lying right in the middle of the mud-gravel driveway near the gate. The paper boy had a good aim. He had avoided the hedge along the right of the path.

Beebee had already got to the newspapers wagging her tail. She looked like a well-fed golden retriever should. She was pleased but surprised that Sundaram had not gone for his morning walk. She ran around the papers in circles when he approached. Time to play 'snatch the paper'. Her eyes watched and waited for him to reach for the papers.

'No walk and no playing today, Beebee,' Sundaram said sternly. Beebee stopped, puzzled. Sundaram was behaving oddly today. No walk. Now, no playing with newspaper. This man was going potty.

There was a slight chill in the air. It was still December, the month when Chennai took a break from the cyclones and geared up for the coming summer. The Tamil month of *margazhi*, when singers were traditionally supposed to go down the streets early morning singing religious hymns. Lilting

Tiruppavai songs in praise of Lord Krishna and songs from his love-struck Aandal. Men and women walked with musical instruments and bells and sang in a chorus with eyes half closed in devotion. The ones in front, however, kept their eyes wide open to avoid oncoming buses and trucks. Over time, things changed a bit. Now they went around on cycles singing film songs. Mostly obscene ones.

The evenly cut hedge on the right of the driveway was the 'December flower' hedge. One didn't know the hedge by any other name. Lakshmi had mentioned its botanical name earlier but nobody was willing to remember a tongue-twister. December Flowers it remained. Elongated blue flowers shaped like a shell. They flowered only in December and with luck lasted till January. Sundaram used them to decorate the pooja room. They flowered for only one month a year. The rest of the year, the hedge lay colourless, coated with dust and grime. It was useful only to find lost tennis balls and Beebee hid an odd bone or two under it. There was no hedge on the left of the driveway. Only a row of potted plants which Beebee knocked down regularly while she looked for her tennis ball. A row of multicoloured crotons grew behind the pots gracefully covering the drab compound wall behind.

The early morning dew clung to the leaves. Sundaram had just a *veshti* and banian on and when he saw the droplets of water, he suddenly felt cold. He adjusted the white sacred thread, *poonal*, peeping out of his banian, bent down, grabbed the papers and hurried inside. A tiny pebble stung the sole of his bare right foot. The gravel in the driveway was a nuisance. It had poked various feet for more than three decades, but Sundaram had never found the time to pave the driveway. All he did was pour some concrete over a small portion in front of the porch steps so that the lady of the house could draw *kolam* on it every day. Every morning the cement patch was decorated with intricate designs of white and a dark red border to keep the *kolam* in. It was an art and consumed much of Lakshmi's time. She bought books to keep her up to date on new designs. Flour on cement was nourishing food for the ants, Lakshmi said. She started the day with a good deed. She fed the ants.

There was no time to waste. Sundaram hurried back. Beebee had lost interest in the papers by this time and bounded off to the sprawling green lawn sniffing. She went right through the December Flowers hedge as if the hedge didn't exist. Sundaram went around the *kolam* and carefully avoided a leech which had left a long glistening track of slime on the cement patch.

The Hindu and *The Indian Express* was Sundaram's menu every morning. It had been like this for almost as long as he could remember. Once he had tried *The Statesman* instead of *The Indian Express*. For all of one week. He was too old to switch to another paper. The only other daily which languished on the table till Sundaram had the time to browse through it in the evening was the Tamil *Dina Thandhi*, literally, The Daily Telegraph. Sundaram eased his portly frame into the cane chair designated for him not officially but by silent acknowledgement by everyone. This was the only one facing the driveway. The others faced the lawn. Nothing would disturb him now. The next half hour was to be spent in a world that had passed by the previous day. Politics, sports, opinions and editorials. He didn't notice the piping hot coffee that Lakshmi had placed on the side table, but he knew it was there. His right hand moved out of habit to grasp the steel tumbler and lift it by the rim. *The Hindu* was firmly clasped in his left hand. Only the crinkling of the paper broke the silence when he turned the page.

Lakshmi heard Amma stir in her bedroom.

The household was up. She made another tumbler of coffee for herself and came out onto the verandah. For a woman in her early fifties, she had remained attractive and graceful. She carried herself with quiet dignity, her measured walk giving her the appearance of a thinking woman, which she was. She was fair. Very fair. For the colour-conscious Tamil Brahmin society, it was this that had clinched her horoscope for the Sundaram family. She hailed from Tenkasi, near Tirunelveli, and that was useful.

Not that they had anything against Thanjavurians. But being from Tirunelveli helped.

The Indian Express lay unopened. Like most Chennai*vasis*, Sundaram picked up *The Hindu* first. It provided facts and got the stories right, he said. *The Indian Express* came later for the embellishments.

'Is this yesterday's milk or today's?' asked Sundaram, without looking up from *The Hindu*. It tasted a bit different, thicker than usual.

'Yesterday's,' Lakshmi confirmed. 'The milkman should be here any moment now. Today you decided not to go for a walk and we had to make coffee early . . .' Before she had finished her sentence, there was the grinding creak of the gate and footsteps coming up the path. It was the familiar, dark, stout, mustachioed Balan, walking in with an exaggerated gait.

Balan the Milk Man.

Balan the Milk Diluter.

Balan the Water Mixer.

He was known by several names. Names called mostly with affection.

Built quite like a bull himself, Balan was following his by now well-laid-out daily routine twice a day. Every morning and evening, he brought an emaciated cow to Sundaram's house and tied it to the gate. In fact, the lean cow was so used to the routine that it ambled over to the house by itself and stood outside waiting for Balan and munching at the leaves across the compound wall to kill time. If Balan came a bit late, the entrance was covered with a generous quota of dung. Black-grey mounds of dung. When left unattended for some time, a swarm of fat flies gathered around it for lunch.

'Hey Balan, can't you keep your damn cow off my plants?'

Sundaram kept shouting. 'And why does it have to come all the way to my house to shit?'

'Sir, what can I do if your plants jut out onto the road for cows to eat? Cut off the branches then, *ayyah*.'

'I will. But your cows have learnt to open the latch with their horns and come in. They eat up all the flowers meant for pooja.'

If you really love your flowers, you should keep your gate locked, muttered Balan to himself.

Balan walked down the driveway, went around the house and took a two-litre aluminium can handed over to him by the demure cook, Revati. Lakshmi insisted that he take the can from her and not use the ones he brought. Or else he will add water and dilute the milk, she said. Several years ago, Balan had designer milk cans with fake bottoms—to hold water. It looked empty to begin with, but when half full with milk, the water was released into the milk. It was neat and effective.

Balan trooped back to the gate.

'Get the milk fast. And don't add water!' Lakshmi shouted from where she was sitting overlooking the lawn and part of the driveway.

'Okay, okay,' Balan shouted back.

He went out, lifted up his red and blue striped lungi over his knee, tucked one end into the folds and settled down by the side of the cow on his haunches. His striped long underpants stood out. The can was tucked firmly between his thighs and the milking began. The first spray of milk hit the bottom of the can.

The cow stood swishing its tail and bored, staring at the gate. It tried licking the paint off the 'Beware of Dog' sign on the gate, but gave up in despair. It was not as tasty as licking a cinema poster off the wall. There were cows standing outside other houses on Clive Avenue. Balan looked around. Yes, his cows were all there. All emaciated and all on time. But the important thing was, the cows were all his.

Balan the Monopolist.

His 'boys' were trooping in. Ramaiah took care of the North Indian's residence, and Gunaseelan after Rajaram's. The others would come soon. There was a look of quiet satisfaction, even pride, in Balan's eyes. He had worked hard to achieve a certain standing in this colony. Everyone knew him well and he had, over the years, not only effectively monopolized business in the area but had managed not to lose his consumers to any other milkman or milk machine.

There had been a time when things had gone horribly wrong for Balan. A milk dispenser had been installed in the colony and this had almost driven him to despair and ruin. Milk became available at any time of the day or night, at a convenient location. Unadulterated milk. It was a new phenomenon. There was great excitement on Clive Avenue at this development. They did not need to buy Balan's water-milk or see his emaciated cows or heaps of cow dung again. Balan's cows lost their jobs and started growing fatter. When he protested, they kept him on only for the mornings. We don't want your milk twice a day Balan, they said with some relish. Balan's business crashed. He looked around desperately for help. It was time for a politician to step in. Politicians could turn any situation around. He approached some well-connected politicians in the ruling party and persuaded them to talk to the officials of the Madras Municipal Corporation to shut down the milk outlet. The officials pushing files in the eighty-year-old Ripon building said no. The outlet would stay they said. It was the minister's brainchild and he was personally interested in its success. He had come across a milk dispenser on his visit to Europe—the first of several visits he had made on government money—and had wanted to replicate it in Madras. Madras had to keep up with the times.

Balan tried to bribe the officials but couldn't pay the price. Balan was in a fix. His fat cows were now idle and the milk was going to waste. He had to dig into his savings to pay his boys.

He sat engulfed by depression and moped around for a while. But not for long.

For Balan was a fighter. When his mother abandoned him, an illegitimate child, outside the Catholic orphanage, he is said to have rolled into the orphanage compound all by himself, and lay there smiling and cooing till the sisters found him. He was promptly christened George Kuriakose lest he grow up as a Hindu. Balan grew up loving Christ till one fine day he decided to exchange his Catholic attire for a Hindu one. Not that he had anything against being a Christian. He continued to love the Lord who was both father and mother to him. He just wanted a more common name. One he could hide behind. One that would not make him stand out in a crowd. So he called himself Balan, the first name that came to his mind. And Balan he remained. Life had not been easy but he had fought hard and long. He never ran away from a challenge. Even as a child in the convent, he learnt to stand up to bullying. But this time, it was the government—a municipality.

He stopped moping around and decided he would take on the damn machine. Balan set in motion an elaborate plan. He lowered the price of his milk and launched a door-to-door campaign arguing his case. How can you buy milk which is not fresh, he asked. The other day the municipal commissioner told me confidentially that they added milk powder. Balan lowered his voice. Nothing like a conspiratorial tone for conviction, to sow the seeds of doubt. Then came the clincher. Fresh milk is a must for filter coffee of the perfect consistency. It will simply not taste the same with milk from the dispenser.

Chennai*vasis* lived and breathed filter coffee. Before Tamil infants developed a taste for mother's milk, they could tell the difference between filter coffee and instant coffee. Its fame had spread all over India and the Tamils were proud of it. North Indians referred to it generically as South Indian coffee which hurt the Tamils no end. But then, to the North Indian, everyone south of the Vindhyas was a Madrasi, and the rest of the south gave up on the North Indians in disgust. To change the taste of this sacred coffee was blasphemy. Balan had found a winning argument. Powder milk in filter coffee? Well, it just wouldn't do. Maybe Balan was right after all. At least Balan milked the cows in front of them and they knew what they were getting.

The Sundarams were thus reconverted to the Balan cause. They even lent him twenty thousand rupees to put his life back on track. With this major coup, Balan set about bringing the others back into the fold. After months of persuasion and pleading, he managed to get much of his clientele back. The milk outlet gradually lost business and died a natural death. Balan was delighted and swore to his loyal consumers that he would never add water again unless absolutely necessary. The 'colonists' soon agreed that the milk tasted better. Squat and stocky, with a bushel of hair sticking out of his ears like a koala, Balan went about enjoying his monopoly.

Balan surveyed Clive Avenue again. Funny name, Clive. Weren't all British relics being changed into national relics, preferably Tamil relics? Edward Elliots Road had become Dr Radhakrishnan Road, Mowbray's Road was now T.T. Krishnamachari Road. Hamilton's bridge had become Ambattan Bridge, and Mount Road had been renamed Anna Salai. Even Madras had become Chennai. So why had Clive Avenue still remained Clive Avenue? Not that this bothered the residents. In fact, they were secretly relieved. The British were not bad chaps provided they kept a distance. Once someone from the Avenue asked the Madras Municipal Corporation about Clive Avenue. The officials had checked their files and replied that it was not on their records. The street didn't exist. So how could one change the name of a British relic that didn't exist?

But Clive Avenue did exist. One only had to ask the House Tax Collector, the Income Tax Officer, the Property Tax

Collector, the Water Tax Collector. They did not need a map to come to Clive Avenue.

Though it was hardly an avenue, Clive Avenue did exist. There were eight residences, four on each side. They were big bungalows, not those hideous flats. The road was not very broad but the street had pavements on both sides giving it the appearance of being broad. Trees lined the sides at irregular intervals, green, and throwing some shade onto the road. The avenue ended in a cul-de-sac and a huge gulmohur tree. At the intersection was a cement pit for dumping waste. But all muck was dumped around the pit in a heap and the pit remained clean. Since the avenue didn't exist, the municipal garbage lorry and cleaners didn't bother to clean and collect the heap. The lorry driver was sure that he could not reverse in a cul-de-sac. Unless, of course, it was Deepavali or Pongal. Then Clive Avenue suddenly came into existence and the lorry came in and reversed as many times as the residents wanted and till the cleaners got their *bakshish*.

While Balan milked his thoughts, the cow kept staring in disappointment at the inedible sign 'Beware of Dog'. To the left of the signboard was a circular marble plaque cemented firmly into the wall with the inscription SABARMATI. In a fit of nationalist fervour, Sundaram had decided to call his residence Sabarmati, after Gandhiji's ashram on the banks of the river in Gujarat. His house had come up first and he could afford to call it whatever he wanted. The others sprang up later with fancy English names like 'The Cascade' and 'Moonlight' or Sanskrit ones like 'Dayadhra' and 'Gokulam'. There was a Tamil one, 'Thenaruvi'. Sabarmati stood out. Sundaram's doctor friends felt that the name reflected a Freudian desire to live in an ashram. One didn't need a doctor to say that. Half of Chennai had the same desire.

Half an hour later, Sundaram got his second tumbler of coffee. He sniffed the aroma like one would test a red wine for its flavour and bouquet, and picked up the copy of *The Hindu* again. Coffee and the papers went together.

'When is the flight coming in?' he asked for the nth time when Lakshmi darted by.

'At eleven o'clock,' she replied patiently.

'I hope the flight is on time. These US flights can be quite unreliable.'

'He is changing over to a British Airways flight in London.'

'All these airlines are the same. Please check the timetable and tell me. By the way, has the driver been told to come at nine?'

'Yes,' she confirmed. 'Selvaraj will be here at nine sharp.'

'Hope he turns up on time. Something important, he goes missing.'

Lakshmi let the comment pass, since Selvaraj was the most dependable driver they had had so far. On the rare occasion he ran a red light or two, but that was all. They had had a rapid turnover the last few years but Selvaraj had stuck with a genial sense of humour. He needed it to work with a man like Sundaram. Selvaraj was paid well and that helped. This was not the time to contradict Sundaram.

'Don't worry,' she assured him, 'he filled up the tank yesterday and has even reversed the car into the garage.'

It was another one of Sundaram's superstitions. When leaving for a long journey or before doing something important, the car had to move forward and not backwards. One cannot start anything by going in reverse first was his impeccable logic. Since the driveway was along a straight line and cars going in had to reverse to get out, Sundaram insisted that his car be reversed in advance and parked in the garage. And when the car reversed out, he forbade anyone to close the gate for a full half hour afterwards.

At least today, Sundaram wanted to ensure that things went right. His son Rajendran—Rajan for short—was coming back from the US after two years. Rajan had completed his Master's in Business Administration at the Wharton School with flying colours and Sundaram was suitably delighted. Initially he had been disappointed that Rajan had not taken after him and done medicine. Sundaram's father Srinivasa Iyer had been both a surgeon and an Iyer, and Sundaram had continued the tradition even though he had left the Iyer out of his surname.

Medicine 'happened' to Sundaram. A stethoscope was stuck into Sundaram's ears by his father when he was barely one. He quickly learnt to differentiate between heartbeats. A good heartbeat, and the one-year-old child smiled. Little Sundaram had frowned when he had heard the heartbeat of his father's sixty-two-year-old uncle. In a few hours, the poor man had died of a massive cardiac arrest. Sundaram's father jumped with joy, not because his uncle had died but because he realized that his son was a medical prodigy. By three, Sundaram could administer an injection or get an injunction. By four, he learnt how to cover up a surgeon's mistakes. His education was complete.

Only once, in his early teens, did he toy with the idea of turning away from medicine and starting a paan shop. He gave up the idea when he realized that he had no money. Not that he was materialistic. He just didn't care much for paan. In some ways, Sundaram was a better surgeon than his Iyer father. He also had more brains. Sundaram had worked hard first as his father's understudy and had learnt all that he could learn from him. This included a few things he need not have learnt. Like picking his teeth with a scalpel.

Rajan found it easier breaking away from his family's caste name than rejecting his family profession. The fact that Sundaram had dropped 'Iyer' from his name made things easy for Rajan to conceal his Brahmin antecedents. 'Rajan' confused everybody. He could have been Rajan the Brahmin or Rajan the non-Brahmin. He could even be Peter Rajan the Christian. In any case, 'Iyer' had, by that time, become a bad word in the

Tamil lexicon. Tamilians who had been honoured by having
streets named after them suddenly found a part of their name
chopped off and their caste names removed. It was like having
half an identity. Kasturi Ranga Iyengar Road became Kasturi
Ranga Road. The proud 'Iyengar' suffix was rudely lopped off.
The great man stood half naked, as if his trousers had been cut
off by an irate mob and made into swimming shorts. The
pioneer of *The Hindu*, which the Chennai*vasis* devoured to this
day, stood without an identity. Because he was of the wrong
caste. It was not a consolation for the great Kasturi Ranga
Iyengar that he had died decades earlier. Rajan was happy to
get rid of the Iyer tag. Sundaram didn't care for it either. But
he prayed that Rajan would become a surgeon. Like Sundaram's
own father.

Rajan, Sundaram felt with a twinge of regret, would have
made a good surgeon since he was bright and talented, and
with his wide contacts he could have helped put Rajan's career
on track. But Rajan had not shown any interest in any science
subject leave alone medicine, and opted for the Commerce and
Accounts stream. When asked why, Rajan's answer was that this
was the path of least resistance. Rajan had a distaste for any
organized field of study. In spite of his distaste, however, he
topped in Physics and Chemistry in school. But that was
because he was bright and not because he liked Physics or
Chemistry. Commerce and Accounts did not tax one's mind
and he opted for it in college. So Sundaram finally reconciled
himself to S. Rajendran CA, MBA rather than S. Rajendran,
MD.

At 7.20, Sundaram was ready and out in the garden with a
cane basket plucking flowers for pooja. Barefoot, white *veshti*
and white, longish *jibba* was his winter uniform. In summer,
he shed the *jibba* and went bare bodied into the garden, his
veshti barely containing his pot belly. Three streaks of yellow

sandalwood paste ran across his forehead with a vermilion dot in the middle. Standing in the lush green lawn in December, he looked like a temple priest lost in paradise. Pooja was central to Sundaram's existence. He had a special room for it. If he had an early morning surgery, he got up an hour earlier to spend adequate time in the pooja room. He believed that it was the unquestioning faith and prayers of his ancestors that had blessed his family with happiness and divine grace, and he vowed to continue the tradition.

Every inch of the four walls of the pooja room was covered with gods of different shapes and hue. There were idols in metal, wood and stone and framed pictures of gods and goddesses. Sundaram went up and down from Madras several times till he found a piece he was satisfied with. There was the elephant-headed Ganesha, round and impressive, in various shapes and sizes. A large mouse *vahanam* supported the Elephant God on its back. There were Guruvayurappan, Shiva, Parvati and Gayathri sitting under a *thiruvasi* of silver. Other bronze idols fought for space. The pooja room was a veritable mini temple inside the house. The smell of agarbattis and camphor numbed the senses.

Sundaram went for the flowers with the glee of a hangman going for the rope. It was always a pleasure to decapitate the stems and throw the flowers into the cane flower basket. It was a sprawling garden and there were so many heads. Chop. Off with the head. The lawn was green this time of the year. Lakshmi tended it with great care and affection. With a Bachelor's degree in Botany, she had been a brilliant student and could remember all the mind-boggling botanical terms even now. *Salix triandra. Zantedeschia. Nelumbo. Gelsemium. Codiaeum. Hibiscus mutabilis* (which, she pointed out, was not a hibiscus, but cotton rose). It was not easy to maintain a lawn in Chennai given the frequent water problems and the soaring temperatures. Once there was even a ban on watering lawns with a hose. The use of mugs was advised. The lawns had all turned brownish yellow then and weeds sprung up rapidly.

It was December now, after two violent bursts of cyclone. The lawn was green and trimmed. The plants were carefully lined on the sides and selected for providing the right flowers for pooja. The gods liked most flowers but not all, even though they had created them. Take the alamanda, for example. The lovely, delicate lavender-coloured flowers were studiously avoided as their seeds were poisonous. Sundaram had remained unmoved even when Rajan had pointed out that the gods viewed all flowers equally. Wasn't it Shiva who had swallowed poison till his neck turned blue? What would the alamanda do to Him?

As always, Sundaram first went towards the flaming red hibiscus. With clinical precision, he guillotined them till their heads lay lifeless in the flower basket with their eyes open. Emboldened, he went for the jasmine. Hibiscus for decorating the outside of the pooja room and jasmine for the offering inside. Sundaram glanced at the basket. It was full of heads. He went across to the tulsi plant and stripped it of its holy leaves till the stem stood naked and raped. A daily ritual he had practised for several years.

The phone rang. It was shrill and cut through the morning haziness. Sundaram liked the volume loud. Even when he watched TV. Lakshmi told him that he should have his ears checked, he could be going deaf, but Sundaram would have none of it. When Sundaram watched TV, the rest of the house went deaf.

Lakshmi picked up the phone. The husky voice of her daughter, Veena, came on the line. She would go directly to the airport, she said. Her four-year-old son, Aditya, was not keeping well and she had decided to leave him behind with the maid. He would be quite uncontrollable at Sabarmati, what with all the excitement on Rajan's arrival.

'Your daughter will go directly to the airport,' Lakshmi shouted out to Sundaram.

'Okay. But she should plan to come here with us from the airport.'

The message was conveyed to Veena. Since her marriage to Jayaraman, Veena had shifted to their company flat across the bridge in Adayar. It wasn't very close to Clive Avenue and she preferred not to keep going up and down. The airport was closer to Adayar.

When the beheading game came to an end, Sundaram removed his *jibba*, went into the pooja room and prayer and meditation took over his being. The violence of the headhunter gave way to the piety of the priest. Prayer was the yoga of the mind. It kept the mind nimble.

The phone rang again. There was no respite from the phone throughout the day, especially since it was a doctor's residence. They had been trying to train someone to answer the telephone, but with the rapid turnover of servants in the house, it hadn't been possible. Lakshmi picked up the phone.

'Hello.' It was the feeble voice of Bhuvana Rajaram. 'Hello Lakshmi, you must be waiting anxiously for Rajan's arrival. I'm happy for you. Two years is a long time.'

'Yes, I am. I am trying to get some last-minute things tied up before he arrives.'

The Rajarams lived on Clive Avenue, three houses down. Bhuvana was a good soul. She was a considerate woman as long as she didn't have to spend money on being one. Her hand of help stopped outside her purse. It was rumoured that this pathological obsession of saving had started on the very night of her marriage to Rajaram, then a bright young civil servant on probation in the Indian Administrative Service. IAS soon became an integral appendage: Where is Rajaram IAS? What is Rajaram IAS doing? Is Rajaram IAS in the toilet?

Sitting in the hotel room, wide-eyed as all new brides are supposed to be and innocent as all new brides are not, Bhuvana had asked, 'What's your salary?'

'Six hundred rupees,' Rajaram IAS had said, puffing out his skinny chest with pride.

'Six hundred?' she had asked feebly, turning pale.

'Yes, six hundred. It will be even more when I finish my probation,' he beamed.

Her last words had been 'I've been cheated', before she passed out and ended their honeymoon rather abruptly.

When they revived Bhuvana, she was a different person. She blabbered incoherently on how important it was to save money for their children and to buy a house. She assured Rajaram IAS that her father, a successful, child-labour-employing match factory owner in Sivakasi, would support them till death, his or theirs, whichever came first. Every month when Rajaram IAS came back from the office with his salary, she promptly confiscated it and put it in the iron safe in the bedroom. That was the last he saw of the money. She didn't trust banks. To get out of her clutches, he started 'hiding' his promotions from her—particularly if it involved an increment. But she always managed to find out, so he gave up trying. Since he was an honest officer, he didn't know where to find that extra money to help him tide over his woes. He remained to this day in a suspended state of hatching plots. She remained her considerate self as long as she didn't have to spend money.

'I thought of sending you some *murukku* for Rajan, but decided against it since you must have already made some yourself,' Bhuvana gave a reason. 'I still remember how much Rajan likes *murukku*.'

'No, I haven't made any *murukku*,' Lakshmi tested Bhuvana's resolve.

'I'm sure you must have made other things,' Bhuvana continued without missing a beat and ignoring Lakshmi's cold repartee. 'Anyway, call me up if you need anything, okay?' She hung up.

Lakshmi had no time to waste thinking about Bhuvana. There were many things to be tied up. She had barely kept the phone down when the doorbell rang. The watchman with the drooping moustache from across the road stood there holding a big, handsome basket. His shoulders stooped a little. It was obvious that the basket was not very light.

'Madam wanted me to come and give this to you,' he said.

Lakshmi motioned him to keep it on the floor and he put it down with a thud. Golden-green *banganapalli* mangoes fell out. There was the sudden gush of ripe mango smell. The best South-of-the-Vindhyas mangoes. A card on top said in delicate handwriting: 'For Rajan—From the Leonards'. The French Leonards family lived in a house diagonally across the road. They had moved into Clive Avenue a year after the Sundarams had occupied Sabarmati and laid claim to being one of its earliest residents. Rajaram IAS and the others had come much later.

'Oh! How thoughtful! Please thank your madam very much. Tell her I will call her up later and thank her personally.'

She had no time for ogling the mangoes now. 'By the way, can you please take this basket and put it beside that door,' she asked the perspiring watchman. He bent down to pick up the basket and carried his girth and the basket across to the door. Then, with a salute, the watchman with the drooping moustache walked out.

It was easy to figure out at what time cooking began in Sabarmati every day. A strong smell of sambhar usually wafted out of the kitchen accompanied by the crackling of mustard seeds bursting in hot oil. There was the hiss and whistle of the pressure cooker that came on and died down after exactly twelve minutes like a steam engine settling down at a wayside station.

Revati was presiding over the kitchen when Lakshmi walked in. Revati was the third cook in six months. The first one refused to continue working when she realized that the Sundarams were not only Brahmins but worse, vegetarians, and that she couldn't fry chicken for herself. The second was fired when packets of cheese and Pepsi bottles started disappearing from the fridge. They had first suspected Veena's son Aditya but soon noticed that even dal and rice packets had disappeared. The latest recruit, Revati, had come a month earlier and had stuck it out so far. Revati wasn't perfect. She was young, inexperienced and looked upon cooking as a sport. If she didn't score well one day, it was just too bad. Lakshmi liked her light-hearted approach to cooking—it was better than constantly complaining about this or that. She only wished Revati cooked better. Sundaram was particular about food in general and so was Amma. But then Revati had been the best under the circumstances. Moreover, she was a Brahmin. And that was vital.

'Lakshmi, get only a Brahmin cook for the kitchen,' Amma had warned categorically. 'I don't want non-Brahmins cooking in the house. Their cooking is very different from ours. They put all those masalas meant for meat and chicken and completely change the taste of our meal.'

It's not easy to get a Brahmin cook in Chennai these days, Lakshmi complained. They charged astronomical rates. And, one just couldn't hire someone without proper references. Just the other day an elderly couple was murdered by their new maid in a flat in Tirumurti Nagar. But non-Brahmin cooks were a non-starter since they cooked and ate meat—the kitchen would be polluted and converted into a graveyard of animals. Amma peered closely at the labels of bottles and tins to even rule out egg preparations.

'Revati, have you given Amma her coffee?' Lakshmi asked.

'Aiyyo! I forgot. I will give it right away.'

'Don't forget these things Revati,' said Lakshmi sharply. 'At eight sharp every day, Amma should be given coffee.'

Amma was Sundaram's mother. She was Amma to all elders and Paati to the youngsters. All those who knew her by her real name were dead.

'Anyway, today I'll make the coffee. You attend to your

work, Revati. Add less salt to the sambhar. Ayyah was upset yesterday. More salt in the beans curry. Green vegetables need more salt. Fry some vadas also.'

Revati nodded, more in confusion than in understanding.

HOMING PIGEON

Even at the best of times, Chennai airport was chaotic. It was so packed, people could hardly move. The European flights normally came in late at night—the Europeans wanted their sleep and sent off their flights to the East when they were awake—and the crowd was generally irritable and eyes were red with want of sleep. Chennai*vasis* went to bed early.

Rajan's flight, surprisingly, was coming in at the decent hour of 11 in the morning and when Sundaram reached the airport at 10.40, it was not crowded. Selvaraj had fortunately come on time, and with Sundaram pacing the verandah up and down like a caged bear, Lakshmi had felt that it was better to leave early than let Sundaram's tension bubble over. There was another more imminent reason why Sundaram had to leave before the clock struck 10.30 that morning. From 10.30 till noon, it was *Rahukalam*, a bad time for setting out on important matters. The Hindu clock ticked differently. There were good times and bad times. And the clock was to be strictly followed if any Hindu valued his or her life. One learnt it by heart—Chennai*vasis* were good at that—even before one learnt multiplication tables. It will save your life one day, Sundaram's father had said.

The Bad Time. The Hindu Bad-Time Clock hung, neatly written in Tamil in Lakshmi's handwriting, just below the calendar with the smiling face of God Muruga. Muruga would have probably had a broader smile if He had not been used to prop up calendar sales.

RAHUKALAM
Monday 7.30–9 a.m.
Tuesday 3–4.30 p.m.
Wednesday 12–1.30 p.m.
Thursday 1.30–3 p.m.
Friday 10.30–12 noon
Saturday 9–10.30 a.m.
Sunday 4.30–6 p.m.

Another set of Bad Time ran parallel to _Rahukalam_—
Yamagandam, the period of Yama, the God of Death.
Yamagandam, though sinister-sounding, was usually considered
to be better than _Rahukalam_, but Bad Time nonetheless. Why
it was better than _Rahukalam_ no one knew. Beside Lakshmi's
neatly written _Rahukalam_ table stood the _Yamagandam_ table.

YAMAGANDAM
Monday 10.30–12 noon
Tuesday 9–10.30 a.m.
Wednesday 7.30–9 a.m.
Thursday 6–7.30 a.m.
Friday 3–4.30 p.m
Saturday 1.30–3 p.m.
Sunday 12–1.30 p.m.

The nights were governed by their own set of Bad and
Good Times. _Eravuguligan_ was the Good Night Time. With
such rigorous Bad Time regimes, it was a miracle that the
Brahmins of Chennai got anything done at all. It was Lack of
Good Time. The Chennai Brahmin potential had remained
untapped for centuries due to it.

It was Friday and, according to the _Rahukalam_ calendar,
Sundaram had to leave the residence by 10.30 if everything
were to go off well. If he missed the deadline, then he could
leave only after 12 noon. Once when he had to go to Bombay
on a Tuesday, to catch a flight leaving at 5.45 p.m., he had had
to leave his residence at 2.45 to avoid _Rahukalam_ and spend
two hours at the airport before the airline counter opened.

Then the counter was opened but the flight didn't take off. His flight finally left at 8.30 p.m. Sundaram swore he would never board an Indian Airlines flight again.

This time, all the signs were good. It was 10 a.m. The car was reversed and parked in front of the porch. He had asked Selvaraj to take the Contessa out. It was white, big, with a spacious boot, reserved for going to the airport and other such chores. Otherwise, his other car, the burgundy Maruti Esteem was suitable for daily use. In an emergency, he could drive it as well. The gate with the 'Beware of Dog' sign was also kept wide open and none of Balan's emaciated cows were in sight. The omens were too good to be true. Rajaram IAS walked in through the open gate.

Even in the best of times, Rajaram IAS closely resembled an ostrich. Long neck, an awkward gait, strong, long legs and a head not quite proportionate to the neck. Today, his head looked all the more disproportionate with a close haircut. Rajaram IAS liked his haircut really short. He believed that one paid for what was removed and not for what was left behind.

Sundaram wanted to strangle him by his lean neck. Why had this Brahmin chosen just this time to walk in? Didn't he know that it was inauspicious for a single Brahmin to come in front of a person who is about to leave? He could have at least come with his wife. A couple was acceptable, in fact, quite auspicious. Now he had come and ruined it all. The damn fool.

'I hope you are not about to leave,' said Rajaram IAS testily when he eyed the car standing in attention and the glowering eyes of Sundaram.

'Yes, I was about to leave for the airport,' Sundaram was cold.

Rajaram IAS immediately understood the import of what he had done. He was also an Iyer Brahmin like Sundaram and knew the holy parameters. He stopped in his tracks.

'Sorry, Sundaram. I was on my way to the office and I

thought I could come and tell you that I am looking forward to Rajan's arrival.'

Sundaram suddenly felt sorry. The poor chap was only trying to be nice.

'No, no. It's fine. I will ask Rajan to come over as soon as he arrives.'

As soon as Rajaram IAS left, Sundaram went in cursing under his breath, filled up a tumbler with water, sat in the dining chair and drank it. This would exorcise the curse.

Sundaram had stopped going to the airport to receive people years ago. He sent his car instead. The only time he went to the airport was when he travelled himself. It was strange to look out of the car. For once he was not preoccupied with work, not rushing to catch a flight or perform a surgery. He had time to see the city pass by. He had not done this in a long time. How Chennai had changed!

The car was going down Mount Road, now called Anna Salai. Shops and showrooms passed by. Textiles and electrical goods. Hotels, 'Boarding and lodging', Hotel Srilekha International on the right. Shops grew in all directions. Arranged like matchboxes, waiting to catch fire in the Chennai summer heat. There were bus-stands with crowds spilling onto the pavement and onto Anna Salai. Policemen in khaki stood with lathis to beat them back but never did. The crowd occupied the side lane meant for cyclists forcing the cyclists onto the road. The cyclists in turn displaced the other two-wheelers. The motorbikes and scooters displaced the auto. The auto the car and so on till the buses came in like a teargas shell, displacing and scattering them all.

Only the cows held their own. Unperturbed and carefree, they just sat in the middle of the road swishing their tails. All of them a uniform dusty white-grey with large grey patches of dirt and grime. Their mouths constantly chewing an imaginary cinema poster licked off the wall and long digested. The buses went around them respectfully. Not because they were holy, but because the bus drivers knew they would be lynched by the milk vendors' union if they killed one.

The Chennai cutouts demanded devotion as well. Monstrous and as tall as ten-storey buildings, they lined both sides of the road shutting out sunlight. The cutouts were as imposing as the gods. Only, these were of contemporary gods—politicians and film stars. Film stars, in varying degrees of undress, intimidated mere mortals on the road. An actress with thighs as thick as oil pipelines in Saudi Arabia—the cutout-makers vied with each other to make their plywood cutout bigger and grander. Sometimes, these cutouts fell and crushed the pedestrians below. Crushed by a favourite politician or actor. Or, luckier still, by an actress' thigh. Unfortunately, in Chennai, only the cutouts fell, not the politicians.

Sundaram sat in the car and took everything in. Chennai had changed. Gone were the days when one could drive the whole length of Mount Road without changing gears. There were suddenly more cars, more people and more of everything. A traffic jam near SIET College held them up. It took all of four policemen to clear it. If the traffic lights had been working this would not have happened. They were mobile again. The bright buses of the Pallavan Transport Corporation jostled against the dirty mufassal buses. Sundaram closed his eyes and sighed.

Rajan saw them first. His parents, Veena and Jayaraman stood scanning the escalator. Rajan waved but they didn't notice since the others on the escalator were waving as well. Some, carried away by all this mad waving, stumbled on the last step, crashing their bulky handbags into the others.

It had been two whole years. Rajan couldn't make it during his break the previous year because Procter & Gamble had offered him a summer assignment that was too good to decline. His parents couldn't visit him given Sundaram's commitments at the hospital; it was also not possible to leave Amma alone and go. Only Jayaraman had stopped by for a couple of days during one of his business trips to Los Angeles. He had filled him in on all the Chennai gossip.

Rajan walked right up to them before they saw him.

'Appa! Appa! Rajan's here,' cried Veena and everyone spotted him at once.

Rajan put his bag down and hugged his father. Then he hugged his mother, Veena and Jayaraman. He noticed that his father was suddenly looking his fifty-five years. The furrows on his brow had increased and his stocky build looked portly, even flabby. His hair had turned completely grey and was thinning. He had, however, managed to keep the chin under control— there were no double chins—and his nose remained as sharp as ever. His mother looked the same, younger than her years. The same gentle eyes and high chin. A longish throat ending just above the border of the cotton saree.

'You have lost weight,' Lakshmi commented.

Why did parents say the same things over and over again when they saw their children. In fact, Rajan had put on two kilos in the last two weeks.

'Amma, don't you people ever change? I have actually put on two kilos.'

'That may be true, but you're thinner than you were two years back. You haven't been eating properly.'

It was pointless to argue.

'I'll go get my baggage. See you all outside.' Rajan picked up a trolley and pushed it towards the conveyor belt.

His two massive bags rolled out onto the belt like two fat Americans on their Harley Davidsons. Picking up and dumping them on the trolley would have given anyone hernia. That was the price for travelling to the US. That and AIDS. That, AIDS and the American accent. Rajan had managed to avoid them all, well, almost all since he couldn't help pronouncing 'important' 'impartant'. Many paid the price only to acquire an American accent. Otherwise their trip was a waste. Even when they went to the US for four days, their accents changed on return. Rounded rs, 'hi' for 'hello', 'howdy' for 'how are you' and 'cool' for 'fine, thank you'. Good Chennai Brahmins began punctuating their sentences with 'Jesus Christ!' All this in four days. Little did they know that all these 'American' words had gone out of fashion about fifty years earlier.

A youngish, lean and hungry customs officer stopped Rajan just before the exit.

'Anything to declare?'

'Nothing. I am a student coming back from the US. I am . . .'

'But your flight was from London,' he interrupted, his eyes narrowing.

'I was on a five-hour transit in London.'

The customs man lost interest.

The ride back was one series of questions and answers. Sundaram and Lakshmi tried to catch up on the past two years in half an hour. Rajan answered them patiently. They all sat in Jayaraman's Zen, squashed and sweating. Selvaraj and his Contessa carried the two US bags.

Chennai was passing by outside. Rajan hardly had any time to look out of the window. He was too busy answering questions.

How was your course? How did the other Indians fare in the exams? Were there lots of Indians in the faculty? What did you do for food? Were the instant packets we sent you useful? You must be starved of Indian food. I hope you have not started eating meat. How is Dr Rajagopalan's brother's grandson doing? Is he planning to settle in the US? Did you get around to meeting Venkatraman's daughter and son-in-law? They are supposed to be in Los Angeles or San Francisco. They have a big house. He's a computer engineer or something like that in a big company.

Chennai had passed by Rajan's window in a blur. They turned into Clive Avenue. The avenue seemed not to have changed. The same dustbins, the gulmohur tree in the distance and two coconut palms straining out of Rajaram IAS's compound wall like the necks of camels. The tar-topped road tapering off into mud paths on the sides. The only addition was a low hedge running right along the compound walls of all the houses. It was a part of Daulat Singh's Clean Clive Avenue drive. Daulat Singh, the sole North Indian in the neighbourhood, had taken on a crusading role in cleaning up the avenue, and even the tight-fisted Rajaram IAS had been won over to part with a monthly contribution to maintain the avenue.

Whenever he entered Clive Avenue, Rajan got the feeling that he lived in a village. It may have been the lethargy in the air, the still gulmohur tree, the lack of traffic, Balan's cows lounging in the shade, or the tar road tapering into mud, he wasn't quite sure what. It was as if an invisible door shut out the bustling, overcrowded, concrete city outside with its ten million people. Clive Avenue was like an ancient black-and-white photo come alive in colour.

'Nothing seems to have changed here,' Rajan said.

'Not too loud,' Veena warned. 'Your mother will be disappointed. She was the one who chose the hedge and tried to green this road.'

Their house stood well ensconced at the corner under the gulmohur. It was odd that even from a distance, Sabarmati always looked as though it required a coat of paint. When one went nearer, this impression was only strengthened. Large patches appeared where the paint had fallen off revealing all the colours used before. The history of Sabarmati could be discovered by peeling it off layer by layer. Light blue peeked out through light green, yellow through blue flakes. In this bleak pastel scenario, the shock of bougainvillea raining down in front was a bright spot. Turning into the driveway, the carefully tended lawn and plants came into view on the right. Rajan had come home.

Lakshmi had asked Revati to keep the aarti ready. Rajan had to have the traditional welcome.

As the car came into the driveway, Revati ran in to fetch the aarti. Lakshmi emerged out of the car first. Veena came out next. Both held each end of the silver aarti plate and brought it down the steps. Rajan came around and stood in front of the plate. Lakshmi started singing and as she sang, they rotated the plate around, the vermilion water inside moved clockwise, in circles. It had to be clockwise three times and then anti-clockwise thrice. The liquid splashed a bit when it abruptly changed direction. Revati had put in too much water, Lakshmi noted. Rajan looked serious. These were the hazards of coming home. You had to do as the Sundarams did.

Beebee had bounded up by this time and had started sniffing Rajan not realizing the gravity of the occasion.

'Beebee, come here!' Sundaram called out from behind.

The dog kept sniffing—the shoes, the pants. Lakshmi could see all this from the corner of her eye. Rajan squirmed trying to keep Beebee away but not wanting to offend the animal. Three clockwise and three anti-clockwise. It was done and there was relief. The plate was taken away by Lakshmi and the contents drained out outside the gate and onto the hedge outside. The effect of all evil eyes was being drained out onto the hedge.

'Rajan, see Amma first. She has been waiting to see you since morning,' said Sundaram as soon as they stepped into the verandah. Rajan had planned to do that in any case, go straight to Paati's room. She was Paati to him.

She was sitting on a straight high-back cane chair, her legs resting on a stool in front. Bright sunlight came streaming in from the windows. She held an open book on her lap. *Kambaramayanam* it said in Tamil. Rajan paused for a second in the doorway. She had not heard him come in. It was a strange moment. It was like picking up from where he had left off two years earlier.

'Paati, how are you?'

She turned and looked at him through her thick glasses.

'*Vaa da*, Rajan . . . so you finally decided to come back from America.'

She was around eighty-five. She had looked eighty-five since she turned sixty. Like all grandmothers, she never changed. The same gentle, caring eyes, the deliberate movement of limbs slowed down by age, a gruff, manly voice, white hair, flabby girth and legs affected by arthritis.

Paati was born on 22 September 1914, the day the German battleship *Emden* let loose a few shells on Madras from the shore. Madras was hit, three died and some were injured. It was India's first encounter with the First World War. There was panic on the streets. There was an exodus. Trains ran full and there was no place to stand on the railway platforms. Paati's family was nervous but they were warned that the child was expected any moment. Don't risk the mother's life, the doctor said. *Emden* was not going to return. But rumours said Madras would be shelled again. Paati's family decided to stay.

Paati was born late that night, at home. Paati's grandmother and their neighbour brought her into this world. She was born into a turbulent Madras. The battleship *Emden* was on everyone's lips. Will *Emden*? Won't *Emden*? Paati became the Emden Papa. The Emden Baby.

Emden Ma, where are you? Emden Ma, come and drink your milk. Emden Ma, have you done your potty?

'Why can't you call her by her proper name?' her father grumbled. But 'Emden Ma' stuck.

Emden Ma soon became Emma for short.

Where is Emma? Is Emma back from school? Emma, your red pavadai *with the gold border is ready with the tailor.*

Soon everyone forgot her real name. She was Emma to all. When she got married and had a son, she became Amma, Mother. Then when her granddaughter was born, she became Paati, Grandmother. The only time people got to know her real name was when her wedding invitation was printed. The invitees saw the name and thought that Emma's sister was getting married.

Rarely had someone who had entered the world amidst such turbulence had a more comfortable upbringing. The family was quite well-to-do, and lived in a palatial bungalow behind Edward Elliots Road at the heart of Madras—a kilometre from Clive Avenue, which didn't exist then. Emma was the first daughter but the third child. Being the first girl child, there was much celebration in the house. She grew up to be strikingly beautiful, leading a sheltered life, and protected—protected from the growing freedom movement outside. It took some time for Madras to warm up to the idea of throwing out the British—they were decent chaps after all—but once it did, Madras was full of freedom fighters. This idea, however, never caught on with the sprawling bungalow behind Edward Elliots Road.

Emma was self-taught and accomplished at music. She was fluent in Sanskrit and quite capable of holding her own in English. Several decades later, when strangers saw Paati as an old woman, they usually took her to be uneducated till Paati startled them with her command over English. Her diction was far better than the later crop of students from English-medium Tamil schools or Tamil-medium English schools. Tamil she had to learn since her family was fanatical about their mother tongue, as all Tamils were. Without a good Tamil education, one was not a complete person. One had to know *Tirukkural* by heart. That made the Tamils happy. Of course it was promptly forgotten.

Emma was taught the violin. She played with grace and understanding and she was quick to grasp the nuances of the art. The great Sabesayyer was her tutor. A gleaming black Chevrolet went to pick him up and bring him to her residence every other day. When she married a handsome boy from Tirunelveli—not that her parents had anything against Thanjavur—and moved to another part of Madras with her husband, Edward Elliots Road became the poorer for it.

Rajan sat on Paati's bed. The cot was higher than usual and had a set of wheels attached—it was easier to move it around, she said. The cot couldn't move beyond the four walls of the room in any case since it was wider than the doorway. But that was an unnecessary detail for Paati.

'Well, what's there to do in America? There was nothing and I decided to come back.'

'What do you mean what's there to do?' Paati challenged. 'What about all the others who refuse to come back? Are they all fools?'

'Well, that's true. But there's nothing like coming home. I have finished with America and have decided to start a new life here.'

'Yes, start a new life. That's fine. To begin with, get married.'

As soon as Paati said 'married', Lakshmi and Sundaram cringed and quietly tiptoed out of the room. They had wanted to broach the topic with Rajan gently but Paati had always believed in getting to the point directly.

'I want to get a job first.'

'That's all right. Get a job. Job will come anyway with all your degrees begrees from America. Get married as well. Both are not contradictory to each other.'

Rajan laughed. 'Okay, Paati. I will take a shower and come back to discuss my marriage.'

'There is a time for studies; there is a time for marriage. If either of them passes, problems start.'

'Paati, I am only twenty-five. In the US, marriage after thirty and forty is the norm. They prefer it that way.'

'That's why their marriages last only two weeks,' Paati let out a hoarse laugh.

'Paati, as someone said, youth is the only season for enjoyment, and the first twenty-five years of one's life are worth all the rest of the longest life of man, even if those five-and-twenty years are spent in penury and contempt, and the rest in the possession of wealth, honours, respectability.'

'Well, if you don't get married, even wealth, honours and respectability will elude you! At eighty-five, I am not so sure whether they are goals worth pursuing anyway,' Paati added.

'Paati, tell me how is your health?'

'So far so good. I have been living on a day-to-day extension for the last thirty years. God has decided that I should live longer and I have decided to accept my fate with resignation.'

Lakshmi and Sundaram had stayed out of sight but well within earshot. They came back now as if they had heard nothing. Paati's health was an easier topic to handle.

'Do you still play chess, Paati?'

'Well . . . I used to play with Veena till last year. Now she has her hands full with Aditya and I have not touched chess for more than a year now.'

'What about bridge?'

'The same.'

'Paati hardly plays chess these days,' Sundaram agreed. 'But once in a while Dominique drops in and keeps Paati engaged. The only problem is that, of late, Paati has started cheating a lot. Whenever Dominique cuts her pieces, she asks her to keep them back on the board begging poor eyesight.'

'Don't start believing them,' Paati retorted. 'Go and freshen up. People will start coming.' And indeed, people had started to come in.

DOMINIQUE

All those who had to know Rajan was back knew. Peter Madhusudan the postman. Balan the milkman. Murugan the cobbler. Devanathan the income tax officer and a host of others, neighbours and Rajan's friends.

When Rajaram IAS dropped by that evening, there were several cars parked outside the house. Veena and Jayaraman had fetched Aditya from Adayar and had decided to dine at Sabarmati. Rajaram IAS craned his ostrich neck to spot Rajan in the midst of admirers.

'Come in Rajaram mama,' Rajan got up looking relieved.

'And now the story reaches a crescendo/He has torn away the siege's torques/The wider world ecstatic it should end so/Crowd in to see the way a hero walks,' said Rajaram IAS smiling.

'I'm hardly a hero, but who was that?' Rajan asked. 'T.S. Eliot?'

'No. You may not know this. Boris Pasternak in "The Victor". Okay, try this one—"Of course, America had often been discovered before Columbus, but it had always been hushed up."'

They both laughed. 'Oscar Wilde,' said Rajan.

Rajaram IAS had seen Rajan grow up—as a sick baby, a cricket-playing boy and a teenager at Vivekananda College. They belonged to different generations and, except for an interest in cricket, didn't seem to have anything in common. It was their love of poetry that brought them together.

Rajaram IAS, not quite IAS then, had done his postgraduation in literature from the once-prestigious Presidency College—another relic of the British Madras Presidency. Overlooking the grand Marina Beach and the Bay of Bengal, contemplation of Shakespeare, Milton and Wordsworth was easier. That explained Rajaram IAS's eccentric outbursts of Shakespeare. He knew practically all the plays by heart and had acted in several of them. He had to give up later since Bhuvana felt that continuing in this vein would not befit a senior civil servant. But Rajaram IAS's interest was not confined to Shakespeare and poetry. Even now, he locked his office door between one and two in the afternoon and lounged on the sofa with a book—any book.

Rajan's motivation was different. He had begun to read poetry in college to take his mind off the drudgery of commerce, accountancy and management, dry subjects that didn't require brains, subjects without emotion. It was easy to hide a book and read while the lecturer droned on. Robert Frost, Byron, T.S. Eliot . . . he read them all. He soon realized that people were impressed when one quoted one from memory. Superficial knowledge was better than knowledge itself.

Rajan and Rajaram IAS had sat together discussing poetry and prose for long hours.

And now the link had been revived once again. They discussed the latest crop of authors and their work. Amitav Ghosh. Salman Rushdie. The latest Gabriel Garcia Marquez.

Then, they got down to other things. Why Rajan came back from the US. What there was to come back to. How he would have certainly got an excellent job there. Whether he had at least applied for a green card. People were willing to pay in lakhs for a US visa and Rajan had come back empty-handed.

And so the visitors came in and went out after seeing Rajan. It was like coming into a temple and having darshan of the Almighty. But then, Chennai*vasis* liked visiting each other, especially if they could do it unannounced. It preserved informality, they felt. Nothing gave them greater pleasure than catching the 'visited' in his crumpled lungi and torn banian and sending the lady of the house scurrying for cover, trying to adjust her saree while she sent her cook to get fresh milk to make filter coffee for the visitors.

It was nearly dinner time when Dominique came in.

'Rajan, are you still in the mood to meet people?' she called out from the drawing room.

Rajan came out of the bedroom where Aditya had been forced to lie down.

'*Comment allez-vous?*' said Rajan, his eyes lighting up.

'*Très bien. Est-ce que vous vous souvenez toujours de votre français?*'

'*Bien sûr*. I had a lot of French girlfriends in the US.'

Both laughed. They placed their hands on each other's shoulder and kissed. The kiss of Westerners. Now spreading fast in the East. Simultaneous kisses on both cheeks. It was not an easy operation unless one was trained at it and had practised a bit. Often one ended up missing the cheeks and kissing the air. No spit could be left behind—to do that was not only impolite but downright rude.

Rajan and Dominique were both Clive Avenue products. He was Vadama Brahmin, she was Roman Catholic. Both were from upper-middle-class families that could be classified as rich. They were born in the same year as well, Dominique three months earlier than Rajan. They had grown up together. For the first few years of her existence, Dominique had thought she was a boy and tried doing everything Rajan did, like peeing into the toilet bowl standing up. She went trotting behind him with a cricket bat. It was much later that she discovered dolls.

Now, Dominique was all of twenty-five. She was tall, slim and small-breasted. Not a classical beauty by Indian standards, but she was very attractive. Indians preferred their women more rounded. Her white skin, however, made up for her thin frame.

'Nice to have you back, Rajan.'

'No beating around the bush. Who is this new guy in your life?' he demanded in mock anger. 'And what have you both been up to when I was not here to check you? Give me the gories.'

'New guy?' she laughed. 'It's good to know that I can still make you jealous.'

'Jealous! That's not the word. Pity him who falls for thee.'

'You won't be frivolous if you actually see him. He is tall and handsome. Quite unlike Frenchmen, who are basically wimps—they are too feminine for my liking. Not this one. He is different. I met him last year in Chamonix when I went for a course in skiing. He struggled with his skis and I with mine and we decided to struggle together. He then came over for a week to India in August and that is when we decided to get engaged.'

'Most unromantic!'

She laughed. 'Not really. Well, to tell you the truth, it wasn't love at first sight or anything. I just found him a very interesting person and we had a good time in Chamonix. He's an engineer and has a passion for painting. We exchanged notes and got to know each other. Then my parents said "yes" when he came over.'

'How did he find India?'

'Well . . .' she hesitated. 'Frankly, he didn't feel too comfortable here. Must have been the August heat. He sat most of the time in the AC room in our house. He hated the Hindi and Tamil movies we saw—crass and garish he said. He liked the people though—at least the ones he met. He thought they were friendly. But he basically stayed at home.'

'Naturally—what else was he supposed to do? After all, he came all the way to see you, not Madras.'

'Well, yes, I suppose that's true. Anyway, he's got a good job with Ariane.'

'Wow! So, when is the big day?'

'Well, some time next year—probably after October.'

'That's a long way off.'

'Yeah. But I want to settle down a little bit in my new job. You know, I've just joined *Le Figaro* as their resident correspondent here.'

'After all that you used to say against journalists? You turncoat! I hope you're not going to dish out those predictable stories about snake charmers and naked sadhus to your French admirers.'

'You can be absolutely sure I will. The latest issue has an article of mine with pictures of pot-bellied, ash-smeared sadhus in their birthday suits.'

'By the way, you haven't told me his name, *s'il vous plaît*.'

'Jacques Blanchemaison.'

'Blanchemaison? White house?!'

She shrugged.

'You French are crazy. Imagine any Tamil calling himself *Vellai Veedu*, White House. He would die of shame. Dominique Blanchemaison indeed!'

Dominique grew up in Clive Avenue. Chennai was her first home. After her Rosary Matriculation School, she did her BA in Economics at Stella Maris College. She spoke Tamil as fluently as French, which often caught people unawares.

Once she and a Danish friend were having filter coffee at Perumal café when four middle-aged Chennai*vasis* sitting at the next table began passing comments in Tamil. These foreigners are all hippies. They have half our brains—they need calculators to add 1+1. We Indians are miles ahead. Westerners think they can get away with anything because they have white skins. Look at these two girls. Can't they wear proper clothes? These foreigners have no morals. They will sleep with anyone. And on and on they went. When there was a pause in their conversation, Dominique called out loudly in Tamil, 'Waiter! We would like another round of coffee please. After that, get us the bill please.' The four men went pale with embarrassment, choked over their coffee, hurriedly paid the bill at the counter and left.

French literature was Dominique's passion. Though she enrolled for a BA in Economics, she was considered quite an authority on French literature. Her papers were published in well-known French journals and she travelled a bit around Paris presenting them. It came as no surprise that, after her Economics, she decided to do her Master's in Journalism from the Madras Institute of Mass Communications. That pretty much ensured her a job. *Le Figaro*, looking for a correspondent to cover southern India, found her eminently qualified. She trained in Paris for a few months and they promised to pay her well.

The Leonards moved into Clive Avenue immediately after the Sundarams did. Guy and Michelle had come to Madras as a young couple. When his company offered him the job of Head of Office in Madras, they decided to grab the opportunity. To become a Head of Office at twenty-five was a good break. They would also get hardship allowance and they needed the money. But Madras? It was not even Delhi, the capital. Madras was near Pondicherry, his well-wishers consoled. A former French colony. It couldn't be all that bad. It should have remained a French territory. He would then have had no problems. Anyway, even now, he could visit Pondicherry on weekends and speak French there. Leonards tried this formula for a few months but found that they were quite happy being in Madras. In fact, they started liking the dust and the smell of Madras. There was no need to seek happiness elsewhere.

The Leonards stayed on. And on. They kept promising their friends that they would return. But they loved Madras. It was so different. Guy's company had also grown in the meantime and he was made Head of Operations for the Asian region. There was no turning back.

'What are your plans?' Dominique quizzed.

'I don't have any.'

'Don't be silly. What about your future?'

'Believe me, I don't have any plans. My first priority is to take it easy. I have studied enough and I have decided to take six months off before I even think of finding a job.'

'Take off? So you do have intentions to work some day.'

'Save your sarcasm. I will take a break for a while, rejuvenate before I start. You guys do it all the time in the West—you even take off for a couple of years. Actually, it's a very sensible thing to do. We tend to forget that there is more to life than scurrying around like rats. Anyway, I'm not too worried about getting a job. I have a CA and an MBA—I should get something.'

'Yes, but have you zeroed in on anything? Any multinational begging at your doorstep?'

'Sometimes, smaller firms are better to start in. There's more scope for learning and making mistakes. I have to decide what field I want to look into. The US is finally looking at India—IT seems to be the buzzword.'

'Are you planning to go back to the US again by any chance?'

'You disappoint me, Dom. Go back to that country which miraculously has gone from barbarism to degeneration without the usual interval of civilization? At least we in India are through with our interval of civilization and are now degenerating with dignity! No, I'm not going back. Read my lips: NOT GOING BACK.'

'Okay, okay, you can cut out the George Bush stuff. You're getting carried away with your own erudition.'

'And what after that?'

'What do you mean?'

'What about after getting a job? Like getting married, for instance—your parents are looking forward to it.'

'Getting married? Now?'

'Yes.'

'Dom, you must be joking! You sound like Paati. For heaven's sake, I'm only twenty-five. You yourself are getting married only at the end of next year. I can certainly afford to wait.'

ASTROLOGY AND
MANAGEMENT

When the astrologer entered Sabarmati, he looked pleased with himself. He knew what to expect and had all the answers ready.

The Sundarams had asked their family astrologer to visit. They had several questions for him. Rajan was due to return from the US in a week and they needed to plan ahead for his future.

Beebee was the first to welcome Chandramouli when he opened the gate and came in. Beebee knew the astrologer by his smell and he always came in smelling nice. His forehead was streaked with *vibhuthi* and vermilion and he sported a strong sandalwood perfume. His legs, however, smelt of old leather. That's what came of wearing ten-year-old Bata sandals every day.

Earlier, astrologers came on bicycles carrying sheaves of papers smeared with turmeric and vermilion and complicated calculations scribbled on them with pencil. Holy astrological calculations. Some carried a parrot in a cage. Chandramouli was a modern-day delight. He came in his 1975 vintage Fiat, chocolate brown and working perfectly. While he wore a *veshti* tied shabbily around his ample waist, the rest of him was in tune with the times. He carried a briefcase full of computer printouts, a Japanese calculator that his son had given him, a cellphone to attend to urgent calls and a pager, a useless appendage, bought at a time when cellphones had not been introduced. He looked professional and credible. Chandramouli was a Ph.D and people were impressed. An astrologer with a Ph.D had to be accurate. Few knew that his doctorate was on India's trading links with the Arab world in the eighteenth century. The Sundarams were keen to consult him, even though his predictions had not always been reliable. He predicted good things, even if some did not come to pass. That was the secret of his success.

If a person had heart problems, 'he will recover soon, don't worry,' Chandramouli said soothingly. If the person died, 'I didn't want to say anything earlier because you would be upset.' If someone was unmarried, 'She will marry as soon as Saturn goes into a more favourable position. By the end of the year if not earlier. Keep looking.' He liked to hedge his bets. That's how he survived.

The Sundarams were waiting as Chandramouli shooed Beebec off, took off his sandals and went into the drawing room with the confidence of one holding Sabarmati's future in his hands. A nylon mat had been spread out on the floor in the centre of the room and Chandramouli plonked himself on it with a sigh. He was getting on in years and would have personally preferred to do his astrology sitting in a chair but sitting cross-legged on a mat somehow made his role more authentic.

'Amma, I have studied the horoscope carefully,' he said and paused for a long time. Drama never hurt anyone. 'When is Rajendran coming back from America?' He liked to call Rajan by his full name. It created a formal, professional atmosphere.

'Next Friday,' answered Lakshmi.

'Good . . . good,' he nodded approvingly, even though he did not hear her answer. But he seemed to endorse the idea of Rajan coming next Friday which made Lakshmi happy. That was what was important in the end. Making his clients happy.

'You should not worry about Rajendran. He will have no difficulty settling down in a good job. He will marry a good Iyer girl of your choice—she will even belong to the same subcaste, Vadama. She will be good-looking, talented and very considerate to her in-laws. The girl and Rajendran will be highly compatible. Her coming into this house will ensure an increase in your fortunes. She will be a goddess of wealth, the Lakshmi of the house. However, the only thing I have to say is that Rajendran must be careful not to be influenced by bad advice given to him by a friend from the West.'

'Boyfriend or girlfriend?'

'Maybe a boyfriend.'

'Why?'

'That boy will try to encourage Rajendran to marry a foreigner. But don't worry. In the end, this will not happen because Rajan is a good boy.'

'I hope he will not marry an American . . .'

'No, no. I don't think so. He will marry a girl from Madras very soon and settle down here.'

'Who is this American?'

'Someone studying with him, I think.'

There was a pause. The Sundarams digested the information. Chandramouli paused to see whether he had hedged his bets enough. Even if some of his predictions had gone awry, Chandramouli was not a fake. A serious student of astrology, his interest in the subject started rather suddenly, a few years before his retirement, when he saw his guru in a dream exhorting him to take up astrology for the good of mankind. He took this to heart and an astrologer was born.

Chandramouli worked full-time at his new vocation. He read book after book and studied related subjects to get a better understanding of how stars behave. When this new-found passion began interfering with his work, he sought voluntary retirement and spent all his waking hours thinking about *Rahu, Ketu* and *Shani*. He sought out other practising astrologers and took their advice. And he realized quickly that even with the best of knowledge, predictions could go wrong. He accepted this human frailty and started hedging. He soon discovered that good predictions went down better with clients than the bad ones—even if they were inaccurate. He practised hard and came into his own after some fits and starts. One day, he predicted accurately the marriage of the daughter of the Chief Justice of the Madras High Court and he became a household name in the Chennai Brahmin circles. Chandramouli had arrived.

Chandramouli had studied Rajan's horoscope carefully. It was a good one. His marriage was fated to be happy—except for a small hitch. He wasn't quite sure whether Rajan would have a traditional marriage. To a conservative household like the Sundarams', unconventional choices were not going to be easy to digest. He decided not to mention it. After all, why create panic when all he had was a mere suspicion.

'I hope Rajan doesn't get carried away. There are so many horror stories one keeps hearing about boys in the US. Just the other day I heard about this boy who kept telling his parents that he was not ready for marriage only to reveal later that he had been married to an American for a good five years and had even had a child, but was afraid to tell his parents,' mumbled Lakshmi.

'Don't worry. Didn't you hear what he just said? There is no need to fear about Rajan marrying an American,' Sundaram tried to convince himself.

'Have you started looking at horoscopes for alliances?' enquired Chandramouli, not comfortable at the turn the conversation was taking.

'Not so far. We had received five or six earlier but put them away since Rajan was still in the US. They are from good families. Now that he is returning, I think it's time to take a look.'

'I agree. Even if Rajendran wants to marry later, we have

to start searching from now on. Give these horoscopes to me if you have them. Today is a good day being a Friday.'

Lakshmi went in and brought out a sheaf of letters that had envelopes with yellow smudges of holy turmeric at the corners. They were tied together with a rubber band.

'Here you are,' she said handing some of them over. 'I agree that it's time we got serious. Tell us whenever you finish whether they are worth pursuing. In my opinion, there are at least two which are worth a second look. Among the ones I have given you is Chartered Accountant Sethuraman's daughter Gayathri. She looks really striking in the photo.'

Chandramouli pulled out a sheet of paper and the photo fell out. He gave it a hard look.

'If her horoscope is compatible with Rajan's, we would be keen to pursue the matter. Like us, the Sethuramans are originally from Tirunelveli and are very traditional. They have a conservative outlook and are also followers of the Kanchi Mutt like us. Even though Sethuraman has a flourishing practice in Madras, they are not ostentatious in their lifestyle. The girl has an MA in Physics and sings and paints quite well . . .' Lakshmi rattled on.

'Let me be frank. I want my son to marry into a traditional, conservative family,' Sundaram said emphatically. 'They should be religious and should have an interest in our culture and traditions. I am not interested in their bank balance only. The girl should be one who can adjust to us, take care of us in our old age and be prepared to bring up her children according to our traditions. If she doesn't know her shlokas, Lakshmi can always teach her later. I don't want Rajan to marry one of those modern girls who spends her time at discos and wants to continue to do so even after marriage. From what we know of Rajan, he is not that type either, unless of course he has changed after going to the US.'

'We are keen on this alliance,' Lakshmi confessed. 'Of course, the horoscopes and other things should match. We can proceed only after you give us the green signal.'

Chandramouli made a note of all that Lakshmi had said about Sethuraman's girl while she handed over the rest of the horoscopes.

'One of these belongs to the daughter of a senior police officer. The girl seems to be good-looking and talented. She too has completed a Master's in Physics. The only problem is that she is of the same age as Rajan, just a few months younger. We would prefer someone at least two or three years younger. The other less important matter is that police officers have such a reputation these days that we have to be doubly sure about the family before we proceed on that horoscope.'

Chandramouli noticed that Lakshmi was holding one back with her.

'What is that one?' he reminded her.

'Oh, this! This girl is from an Iyengar family. We don't have to consider alliances from Iyengars right now. We would like to look at good Iyer girls first. Actually, we are not at all keen to consider Iyengar girls . . .'

'Let me clarify,' Sundaram hastened to add, squirming at Lakshmi's blunt declaration. 'We have nothing against Iyengars, or for that matter, any other type of Brahmins. My uncle's second son married a Marathi Brahmin and is settled in Bombay quite happily. My father himself dropped the "Iyer" from our surname since he thought it was an unnecessary appendage. But looking at it practically, an Iyer girl has a better chance of settling down in a family like ours than someone who is used to a different type of upbringing.'

Chandramouli nodded his head vigorously. These were sensitive issues and he was not going to waste his time giving his opinion. It hardly mattered to him whether the girl was an Iyer or an Iyengar or even a Manipuri Brahmin as long as the horoscopes matched and his clients were happy with the choice.

'When do you think you can give us a feedback?' Lakshmi interjected.

'A couple of days are enough. I have all the data in my computer and I should know immediately.'

'Don't depend too much on your computer. I am interested in your intuition,' said Sundaram, wary of fancy gadgets being used for something as vital to human existence as astrology.

'No, no. I do it myself first and match the results with the computer's. Usually they match. It even gives percentage of compatibility—67 per cent, 74 per cent, 82 per cent . . .' Chandramouli tried to impress and reassure his clients.

He had exactly the opposite effect on Sundaram. The more Chandramouli extolled the virtues of the computer the less convinced Sundaram became of Chandramouli's ability to read horoscopes and come up with an accurate match. 'I think we should consult another astrologer as well just to cross-check and make sure everything is all right,' he mumbled to Lakshmi when Chandramouli left.

Rajan walked into Sabarmati a week later blissfully unaware of these machinations. He went about meeting old friends. Rajan had come all the way from the US to settle down in Chennai to find that most of his friends had left for the US, the land of milk and honey. Scattered all over the US and submerged in anonymity. Wherever he went, he was met by the parents. 'Oh, Sridhar went off to do his Master's in Law from Michigan last year. I hear the university is one of the best in the States.' Even Rajaram IAS's son Kartik had left to do computer engineering in Australia. Rajan and Kartik had been close even though they had studied in different schools and Kartik was a year older. Taking advantage of the dead-end in Clive Avenue, Rajan and Kartik had put together a band of dedicated cricket lovers who played come sun, wind or rain. They had left no window unbroken in Clive Avenue.

Only CV was still in Chennai. Rajan couldn't believe his luck.

'Why haven't you gone to the US?' Rajan asked as soon as he met him.

'Someone had to be here to receive you!'

They laughed. CV was C. Vaidyanathan. Rajan and he had been classmates and best friends. They had studied together from class one right up to graduation, played cricket in the same team and wasted each other's time discussing its pros and cons. And chased the same girls.

CV lived with his parents in T. Nagar, in the heart of Chennai, in a narrow lane full of shops and vendors, cycles, pedestrians and cows. But CV's family had never thought of leaving T. Nagar. The house was lucky for them they said. It had seen several marriages, and their business had flourished. So they continued to live there even while the cars got bigger and the roads smaller.

It was late evening when Rajan reached CV's residence. Sitting under the stars on the open terrace, Rajan was full of questions. He had left Madras as a confident student and had returned to Chennai as an unemployed postgraduate. There was a big gap that needed to be filled.

And CV was just the person to fill him in on all that he had missed. CV had joined a flourishing leather company soon after he graduated and had risen to the level of a director in a couple of years. The fact that CV's father and uncle owned the company had helped of course.

Like in all business families, CV was married off to a girl from another business family soon after his BCom. Both families waited eagerly for an heir but CV and his wife had not obliged as yet.

CV was delighted to have his friend back. He had never quite believed that people could actually come back to India from the US for good. They exchanged notes on all their friends. Where were Venu, Paul, Trips, MR? What were Sharath, SK, Akbar up to? Why was KB in such a hurry to get married? Is Akbar still the same even after his Ph.D? Where had Mani disappeared? They discussed the idiosyncrasies of their former teachers, in school and in college. Did Professor Manikkam still dig his ears with his ball pen? Then, they discussed jobs.

'Boss, I'm taking off for about six months before I look around for a job. I've had it up to here with studies and I want a break.'

'So the US bug has bitten you as well. The Americans are perpetually taking a sabbatical somewhere or the other.'

'No, no,' Rajan protested. 'This has nothing to do with that. I just feel like taking a break before settling down. And I really don't think finding a job will be that difficult—especially with a CA and an MBA.'

'That may be true,' agreed CV. 'But, somehow, I am always uncomfortable with this taking-a-break business. One never knows when the right opportunity will come, and if you happen to be taking a break then, you miss out on it forever.'

Rajan was silent. He wasn't convinced. CV was too much of a businessman to appreciate the value of 'taking off'.

'CV, you're always so linear in your thinking. There is more to life than shedding college clothes for a business suit. And it's not as if I am planning to do nothing for a lifetime. By the way, what sort of jobs are going around these days?'

'Why? Haven't you got any offers already?'

'Yes. I got several in the US. After I decided to come back, one or two Indian companies also contacted me.'

'Like?'

'Hindustan Lever and Infosys.'

'Great!'

'I am not sure whether it is great. What I am looking for is a job which will enable me to do cross-functional work as well as build on my subjects of specialization, accounts and management. I wonder whether I should go in for a big multinational. What about financial institutions? Infotech? Software?'

CV was silent for a minute. When he was thoughtful, his eyebrows knitted together and forehead creased with furrows.

'I think I see your point. However, first decide what line you're planning to get into. Banking? IT? Manufacturing companies? Heavy industry . . .? You have to take a decision. Given your background, I don't think you should go in for a specialized job but one which will use your skill more holistically. You could take up a smaller company to begin with. There are many now, particularly post liberalization. Some folded up quickly, but many have survived. In any case, Indian companies and their practices are not as advanced as in the West. Get a feel of the Indian corporate scene and then decide about shifting to a bigger concern. How about Bharat-UK Computers?'

'*Arey*, you even have a company ready? Does it belong to one of your numerous brothers-in-law?'

'No. They are looking for a Deputy Financial Adviser and you fit the bill perfectly.'

'So you know them.'

'No, I don't. I heard about it from one of their employees who is a good friend.'

CV's advice was always invaluable.

'Shall I put in a word with someone? The other day Varadachari was also asking about your plans. He is still with Reliance. He will grab you if you say yes,' Sundaram asked.

The Sundarams were obsessed with Rajan settling down. It was the duty of all parents to settle their children. It said so in Tamil literature and its virtues were extolled by one and all.

Rajan was not about to rise to the bait.

'Appa, I've told you I genuinely want to take a break for a few months before taking up a job. Please don't insist on jobs right away. If I need your help, I will ask you.'

Rajan was a bit of an idealist and Sundaram was only too well aware of this. He wished that his son were more practical.

'Rajan, sometimes I feel that you left behind your brain in the US. Nobody sits idle in India. This is not America. The job market is a jungle here and man eats man.'

'Appa, I realize that. But I am sure that even in India, with a CA and an MBA I should be able to get something easily.'

'You exasperate me. They are not sitting outside the house waiting for His Excellency to make up his mind.'

'Appa, take it easy. Six months is too short a period in one's lifetime to worry about.'

'Say that to the company managers,' snapped Sundaram. 'If they had been "taking off", there would have been no Tata or Birla.'

'You are getting unnecessarily worked up. My life is not going to be ruined just because I begin my career a few months later.'

'If you try a multinational or even some of our own Tatas and Birlas, you can settle down straightaway. It's not good to keep switching. What does CV say?'

'He agrees with me.'

'Rajan, remember that he can afford to agree with you since he has his own family company. You don't have one. You should aim to get the best available job. We are not a business family so don't use CV's yardsticks.'

'No, I'm not. It was actually my idea. Anyway, let me think about it. You will have to feed me in the meantime and keep me clothed.'

Sundaram was trying his best to control his anger.

'It's not as if India is full of jobs waiting for you,' Sundaram said sharply.

Rajan kept quiet not wishing to provoke Sundaram further.

'Have you spoken to Jayaraman?'

'Yes, I have. And he agrees with me as well. In fact, he has suggested a few options.'

The conversation was not taking a very happy turn. It seemed Rajan had spoken to everyone and he was still not seeing sense. Sundaram didn't want to start an argument. Neither did Rajan.

'Have a word with Rajaram. Even if your desire is to sit

twiddling your thumbs, you will at least get the government's point of view about which industry is doing well and which isn't.'

'I think that is a good idea,' agreed Rajan ignoring the sarcasm and grabbing at the opportunity of finally agreeing to something. 'But you must realize, Appa, that our government doesn't have a point of view.'

Sundaram was relieved. He had managed a temporary reprieve. He decided to have a word with Rajaram IAS and ask him to put the right ideas into Rajan's head.

Rajan met Rajaram IAS in his office at Fort St George in keeping with the serious nature of Rajan's visit. To meet Rajaram IAS at home would have meant interruptions from Balan the milkman, Peter Madhusudan the postman and a host of others. At Rajaram's office only the Honourable Minister could interrupt him.

Fort St George had seen better days. The British wouldn't have ruled over south India were it not for Fort St George lording over Madras. In fact, it marked the beginning of British rule over this part of the Coromandel coast. A series of stately red-stoned buildings came up around it on Sydenham Road and Poonamallee High Road, George Town and Park Town sprang up. Soon, the Ripon Building, Moore Market building, High Court, Town Hall, Central and Egmore Stations all came up, cold, imperial and impervious to the natives. While little hamlets and villages dotted the landscape, the Madrasis considered it a privilege to be colonized by the white Englishmen. But Fort St George now stood colonized by bureaucrats and politicians—natives closely resembling the British.

Everyone from the security guard to the peon to the private secretary was supremely courteous to Rajan. 'Saar has gone to the minister. Would you like to have Thums Up?

Fanta? Would you like some hot coffee? *Arey* Munuswamy, speak softly. Saar is here. Is the AC too cold?' The wait in the anteroom must have been barely ten minutes but it was enough for Rajaram IAS's staff to pay their respects to Rajan who, they were sure, would praise them to Rajaram IAS. Their backs seemed to be perpetually bent, thanks to generations of servitude to their masters, the English first and then the brown sahibs.

Rajan's chat with Rajaram IAS proved useful. Since he handled the industry portfolio in the Tamil Nadu State Government, Rajaram IAS knew all there was to know about TVS Suzuki, Sundaram Fasteners, SPIC, Satyam Computers and MRF. Rajan listened attentively and took notes. At least that's what he pretended to do while he doodled. He drew a palm tree and added a hut and a moon. Then he drew a series of squares and crossed each one out making a pattern. This could be used for tomorrow's *kolam*. Nothing like taking notes to please another's ego. Rajaram IAS was pleased—Rajan was a good, meticulous boy who took notes. Rajan converted the crossed-out squares into a house, a dark haunted house. He added a black crow and it was a masterpiece. It was a long time since he had doodled and Rajan was enjoying it.

So, where could one look for a dynamic growing company? Rajan realized that Rajaram IAS was talking to him. Tamil Nadu was the place now. Rajan nodded, trying to look suitably enlightened. Rajaram IAS, remembering Sundaram's request, exhorted Rajan to think seriously about joining a big multinational. All the top US companies were setting up shop in Tamil Nadu and this was the time to grab opportunities. Ford, Mitsubishi—sorry, that was Japanese—GM, they were all looking at Tamil Nadu. My father has briefed him well, Rajan thought. I should stick to poetry with him.

'This Rajan is an idiot. It's almost a month since he arrived and all he wants to do is eat and sleep. He thinks he has all the time in the world to settle down. If he procrastinates too long, the Tatas and Birlas will lose interest in him,' shouted Sundaram. He didn't have the guts to shout at Rajan. Not yet.

Big business for Sundaram meant the Tatas, Birlas and Ambanis. Multinationals also meant Tatas, Birlas and Ambanis, even though he was reminded that the Tatas, Birlas and Ambanis were homegrown products.

'Ena, take it easy. He will come around soon. You are getting unnecessarily upset,' Lakshmi consoled, trying to keep her voice calm.

'When? When will he come around? This is not a game—he should understand.'

'Don't worry. I will talk to him and find out what's on his mind. The astrologer also said that he would settle down in a very good job. And Rajan did take your advice and agree to meet Rajaram, didn't he?'

Sundaram calmed down a bit. Yes, Rajan had indeed gone to Rajaram IAS on his advice. He would soon find out what happened. Why couldn't Rajan have done an MBBS and become a doctor—that would have prevented a lot of headaches.

'Fine. Speak to him. He must realize the seriousness of the matter. This is not America. India is different. Even Madras is not the same as before. Jobs are disappearing even before you can bat an eyelid and he is talking some nonsense about learning in smaller companies, then middle companies and going on to bigger companies! He is not Bill Gates—companies are not waiting to grab him at fabulous salaries.'

'Bill Gates doesn't work for anyone,' reminded Lakshmi. 'Anyway, don't waste your anger. Talk to him calmly and he will see sense. Rajan is not a fool. He did his CA and articleship here so he is quite aware of the situation. Two years in the US doesn't make him a foreigner.'

'In the meantime, think about what we are going to say to the fathers of prospective brides when they ask what Rajan is doing. We can't say "he is taking a break". That is the surest way of certifying that our son is a good-for-nothing.'

On his way back from Rajaram IAS's office, Rajan chose to drive down South Beach Road, now known as Kamaraj Salai. The Marina Beach came into view on the left and it was magnificent. Golden sands merged into blue waters. The statues on the left—starting from George V on a handsome stallion to Kannagi the angry queen to Kamaraj himself—all had their backs to the beach, which was a pity. Not only did they not enjoy the majestic Marina skyline and the golden sands they actually destroyed the scenic beauty of Marina. But the tranquillity of the distant sea perforated at regular intervals by these dark sentinels assured Rajan that all was well with Chennai. Like the ceaseless waves lapping the sands monotonously, Chennai had a rhythm. Steady, regular, unhurried, uninterrupted. It was like Carnatic music. The patterns of the raga changed but the *talams* stayed the same.

The Sundarams were away when Rajan came in. He went up to his room and lay down staring at the ceiling. He tried to go over his conversation with Rajaram IAS but his eyes kept going to the wet patches on the ceiling where the water had seeped through the roof from an earlier rain. They formed patterns. Ganesha's trunk, a violin, an apple with a worm crawling out.

He could hear conversation downstairs so he went down expecting his folks to be back. It was Dominique leaving after borrowing a sachet of coffee. Rajan asked her to stay back and told her why he had been to Rajaram IAS's office.

'I think it was a set-up job planned out carefully and executed by Appa,' said Rajan. 'But it was interesting. Rajaram was like a lion in his lair. Half a dozen guys running around him like rabbits catering to his whims and fancies, ministers calling him every now and then . . . it was certainly impressive.'

'Rajan, I think there is some sense in what your father's

saying,' Dominique said, squatting on the parapet of the verandah and resting her chin on her right palm. 'You've got to grab opportunities! Don't keep sitting on your backside expecting opportunities to arise whenever you want them to.'

'Dom, has my father set you up also?'

'Rajan, stop being cynical. You're just being foolish. And stubborn.'

'I've spent my whole bloody life in Madras—I'm not green, you nut. I am well aware of what I am saying. Moreover, I had a chat with CV and he agreed with my . . .'

'It's all very well for him—he runs his father's business,' she interrupted.

'There you go again, you sound just like my father. Dom, you've spent far too much time with my parents.'

Dom gave up and walked away throwing a few invectives in his direction.

Dom put behind her the anxiety to push Rajan into finding a job and prepared to concentrate on reviving their friendship. Rajan was equally keen to hang out with his old friends. Theirs was a childhood friendship interrupted for two years. They realized soon enough that they could start where they had left off two years earlier. Dom was all excited about the new gym on Sterling Road and forced Rajan to become a member. They began to go to the gym together every other evening. They came back after a good workout, sweating and happy. Better stay in shape, at least till your marriage is fixed, Dom warned him.

These days Rajan had the freedom to get out of bed and then decide what to do. It was fun. His life lacked rhythm and he was enjoying it.

Rajan was surprised at how drastically his father's demeanour had changed over the last few days. There was hardly any conversation between father and son and Sundaram seemed snappy all the time—not at Rajan but at Lakshmi. He was moody and distracted. It was not the hospital—for Sundaram had the reputation of performing the most complicated and arduous operation and coming out smiling. It was Rajan's future. He was unhappy with Rajan and let everyone know it. Rajan's efforts to talk elicited only grunts. It wasn't strange that Sundaram and Rajan couldn't talk things over more like friends. In Tamil Nadu, father and son were not necessarily friends. The son respected his father, took his advice, exchanged views and maintained a distance. He almost never put his arms around him, patted him on the back or sat down to have a peg or two with him. It just wasn't done. They usually needed an effective interlocutor when it came to things of an intimate nature. The mother and wife was usually the buffer, on whom both relied, for emotional support and effective communication.

Word spread that Rajan was 'taking-off'.

'Taking off from what?' asked his sister Veena.

'Poor Rajan, he deserves a break,' said Sundaram's distantly related, seventy-five-year-old Uncle Gopal who was the first in the family to have studied in the US. With his walking stick barely holding him up, Gopal saw Rajan as a member of an exclusive club of two.

'Take off or not. Rajan should first get married and settle down. Everything else can come later,' said Paati quite categorically. 'If you procrastinate too long, people will seriously think that there is something wrong with him.'

'Like what?'

'AIDS for example. They may think that Rajan has come back with AIDS and all of us are trying to cover up.'

'Paati, how on earth do you know about all this AIDS nonsense?' Rajan demanded.

'Why? The papers are full of it.'

Lakshmi's friends felt sorry for her and told her as much.

'What's come over your Rajan, poor boy? I hope his health is okay. Maybe he didn't want to come back—did your husband force him to?'

Lakshmi was fed up.

STAR-STRUCK

When Lakshmi went to the Kapaleeshwarar Temple that evening, she had more than one thing to sort out with God.

The towering 120-foot *gopuram* stood at the centre of Mylapore, the Town of Peacocks, with four overcrowded, perpendicular roads girdling it. The *gopuram* rose up like a small mountain covered with stucco figures. Gods and demons jutted out of this man-made tower, painted in contemporary Tamil colours, a hideous combination of all possible shades. A large lily pool lay to the west of the temple, bone dry, and the steps led down to its moss-covered floor. Pedestrians and pavement hawkers fought for space on the four roads bringing everything that moved to a standstill.

Lakshmi asked her driver to park the car a kilometre away, and walked briskly to the temple. The tar road pricked her bare feet but her mind was elsewhere. On Rajan's marriage. On Rajan's job. On how to avoid the impending clash between father and son.

She did not forget to buy a small wicker basket overflowing with flowers, two coconuts, six betel leaves and two tablets of camphor. Then, wading through the Friday crowd, she entered the temple through the imposing front gate facing the east. The main deity Kapaleeshwarar, however, faced the smaller entrance in the west. Why this was so remained an unsolved mystery. The deity was traditionally supposed to face the east. But the devotees didn't seem to mind where the deity faced as long as the God solved their problems. Lakshmi stopped for a moment in silent prayer and went in past the 'Only Hindus allowed' sign put up by the temple management to keep away unwanted tourists, particularly foreign ones. She was soon engulfed by the Friday crowd. As she stood in front of the sanctum sanctorum of God Ganesha, the bare-bodied priest immediately recognized her and motioned to her to come into the special enclosure for VIPs. The Sundarams were a well-known 'God-fearing' family and visited the temple regularly. A pious family deserved good treatment. They also gave nothing less than a ten-rupee note when it was time for collection and blessings—this helped of course. The smell of camphor and stale oil wafted out of the sanctum sanctorum. The idol was barely visible. That didn't matter as long as the people outside were brightly lit and God could clearly see who had come to pay their respects. The priest went in to begin his prayers to Ganesha. Lakshmi knew the prayers and silently mouthed the words. Soon the bell rang out and the camphor was lit to reveal clearly the shining face of the idol. Shining, bright and black, the Elephant God appeared briefly as the fire from the camphor reflected off His face.

'Ganesha, everything should come to a successful conclusion,' she brought both her palms to her cheeks and tapped them in prayer. 'I'm starting my requests as always, with You.'

When the priest came around, she placed her customary ten-rupee note on the expectant plate.

'Saar doesn't seem to have come today,' the priest enquired.

'No. He has still not come back from the hospital.'

'Poor saar, he has so many things to do. Ganesha's blessings are always with him.'

After seeking Ganesha's blessings, Lakshmi walked around the temple. Her feet sank soothingly into the soft sand brought in from the beach to cover the path around the temple. She went around to the hall of granite pillars and touched with reverence the image of Hanuman carved out on one of the pillars, shining, white and covered, as the God was, with butter spread generously all over by the devotees. Some of the butter stuck to her fingers. She hesitated for a moment not quite sure whether she should lick it up as a blessing from Hanuman or wipe the stickiness away and incur the wrath of the Monkey God. She looked around, and seeing no one was watching her, did the latter.

Kapaleeshwarar's inner sanctum was usually thinly populated while there was always a huge crowd waiting to enter the sanctum of His wife, Karpagambal. Today was no different. Lakshmi backed into the hall of pillars, found a spot from where she could see the inner sanctum of both the gods, closed her eyes in prayer and folded both her palms in front of her. You have always looked after us and given us no cause for regret, she prayed. Now I come to You again. Rajan's happiness is in Your hands. Give him the good sense to choose what is right. Get him a good job and a good wife. After that, our duty will be over. Then, he will be completely in Your hands. Remembering that even now Rajan was completely in His hands, she quickly added: even now he is entirely in Your hands. So help us.

Just then the bells rang out loudly from one of the inner sanctums and Lakshmi took it as divine consent to her wishes. Instinctively, she brought her palms together in prayer. Thank you, God!

'Saar hasn't come today?' someone cut in and broke her reverie.

Lakshmi looked up startled. It was Ganeshan—not the God but the man.

'No. He was held up at the office.'

Ganeshan was Sundaram's schoolmate and a certified chatterbox. Lakshmi looked desperately for a way to beat a dignified retreat.

'How is Sundaram? I hear Rajan is back. How is he? Did

he like America? You must now be looking for a good girl for him. Or have you already decided on one? In fact, I have some horoscopes that I would like to suggest. They are all from very good God-fearing families. I must come one of these days and hand them to you. I have also asked the girls' families to write to you directly.' He said it all in one breath and running out of oxygen, he had to pause.

Realizing that she would not get another opportunity, Lakshmi cried, 'Come anytime. I'm sure my husband and Rajan would look forward to meeting you. But pardon me now, I have to join the queue to see Karpagambal, otherwise the queue will just get longer.'

Lakshmi hurried away putting as much distance as she could between her and Ganeshan. She took one look at the queue, which stretched right till the peacock's cage, and decided against joining it. She needed to get home. Her prayers had in any case been answered.

There was great excitement at Sabarmati. At least two horoscopes had matched, one of them very well indeed. Chandramouli's computers had confirmed compatibility and he had left after triumphantly pronouncing his verdict. Chartered Accountant Sethuraman's daughter Gayathri's horoscope had matched best of all—87 per cent compatibility.

'I had this feeling all the time that Gayathri's horoscope would match well with Rajan's,' Lakshmi told Sundaram, sounding relieved. She peered once more at the calculations worked out by Chandramouli. 'The family suits us best. And she herself is very talented, I believe.'

Sitting on the floor in the middle of the drawing room, Sundaram and Lakshmi took turns to look at the astrologer's calculations and observations.

'What is she doing now?' Sundaram asked.

'I don't know. Now that the horoscopes have matched, we can ask a few people and get to know more about her.'

'Don't we need to cross-check with another astrologer? You know, with all these fancy computers, I'm not quite sure about the results. Computerized calculations confuse me. It doesn't seem right to first talk to the girl's parents and then discover that the horoscopes don't match.'

'No, no. I don't think that will happen,' Lakshmi added with alacrity. 'We've known Chandramouli for such a long time. I don't know why you're so suspicious about computers— you use the latest computerized equipment in your hospital labs and I don't think more patients are dying there.'

Sundaram didn't think it was funny and answered her seriously. 'That maybe true. But astrology needs intuition and that is one thing a computer can never provide.'

Lakshmi was not about to give up now. She had been eyeing Gayathri for some time and did not want Sundaram ruining a good match. 'Don't get so worked up. Even intuition fails sometimes.'

Sundaram did not look too convinced. He looked up briefly and found her pleading eyes.

'Okay, fine. I am willing to take Chandramouli's analysis at face value. But how are we going to bring Rajan around? First, he must agree to get married. I have had enough of his "taking off". It's time he decided about his future.'

'I'm sure once we have a serious talk with him, he will see reason. For all you know he may be perfectly amenable to the idea.'

'Perhaps. But if I know him, he is going to be perfectly pig-headed about it. I hope the US has mellowed him a little. Further, he should agree to sitting through a "girl-seeing" ceremony at Sethuraman's house. We should follow custom, even if it may not be to his liking.'

'First let him get used to the idea of getting married. Then we can talk about "girl-seeing", Lakshmi cautioned.

Lakshmi was mandated to broach the topic with Rajan. A

visibly relieved Lakshmi went into the bedroom to put away the calculations.

There was someone banging on the gate outside. 'Saar, Saar . . . Iyeray.' Sabarmati woke up with alacrity. It was past 11.30 at night. Sundaram put on the lights, took the keys and walked towards the gate. It was ekadasi, and with the new moon, he could barely see the outline of a figure in the dark. Getting closer, he saw a thin frame waving his right hand. The outline of a cycle rickshaw loomed behind.

'Who are you?' Sundaram demanded. Rajan had followed him close behind.

'Saar, this man was found drunk on the pavement. Your address was found in his pocket, so I brought him here.'

'It's Paramesh Uncle.' Sundaram seemed to have no doubt. He quickly opened the gate and went out. It was indeed his Parameshwaran Uncle, slumped at an angle on the rickshaw seat, drunk and dead to the world. Sundaram and Rajan rushed to pick him up and carry him inside.

'Thank you pa! He is my uncle. Here, take this.' Sundaram gave him a hundred-rupee note.

'Saar, I have brought him from Adayar,' the man with the rickshaw mumbled. 'A little more . . .'

Sundaram dug out a fifty and the rickshaw man blessed him, his family and the generations to come. They managed to dump Parameshwaran in the guest room bed, where he lay undisturbed in drunken slumber.

Parameshwaran was Paati's younger brother, younger by more than eight years. He was still pretty old. But he was a die-hard Communist—qualification enough to remain young, wear a Badge of Youth.

Parameshwaran was Paramesh for short, now Paramesh thatha—Paramesh grandfather—to one and all. He was in his teens in the forties when, as a youth member of the Communist Party of India, he was one of the many who took to the streets after the Quit India call—to fight the British, or so they thought, till they realized that all they were doing was fighting against their own kith and kin. In those troubled times, when the restless mobs could barely spot a white man, Paramesh not only managed to spot a Britisher, but knocked off his hat and a little bit of his head as well. He became an instant hero. A Communist hero. A rarity in the sea of Congress heroes and Muslim League heroes. He was arrested and locked up in the Andamans Cellular Jail. He wasn't tried. The Communist Party made him their mascot and a member of their inner circle. Paramesh the ideologue had arrived. There would be no compromises on principles. We want an egalitarian India and Communism is the only way.

When the Communists tasted power for the first time in Kerala, the party leaders started having second thoughts about their chief ideologue. To stay in power was not easy. Compromises had to be made. Paramesh the ideologue hated compromises. He was in the way.

Paramesh never made it to the politburo. He left the Party. He didn't need them. The Party didn't need him either. However, his friends remained friends even when they crossed over to other bourgeois parties later on. He was a singularly erudite and delightful personality after all. He also had a constant supply of whisky. Some of the younger Commies in his house who were influenced by him had later joined some of the so-called Tamil Dravidian parties. We will win the war against the Aryan Brahmins and bring about a social revolution, they chanted. Paramesh wholeheartedly agreed with them but differed with their methods. You people will sleep with anyone to achieve your ends, he thought.

'What have the imperialists taught you?' was the first question he asked when Rajan had visited him soon after his arrival.

'For one, they have taught me to ignore questions from the proletariat, to begin with,' he replied.

'Touché, my boy, touché.' The old man's frail body wracked with laughter.

Paramesh thatha was a solitary man in the large house. He had a gardener as old as himself to stay after nightfall. Who gave security to whom, people wondered. He had fallen in love thrice but had never managed to get married. He remained a bachelor till loneliness overpowered him and he started drinking heavily. He boasted how he could, like the Russians, down drink after drink and still go about his business. What business he went about nobody knew or remembered. His body had called it a day, but his drinking continued. He was not indiscriminate. He only drank Black Label or Chivas Regal. Apart from liquor, his only major weakness now was his readiness to take up causes—vital socio-economic causes, as he referred to them. His current passion was dowry and its evils. He was not only willing to lend his name to NGOs but was willing to contribute as well.

His old house stood stately and run down on D'Silva Road. Mylapore Club, Alwarpet corner, Isabella Hospital and the Alwarpet pharmacies were all a five-minute walk away.

'What do the capitalists have to say?' He would have said 'capitalist pigs' in the old days.

'They say that the last Communist is going to be an Indian. I told them I already know it is Parameshwaran.'

'Rajan, believe me. There is a social revolution coming. South India started the process several decades back and is succeeding. The north has a lot of catching up to do and is trying to compress history into a shorter and shorter time frame. It won't work. The moment literacy increases, you will find a mini Kerala everywhere. A silent revolution. You, who have come back with such high qualifications, cannot afford to ignore the realities of rural India. Don't be an elitist like everyone else. Look around, be alive. You will never regret it.'

When Paramesh recovered from his drunken slumber the next day, he went home. He had no apologies. No excuses. Only thanks. That's how he lived. Without compromises. Sundaram and the others took care not to inform Paati about his bouts of drunken stupor. That was Paramesh thatha's only request. He was worried what his elder sister would say.

The one thing Lakshmi didn't tell Sundaram was that Gayathri's horoscope contained a flaw. There was a *dosham* in the horoscope. When coupled with Rajan's, there was a threat to the bridegroom's health. This was a *dosham* that would have made people less determined than Lakshmi hesitate to proceed further. But not Lakshmi. She was a bit too keen on Gayathri to let a flaw come in the way. Chandramouli, aware of this, had assured her that the flaw could be overcome with a special pooja and *homam*. Lakshmi was relieved. It was just a minor *dosham*. The more Lakshmi thought about it, the more minor it became. She set out to 'manage' Rajan.

Rajan became a sought-after 'consultant' whether he liked it or not. All those aspiring to go to the US for higher studies came to him for advice. Friends and acquaintances of Sundaram, Lakshmi, Veena and Jayaraman wanted to bring their sons and daughters, nieces and nephews, grandsons and granddaughters to talk to Rajan before or after applying to American universities.

'I am bringing my niece Sonia tomorrow. She's here from Delhi and has come to say goodbye. She's got admission into a university in California. Will you give her some tips before she leaves?' asked Daulat Singh Sondhi, their neighbour.

Sonia was all wide-eyed and excited about going to the States. She rattled off all she knew about LA, NYC, UCLA, UPenn, NBC and other abbreviations Rajan didn't get, and she even had a slight accent. Most importantly she had managed to get a US visa. Getting admission was not the issue; getting a visa was. Hordes of visa-seeking students came back shattered after they were rejected by the US consulate.

'She was actually rejected the first time,' Daulat said, getting worked up. 'The lady at the counter—Indian, that too—did not even look at the application form or the supporting documents. Unmarried! You will never come back, she had said rudely, the bitch! How can she behave like that with another Indian! Sitting at the US Embassy, they suddenly become Americans! Anyway, after this, we approached the Minister of External Affairs and several prominent businessmen for recommendations. At least the second time, they weren't rude. They still asked her for several documents and they gave her the visa after three or four days' wait.'

Female, Sikh, unmarried and with admission into the Master's programme in Advertising. Rajan told her that she was indeed lucky. He would have rejected her if she had come to him for a visa. In Chennai, everybody seemed to be sending their kids to the US. For a better future, they said. They took loans, mortgaged their lands, borrowed from kith and kin, or just got rid of their black money. A few lakhs a year was not a small amount, even for the affluent. Not the least for the Chennai-Brahmins-of-limited-needs, for whom stitching a suit was extravagance. To spend a few lakhs a year was criminal. But spend they did—for a better future for their children in the United States of America.

Rajan had seen it coming and had decided to be patient when Lakshmi broached the topic. He gave her a fair hearing. He was not averse to the idea at all but gave the appearance of being uninterested lest people started thinking that he was eager to get married. Give me a few months and I will be ready, was all he said. After all, I can hardly settle down with a wife without a salary.

Lakshmi was surprised at Rajan's feeble resistance. She had expected him to put up some fight, not realizing that Rajan had come to the conclusion long ago that if he was not capable of finding a mate by himself, he would let his parents find him one. In sheer relief at Rajan's acquiescence, Lakshmi promptly agreed that finding a job was priority right now. Not yet, Rajan added. After I take off for a while. But shouldn't we start considering some horoscopes, asked Lakshmi. Rajan wasn't sure. Emboldened by his hesitation, Lakshmi casually mentioned Sethuraman's daughter. Rajan almost missed it. Sethuraman what? Chartered Accountant? He has a daughter? And you have already compared horoscopes? You guys are crazy.

No, Rajan. If you are sure of getting married in a few months, then you should start seeing some girls. Good girls don't drop out of the sky. Madras has changed from the time when we knew many well-established and well-known families. We are out of touch with most of them now and we hardly have any information about the sort of girls one is considering. The other day, Venugopal's grandson got engaged to the great Chidambaram's granddaughter but it had to be called off when the girl confessed that she was already living with an American who was doing a Ph.D at the same university. One just cannot take things for granted these days. It would be silly to let go of some good horoscopes from respectable families that happen to come our way.

Winter in Chennai had turned to summer without so much as a notice. In fact, Chennai winter had always been autumn, winter, spring all rolled into one. It was March and the temperature was touching 35 degrees Celsius. The elongated, blue, shell-shaped December Flowers were long gone. The *pongal* festival and the cricket matches at Chepauk were over. The singers who went around singing hymns in praise of Lord Krishna in the early hours of the month of *margazhi* had long disappeared. They were replaced by cobblers, paperwalas, vegetable and fruit vendors and the ironing man who went about singing hymns in praise of their wares and looking for the first customer of the day.

It was the season of sweat. The Chennai*vasis* woke up to a hot morning and sweated right through the day to a hot evening. When the sea breeze used to come in from the east around 3 p.m., Madras used to cool down. These days the sea breeze set in dutifully at 3 p.m. but all it brought with it was hot air from the shore. Concrete and pollution had made Chennai summers worse.

Sweat was the great leveller and helped create an egalitarian Tamil society. The Chennai business tycoon, the cycle repairman and the bureaucrat drank the same coconut water or bottle of Pepsi to quench their thirst. Whether it was a safari suit or a sleeveless banian, the sweaty bodies emanated the same body odour. And when they went back home, they were all exhausted from the same heat and humidity. Since electricity was erratic, fans and air conditioners stood like silent relics of a bygone era. The Chennai*vasis* became irritable. Tempers were high till 3 p.m. and went down as the mercury dropped in the evening. Anna Salai was packed with cars as drivers forgot the rules of the road. Festive banners with plantain leaves lay crumpled and dried up in the heat. It was the season for the crows to build nests and beget smaller crows. The Chennai Brahmins fed them rice on religious occasions.

According to the Hindu Marriage Clock, the no-marriage season was also long over.

No girls could be seen between 15 December and 15 January. That was the time for God Krishna to see his divine lover, Aandal. No girls could be seen between 15 July and 15 August. And if one did manage to see a girl at all, no marriage was permitted between 15 September and 15 October. All because of the Hindu Marriage Clock.

It was March and Lakshmi realized the urgency. She had to get moving on Gayathri. Otherwise, they would run into April, May and, before one knew it, it would be September.

'Dom, you should talk to my mother and try to convince her to see my point of view,' Rajan pleaded. 'I just can't afford to take on an added responsibility now. I must concentrate on getting things sorted out before I think of anyone else. As it is, I am being bullied by all and sundry about a job.'

Dominique lent a patient ear, sitting across him in his room. Rajan put his feet up on the study table and she stretched hers out on the bed. She was used to Rajan's monologues. He wasn't afraid to share his thoughts with her since she was not only the sole person in Clive Avenue his age but she communicated easily with his parents as well. Rajan also knew that Dominique knew when to keep her mouth shut.

'I just need some time for myself now, Dom. What's the hurry? Chartered Accountant's daughter! I'm just not in the frame of mind to sit through a girl-seeing ceremony in some Chartered Accountant's home. And those days are over when the girl used to deck herself with flowers, bring *sojji-bajji* on a tray and sing in front of everyone. Why can't these people move on?' He paused, looking out of his room at the terrace outside and the terrace of the house beyond. 'I need a bit of time. I'm not saying no.'

There was the familiar stillness of siesta. The only noise came from a solitary crow sitting across the road on a telephone line.

'You don't by chance have someone in mind, do you?' Dominique asked suddenly.

Rajan looked sharply at Dominique. His eyes met hers. He looked hard and searched her eyes. She wasn't being frivolous. She had asked in all seriousness.

'Why do you ask?'

'Your parents wanted to know.'

He was startled by her frankness.

'Thanks for telling me,' he smiled. 'The answer is no. If you had asked me the same question last year the answer would have been different. It's all over now. I have no one in mind.'

There was a silence again. Then another crow came, sat

nearer the windowsill and crowed as though a piece of chicken had caught in its throat. Dominique looked down at the square pattern of the mosaic floor and waited for Rajan to say more if he wanted to.

Rajan looked out of the window. It had happened just a year ago but now it seemed like a distant dream. A rush of blood and youth had thrown them together and they had fallen in love straightaway. Two alien souls from two different cultures, a Mexican and an Indian, both in the US for the first time.

'It's strange when I think of it now, sitting here many thousand miles away. In fact, I was involved with a Mexican the year before last, the year I joined the course. I think we were literally thrown into each other's arms by the American set-up, the atmosphere, the life—everything about the US was so new. She was exciting, quite different from anyone I had ever met. I had never felt anything like this before and before I knew it, I got carried away.' Rajan smiled silently at these bottled up memories. 'It lasted all of four months. We even lived together for a month. It was just as well that we realized quickly enough that we were too different, culturally, mentally, our backgrounds and even our attitudes to life. It was just physical attraction I guess. Both of us seemed exotic to the other. Anyway, we parted, fortunately, as friends. Now she's just a good memory. It seems so long ago, my past.'

He could feel her beside him. That light perfume and the warm body. Her hands were soft. Like the rest of the body. It surprised him that a woman so strong could be so soft. Her brown eyes were full of questions. The first time they met, he remembered her choking over a cigarette. She had just started smoking—to throw away the yoke of Mexican society. And he, to discard the yoke of a Brahminical upbringing. They began on a voyage of discovery together, not knowing where it would end. She made heads turn when she walked into class. Rajan watched her with quiet pride. He could never quite fathom what she saw in him but he knew he was different from the rest. They broke up just as easily as they had moved in together. It was not as if they wanted to leave each other. They just couldn't carry on. It just wouldn't have worked.

Dominique looked up. There was sadness in his eyes. Rajan was one of those people who could mask his emotions very well and she realized that he had not bothered to do so now.

'You loved her, didn't you?'

'Yes, I did.'

'I'm sorry, Rajan. I'm so sorry.'

Their eyes met.

'Believe me, Dom, she is just a name now. I've changed as well, don't forget. Even if I had had the slightest doubt about what I feel for her I would have told you. And I have the balls to tell my parents about it if she mattered. But she doesn't. My past is my past. Over and done with.'

'I understand. You don't have to convince me, Rajan. I know you better than you think I know you.' She smiled. Rajan smiled back.

'I knew you would understand.'

Dom came over and sat beside him. She put her arms around his shoulder. They sat silent, Rajan lost in thought. She bent over and kissed him on the right cheek. His day-old stubble tickled her lips. She could smell him, his aftershave and sweat.

Rajan turned around to face her, he put his arms around her and their bodies pressed against each other for a brief moment as he hugged her tight. He kissed her on her forehead.

'Thanks, Dom. I don't know what I would do without you.'

They let go of each other.

'You haven't asked me her name,' Rajan smiled.

'Should I?'

'Arantxa.'

'Arantxa Rajan . . . hmmm . . . not a bad combination.'

They laughed.

'You know, if you hadn't told me about this, I wouldn't have believed you. Strangely, my Christian upbringing has been as conservative as your Brahmin one and I still have no idea what sleeping together is like. Funny, isn't it?'

'What about your fiancé? You must have spent time alone together,' asked Rajan.

'Oh, him! Actually, we haven't gone much beyond petting! Sounds old-fashioned, doesn't it?'

'Not just old-fashioned, it sounds improbable.'

'You know something Rajan, my mom and dad met hardly for an hour before they said "yes". Something like your girl-seeing ceremony!' She paused. 'What about the plans your parents have for you? You should start giving some thought to that now,' Dominique persisted. She had been entrusted with a task and she had come to perform it.

'I'm not saying no. In fact, I never said no. I just want a bit of time to get a decent job before I get hooked to someone. I think that is reasonable. Moreover, I don't have a clue about what I should expect from a future wife. What qualities she should have. What qualifications. Doctor? Housewife? Teacher? Businesswoman? I have no clue. I just haven't thought about these things.'

'Then start thinking about them. Your parents want you to see Sethuraman's girl soon and preferably approve. I don't know what sort of girl you will finally choose for a companion, but your parents certainly seem to think very highly of her. Whether she approves of you is an entirely different matter.'

'I leave it to you to put forward my views to my parents. Dom, for once in your life, act as my agent and convince my father. I will be eternally grateful to you.'

'You are giving me a task that's impossible, Rajan,' she giggled. 'Okay, I'll try. I will convey this to your parents. But I have a proposition. I will informally check out Sethuraman's daughter, Gayathri. If she is okay, I will tell you. You must then promise to go through the girl-seeing ceremony without making a fuss.'

'Girl-seeing ceremony? What a lot of crap! These traditions are anachronisms now. It's silly the way we try to cling to them.'

'Rajan, these are not traditions but symbols of tradition. There's no point in trying to change them, however silly they may seem. In the long run these symbols don't matter and they will change with time. They are not even important enough to fight against. What should worry you is that true and genuine traditions are being broken down without any to take their place. This is as much true in India as it is in France. I sometimes worry when I see guys like you trying to be pseudo-rebels. Be rebels with substance. There are so many substantive things to fight against and all you can think of is abolishing the girl-seeing ceremony.'

'My dear grandmother, let's think about the girl-seeing ceremony later. First, I need some space. What I need is—'

'So you want me to check out the girl.'

'I am now convinced that you are far more keen about my marriage than my parents are.'

'I take that as yes. Thanks for your kind permission. Frankly all you men want is just 38-26-38.'

'And here, while you're at it, you might as well take this measuring tape.'

THE MATCH

There was always a crowd in front of house No. 7, a red and dark grey house that lay just across Daulat Singh's. It belonged to the famous actor Selvan.

It hadn't always attracted so much attention. Its original owner had been Krishnakumar, a businessman, who had built it after having consulted some of the best architects of Madras, and he had nurtured it for more than a decade. But its relationship with Krishnakumar ended rather abruptly when his company folded up and he had to file for bankruptcy. A rich Telugu Brahmin with extensive farms and landholdings in Andhra struck a deal and No. 7 soon became a guest house. Telugu guests flitted in and out of Clive Avenue for almost a decade. The house was mostly used to break journey on the way to and back from Lord Venkateshwara's temple at Tirupati. Some came to visit the Marina Beach, wet their feet in the Bay of Bengal, eat hot peanuts and *murukku* wrapped in old newspaper and litter the beach. A few foreigners were also seen at No. 7 who were later spotted trying to keep the beggars away at Santhome Church and Kapaleeshwarar Temple. And so it continued for another decade until there was news that the old Telugu Brahmin had died. Selvan, the up-and-coming film star, looking, what some said, to spend his black money, bought No. 7 without batting an eyelid. And he christened it Moonlight.

To have a film star in the neighbourhood was not always a blessing. In fact, it was not a blessing at all. Hordes of starry-eyed Tamils came at all times of the day 'to see our Selvan's house', a sort of pilgrimage. Initially, tourists coaxed reluctant tourist bus drivers to take them through Clive Avenue. 'Please, you don't even have to stop. We will see the house from the outside. We have come all the way from Thanjavur to see it.' The bus drivers demurred since there was no place near Clive Avenue to park vehicles or even make a U-turn. It was a nuisance. Not that they had anything against Thanjavurians. Clive Avenue was just too narrow a cul-de-sac.

The tourists won in the end. The agencies saw a good opportunity to make some easy money and added another twenty-five rupees to the tour charges to stop briefly at Clive Avenue. If you are lucky you can even see Selvan driving out, they said and the tourists hoped they would catch a glimpse some time. But all they saw was the guard with an old rifle standing outside and a gardener moving about inside tending the sprawling lawns. Selvan was rarely in. He owned several houses and No. 7 Clive Avenue was not his favourite.

Stopping in front of Selvan's house was good for the tourist agencies and good for some tourists as well. They took this opportunity to urinate against a wall, relieving themselves.

It was on one of these occasions that Devanathan, the income tax officer, parked his scooter and walked past a row of Selvan admirers making watery patterns on Daulat Singh's compound wall. He waded through the crowd of tourists towards Sundaram's residence. After that, he was seen entering the house of Rajaram IAS. Then he visited a couple of other houses on Clive Avenue and on the adjacent road.

Income Tax Officer Devanathan may have been an innocuous-looking man, pot-bellied, short and clad in dark trousers and a white shirt barely covering his belly-button, but wherever he went he was given a cup of hot coffee and an envelope containing some crisp cash. He didn't care much for the coffee but drank it anyway. The residents of Clive Avenue and the adjacent areas cursed him, not on his face but under their breath, whenever they saw him. Like clockwork, at the beginning of each month.

For several years now he had been a familiar figure. A regular. Like Balan the Milk Man, Peter Madhusudan the Post Man and Murugan the Cobbler.

This time too, not many noticed him going about his monthly ritual and it would have remained that way had it not been for a team of three officials waiting patiently at the corner of the adjacent road. In mufti. As Devanathan drove out in his scooter carrying the loot, they stopped him, searched his personal belongings and arrested him for carrying on his person envelopes of money that he couldn't explain.

It was not easy to plan for a 'girl-seeing' ceremony. Every detail had to be planned carefully. Who in the house should greet the guests first. What should be served to eat. Where the guests should be seated. What time the girl should come out to greet the guests. Where the girl should sit so that she is not too close to the boy. When should both sets of parents move away discreetly to give the boy and girl time to talk. How much time they should be given alone before they could be interrupted. All the thinking and planning had to be done by the girl's family. All that the boy's family had to do was wear good clothes and appear at the girl's residence.

Sundaram wore his silk *veshti* and silk *jibba*. Lakshmi wore her best Kancheepuram silk saree with a handsome rust and zari border. Rajan wore grey trousers and a long-sleeved white shirt with blue pin stripes. Paati was not accompanying them though she looked as nervous as the rest.

'Rajan, talk softly and don't scare her with your ideas,' Paati warned, calling him to her room. 'Behave yourself. Remember, she will be as apprehensive as you are.'

'Don't worry, Paati. If she does not startle me with her ideas, I will be happy.'

'Stop being flippant,' she admonished. 'You should make a good impression not only on her but on her parents as well. They will be watching you very closely and making careful note of what you have to say.'

'It's about time someone took careful note of what I have to say. Anyway, I already feel like a lamb getting ready for slaughter.'

'Exactly, that's how you should feel. Be sober and careful of what you say. I hear Gayathri is a fine girl, so don't waste this opportunity by being flippant. Remember, good girls from good families are hard to come by. If you go and blabber something there, the girl is going to refuse you. And remember, it is very disheartening for a girl to be seen and rejected.'

'On that, I completely agree with you, Paati. For once you are actually making sense.'

'If you agree with me, then you should logically have no option but to say yes to her,' Paati laughed. Rajan noted that Paati's logic was sound.

Dominique had checked an hour earlier with Lakshmi whether everything was going according to schedule. It was. Rajan has been quiet. He had, however, refused his father's suggestion to wear a traditional *veshti* and had opted for a pair of grey trousers instead. That was not a heavy price to pay and Sundaram had readily agreed to buy peace. It wasn't *Rahukalam*, nor *Yamagandam*. The Hindu Bad-Time Clock had okayed the time of the girl-seeing ceremony.

Sethuraman's house was old-fashioned but big and cosy. A banyan tree occupied a corner of the lawn spreading its cobra hood all over. The boy's side was welcomed by Sethuraman and his wife and taken into the drawing room. Gayathri, escorted by her aunt, joined them a few minutes later. The girl-seeing ceremony had begun.

Rajan found himself sitting diagonally opposite Gayathri. She was good-looking and had a pleasant countenance, he noted. He didn't want to stare and tried his best not to look in her direction. He hardly heard what the others were saying. Why can't all of you shut up and leave us alone? I have several things I want to ask her and I'm sure she has several questions for me herself, he thought. The conversation around him went on. He answered a few questions that Gayathri's father asked him. Rajan's mother in turn asked Gayathri a few inane questions which she answered with the right amount of respect. A round of fried *bajji* and *mysore pak* made their appearance. Rajan hated oily *bajjis* but knew that if he refused they would fuss over him and there would be a scene. He put two on his plate and glared at them wishing they would disappear. Hot filtered coffee was brought in and served in steel tumblers. Rajan was fast losing patience. Why can't you guys disappear?

And suddenly, people started drifting out and he realized that he was sitting alone facing Gayathri. He looked at her and realized that she was waiting for him to take the initiative. He had had several questions for her. Now, he wasn't sure where to begin.

'Well, I'm not quite sure what I should be asking you. It's so strange that without as much as an introduction I must start asking you all sorts of personal questions.'

Gayathri smiled. She did have a lovely smile.

'I know. I agree. These ceremonies are silly.' He heard her voice clearly for the first time, and it sounded even and measured.

'You agree? Anyway, parents always seem to win in the end,' he chuckled. Both laughed nervously and there was a brief pause. Her nails were trimmed and had a light nail polish on them. It was not the bright red his sister was partial to.

'Gayathri, I don't want to push you in any way. I am just curious to know why you have decided to get married now. I hope your parents are not forcing you.'

She smiled again. It was such a sweet smile. Her lips were well proportioned. For a moment he stared at her lips and then quickly looked away.

'In a way, yes,' she answered, her smile disappearing. 'My parents were very keen that I meet you since they felt that boys from good families were hard to come by and that I should not let this opportunity go. Your credentials were obviously impressive and our horoscopes matched and they talked me into seeing you. In fact, you are the first person I am meeting in this fashion.' She was frank.

'Really! Strange you should say that. My parents sold me the same story and you are my first as well. Actually, I had told my parents that I wanted to take off for a few months before settling down but my parents had their own ideas and so here I am!'

The ice was broken and they started talking. They talked about why they didn't want to get married now. Then they exchanged notes on each other. How he hated Science and took Commerce instead and how she hated Commerce and took Science. How he liked poetry and she didn't and she music and art and he didn't. She was crazy about art and had arty friends. His friends couldn't differentiate a painting from a sculpture. How he was short-tempered and she wasn't. Both loved reading. Both enjoyed watching *One Flew over the Cuckoo's Nest*. Yes, Jack Nicholson deserved the Oscar. By the time they discovered shared interests, the others came back into the room. Timeout.

'Did you like her?' was the question everybody had for him. Sundaram, Lakshmi, Veena, Paati, Dominique, Rajaram IAS. Did Rajan 'agree' to Gayathri? Rajan merely shrugged. She was good-looking. She was slim but not thin. She had a nice smile, spoke pleasantly, directly, and seemed to know her mind. She could sing and had done well in her studies. Rajan liked her. But was she the person he was willing to spend the rest of his life with? He hadn't a clue. How was one to judge a person after just a brief conversation over a plate of *bajji* and a tumbler of coffee? He wanted to meet Gayathri again, alone, before taking any decision.

No, Rajan, it's not possible or proper, Lakshmi ruled it out. Now that you have seen her and talked to her, you must decide. In any case, one cannot go on endlessly like this. Don't ask for another meeting. That would be embarrassing, most of all for Gayathri. But this meeting was hardly enough to decide on a life partner, he protested. No, you can go out alone with her only after you decide. But then, if I said no, I wouldn't have to go out with her in any case. If I said yes, I could go out with her later whenever I want to. That doesn't help. It's now that I want to meet her—before deciding. No, Rajan. Your father and I barely spoke to each other before our parents decided to marry us off. We've got along pretty well all these years. Don't you remember? I met Jayaraman only once over *sojji* and *bajji* like you, added Rajan's sister Veena. I think that the half hour we had to talk to each other was quite sufficient to gauge each other. And it's not as if you don't know anything about her. You've heard others telling us what she's like. They have all been uniformly complimentary. You have enough inputs to take a decision, Rajan. Veena was serious and when she was serious she was convincing.

Rajan mulled over it that evening. Well, what the hell. He had seen her and knew a bit about her. He could probably get to know her a bit more over another round of talks but not substantially more. In any case, all these things were a shot in the dark. Gayathri didn't seem a bad choice. Maybe she was low on sense of humour but then there was no time to discover that. Even though she had completed her Master's in Physics a few months earlier, she was not doing anything in particular. But then neither was he. He could hardly crib. He agonized over the whole thing again. And again. Dominique did mention earlier that Gayathri's reputation was good. And that people liked her. Rajan, take the plunge, he told himself. You don't have anyone in mind and she seems okay. But was she really okay? Should he see a few more girls before deciding?

'What's your problem?' asked Dominique exasperated.

'Don't you think I should see a few more girls before I decide?' Rajan asked.

'See more girls? Just the other day you dubbed all girl-seeing ceremonies as crap! Now you seem to be enjoying it. In my opinion, Gayathri seems fine.'

Paati had heard about Rajan's dilemma. Late evening, after dinner, when the house was relatively quiet, she called Rajan to her room. He sat at the foot of her bed and started gently massaging her legs. One was frail and the other fat with arthritis. As a school-going child, Rajan used to sit at her bedside every night, place a book on his lap and massage her legs while he read. This had been a daily ritual till Rajan joined college. Then it became weekly. When he went to the US it stopped. It was quiet, save for the whirring of the ceiling fan above.

'Rajan, I know marriage is not a joke,' said Paati, coming straight to the point as usual. 'I agree that by meeting a girl and talking to her at length, one tends to learn a whole lot and that it's useful to know the girl well beforehand. But to get to know the girl well is not all. Many a time it happens differently, and believe me most couples are none the worse for it.

'I must tell you something interesting,' Paati went on. 'Your grandfather . . . well, he almost didn't become my husband! Since my childhood, I had grown up with my brothers and my father's cousin's son Vishwanathan, who was three years older than me. You know how it was in those days, as soon as I was born, they had decided that I was going to be married off to Vishwanathan, Vichu as he was called. I don't know whether you remember him—a lively, intelligent and friendly chap, who died about ten years ago. And so the die was cast as soon as I was born. Vichu and I didn't know then, but the whole of Madras knew that we were booked for each other! Vichu and I were the best of friends and spent much of our childhood together blissfully unaware of our impending marriage. When I turned fourteen, they started looking at auspicious dates for the wedding. It was a strange feeling. One day we were friends and the next day we were told that we were to be married to each other. Then out of the blue came your grandfather. He was about twenty-three then, a doctor, and had just returned from London armed with his degree. He went straight to my father and asked for my hand! Just like that! He told my father that he had seen me several times and had fallen in love with me. The gall he had! He also assured my father that he had come to India for good and had no intention of going back to Britain. The Independence movement was gathering storm and he said that he was going to stay put in India and work for her people—just as you are telling all of us that you have come back to India for good. But that was not the issue. A boy approaching the girl's father directly for her hand was unheard of then. It created quite a stir in the house as you can imagine. My parents had never heard of anything like this before. My mother was not amused and felt that your grandfather had acted impertinently and his confidence bordered on arrogance, but my father was surprisingly quite nice and understanding about it. He thought about the matter for a full day and made some discreet enquiries about the family. He spoke to the boy's father who supported his son's choice even while they were apologetic about the directness of your grandfather's approach. Then my father came over and asked me for my opinion. I had seen your grandfather come in and had observed him through the railings in the staircase while he was talking to my father. I bet he knew I was there but his back was to me. When my father asked me for my opinion, I don't know what came over me, but I said "yes" to this perfect stranger. Well . . . that was that. That's how I ended up getting married to the wrong man! Vichu's parents never spoke to my parents again even though Vichu and I remained good friends till the very end.

'Well . . . that's an old story,' laughed Paati coarsely, the memories still seeming to hurt a little. 'Even though I married your grandfather without having spoken a word to him before marriage, our marriage went off well. It's one thing that he died young, but in our thirty years of married life, he was the ideal husband—loving, caring, supportive. He was the one who encouraged me to study after marriage when all the other girls stopped studying after school. I finished my BA and even did one year of a Master's. Anyway, the long and short of the story is that talking at length to the girl is not a prerequisite for a successful marriage. Of course, it's better if you can both talk things over. But even a few minutes with her—or for that matter with anyone—will give you an indication of her nature. You managed to spend some time together. That should be sufficient for making a judgement. In fact, the great Tamil poet Kamban described the first meeting of Rama and Sita, after their marriage: "Those who were together only a little while ago came together again, and there was no need for any elaborate ritual of speech between them."'

Rajan listened quietly. His mind was clearing up.

'You may feel that all this is not relevant any more,' continued Paati. 'But human beings haven't changed one bit. They remain the same. You should have faith in yourself and in human nature.'

Rajan slept peacefully that night.

Next morning, Rajan went straight to Lakshmi and told her that Gayathri was fine with him.

Lakshmi was delighted. So was Sundaram. Gayathri had

always been their first choice and their prayers had been answered—with a little assistance from Chandramouli. Lakshmi quickly darted into the pooja room and thanked the neatly arranged rows of gods. Sundaram followed suit. The gods—all of them—smiled back.

Sundaram patted Rajan warmly on the back and after nearly a month, Rajan and Sundaram were back on talking terms. Rajan was quite surprised how his father's demeanour changed and Sundaram wondered why he had ever got annoyed with Rajan in the first place. Paati was relieved that her grandson had finally seen sense.

'Congrats, Rajan!' Veena shouted over the phone.

'Finally!' sighed Dominique. 'It was high time you decided on something. I wonder what it was that finally helped you make up your mind.'

Even Paramesh thatha seemed happy at the news. 'This is one subject I can't give you any advice on,' he chuckled. 'But for heaven's sake, don't take dowry. Don't go about asking for cars, TVs and washing machines from your father-in-law—even if he can afford them. You give whatever you want to the bride—gold necklace, saree, silver cutlery, but that should not give you the licence to ask them for anything.' He knew Rajan had no such intentions.

'I'm happy for you Rajan. I don't think you will regret the decision. At the end of the day, a good Iyer girl with a decent family background is what will ensure happiness in the family,' Lakshmi said delighted.

Rajan was tiring of all this euphoria. 'Now that I have made the decision, you can ring them up and tell them that it's fine with me.'

'Rajan, not so fast. We will first have to wait for their answer. It doesn't look nice if the boy's side says yes first. The girl's side should get back to us first. We then have to take a bit of time, before we say yes.'

'You people are mad,' was all that Rajan could mutter.

That afternoon, Gayathri's parents rang up and said yes. Gayathri had agreed. Later that evening, Lakshmi rang up Gayathri's mother and said that Rajan had also agreed.

CONCRETE PROOF

INCOME TAX OFFICIAL HELD, screamed *The Indian Express* front page. *The Hindu* was more sedate and carried the news on the inside pages. Some didn't carry it at all. Corruption wasn't news anymore.

The Chennai*vasis* glanced at the news item with scepticism. Every income tax officer should be held, they thought. Why only Devanathan? In any case, he would be let off in a few hours. He would go scot-free. Charges would be dropped. The loot would disappear or would somehow be accounted for. Who cared?

Devanathan was kept in custody for all of three hours. He was then released on bail and went scot-free just as the Chennai*vasis* had anticipated. The loot was left behind and Devanathan promised to account for it. He promised to account for all his ill-gotten assets as well. One bungalow and three flats on Nugambakkam High Road, the heart of Chennai. And two Marutis. Deluxe models. All acquired under different names. All bought on a monthly salary of fifteen thousand rupees.

It wasn't easy to convict him or anyone else for that matter. Evidence was required. They needed concrete proof. To say that he could not have bought even half a flat on Nugambakkam High Road on fifteen thousand a month—even if he saved for five years—was not concrete enough. To say that he was caught red-handed with unaccounted cash was not concrete enough and it really wasn't relevant that he always entertained in five-star hotels. And paid in cash.

'Saar, there is a group of people in my department who are after me,' Devanathan explained to Sundaram.

It was a warm Sunday afternoon. Sundaram had been startled when Devanathan turned up at Sabarmati. He had been let out on bail and had taken the first opportunity to come back to Clive Avenue. Lakshmi and the others were out and Sundaram cursed him for interrupting his Sunday siesta, the only one he took during the whole week. Sitting in the low cane chair on the verandah, it was difficult to imagine that Devanathan had been arrested only a couple of days earlier.

'After all, it's only a small amount I get from all of you to run my family. It does not hurt you, but it helps us. How can I be expected to live on fifteen thousand a month, in the small hole which the Government provides as accommodation? It's impossible.' He paused, looking for support. Sundaram kept quiet. What was he supposed to say? 'I have deliberately been singled out and caught because there is a group after me,' he repeated. 'They belong to the other faction that's close to the Commissioner of Income Tax; they are dead against us.'

'Us? Who is us?' asked Sundaram, feeling the need to say something.

'Saar, I am supposed to be close to the minister. The commissioner and the minister are against each other. They are out to get each other and a small man like me is caught in the middle. That's what has happened.' Another pause. It would have been a lengthy one but for two tumblers of hot coffee brought by the cook and placed beside Devanathan.

'Please have some coffee,' urged Sundaram, glad at this brief interlude. The last thing he had wanted on a Sunday afternoon was the corrupt crook of an income tax officer pouring out his story of woe.

'Saar, it has become a CBI case, but in the end, I'm sure that justice will prevail and that all the charges against me will be dropped. I won't bore you with my woes,' he continued. 'You have always been kind and understanding towards me. I can hardly ask for more.'

Sundaram mumbled something which sounded sympathetic.

'I am counting on your support, Saar.'

'I will pray to God to give everyone good sense,' Sundaram told him truthfully. He did that every day during his pooja anyway.

'Your prayers and strong support are required,' he repeated.

'God's support is required, not mine.'

'No, Saar, yours also.'

'Mine?'

'Yes, Saar. They are bound to come to you about my case. They will ask for a statement from you. All I ask you is not to give any statement. They will use anything you say as evidence against me. I am just a small person caught between two elephants—the minister and the commissioner. I have a family to support and children to feed. If anything happens, it will result in disgrace to my family.'

'Whatever happens, happens for the best, Devanathan. You should not worry,' Sundaram said.

Devanathan went to work on his other clients in Clive Avenue, to deliver the same message.

Rajan had woken up the previous morning with his mind made up about Gayathri. But by the time the decision was conveyed to Gayathri's parents late that evening, he wasn't so sure. Should he have insisted on another meeting with her before deciding? He had gone back to bed that night a troubled soul, plunging wildly from self-confidence to gnawing uncertainty. Gayathri's parents had been informed. One couldn't go back on that. But what if she wasn't the right person?

When he woke up, the first thing Rajan asked Lakshmi was, 'Am I allowed to talk to Gayathri over the phone?'

'Of course. Nobody is stopping you. Why do you ask?'

'I'm planning to take her out for dinner today.'

'Well . . . why don't you take her out for lunch tomorrow rather than dinner today? Going out late at night . . . I'm not sure whether Gayathri's parents would approve.'

Rajan sat down at the dining table in exasperation.

'Talk to her all you want on the phone,' Lakshmi hastened to add. 'But I would prefer a lunch to a dinner.'

'Why don't you guys come out of the dark ages?' This was not the time to contradict his mother. In any case, once he started meeting Gayathri, events would take their own course and the last thing the parents would be bothered about was whether they were meeting each other for dinner or lunch. Rajan headed straight for the phone. He rang up and was told that Gayathri wasn't in. She would ring back.

When the enquiry got under way, the officials of the dreaded Central Bureau of Investigation came knocking at Sundaram's door. Three serious-looking men from the CBI were enough to intimidate anyone. Sundaram was leaving for the hospital and asked them to come back later in the evening. The three CBI officials looked surprised that anyone could dare to turn them back. But Sundaram had done just that. They came back in the evening. They sat in the verandah like three expectant wolves. 'Don't worry about us,' they said. 'We'll wait for him to come home.' Revati served them coffee. When Sundaram came back, he didn't think twice about giving a written statement about Devanathan's nefarious activities. The demands, the crisp notes that had changed hands, Devanathan's blackmail. It was all there in the statement. Rajan sat nearby and listened quietly. He was appalled and disgusted. Could his father have been such an easy and willing victim of such skulduggery? Sundaram had not breathed a word to anyone but had paid up. That too, just to ensure that Devanathan did not harass him. The officials went back, clutching their leather bags that contained precious documentary evidence. They finally had it, concrete proof.

'This Devanathan. He must be ashamed to call himself a Brahmin. Vedas can be relearnt; but bad conduct debases a Brahmin at once as Tiruvalluvar said,' a disgusted Sundaram muttered after they left.

'You should have told us about this, Appa,' said Rajan.

'If I had told you, what would you have done?' Sundaram asked in return.

Rajan was at a loss. 'We could have done something about it. Don't tell me that with all those clients of yours, there is no one who can pull up a guy like Devanathan?'

'No.'

'Come on Appa, there must be someone who can take on the slimy bastard.'

Astrologer Chandramouli was back at Clive Avenue. And Balakrishna Shastrigal, the family priest of the Sundarams, was summoned as well and mandated to find a set of auspicious dates for the engagement ceremony.

Balakrishna Shastrigal had seen three generations of the family. Being a *shastrigal*—a Brahmin priest—was his profession but it soon became his surname. Balakrishna Shastrigal. His bulky frame, maintained by feasts at Brahmin households, could barely fit into the cane chair in the verandah. Bare bodied and glistening with sweat, he lifted up his white *veshti* above the knee, folded it around his legs and sat down. A big tuft of hair stuck out of the back of his head. It was impossible to decide on any religious event without him. With a horde of new *shastrigals* descending on the Chennai Brahmin scene, the Sundarams found comfort in this old man. He was reliable and credible. He knew his trade and his shlokas. He was sober and even-tempered. The only thing he did in excess was eat, but that was part of the job description of a *shastrigal*. To feed the Brahmin was a virtue, according to Hindu scriptures. Clutching a sheaf of vermilion-tipped papers, he took out a broken ballpoint pen and made a few calculations.

'What is Saar's *gothram*?' he asked after a few minutes and, on being told, went back to his papers. Chandramouli looked over the *shastrigal*'s shoulder at the calculations and nodded.

The *shastrigal*'s role was crucial and he had the last word when it came to the dates. Holidays, travel plans of relatives and friends were all to be worked around the dates pronounced by him.

'The best dates are 15 June, 23 June and 3 July,' the shirtless Brahmin declared.

'Are there no dates before 15 June?' Lakshmi asked anxiously.

'There are some dates, but not as good as the ones I have told you. Since his star is *poorattadhi*, there are not too many dates in May.'

'I actually wanted to have the engagement now, by May itself, and the marriage by June–July. Anyway, 15 June seems fine. We will also have to ask the girl's *shastrigal* to confirm the date.'

'Alternatively, you could straightaway plan for the marriage on 23 June and keep the engagement for the previous day. That should take care of the problem and the marriage will take place early. June–July is also a convenient time for relatives and friends because of the school holidays.'

'That's true,' agreed Lakshmi readily.

Sundaram nodded. 'I only hope that the main marriage halls have not been booked for these dates. In fact, even before we consult Gayathri's parents about the dates, we should first check whether any of the marriage halls are available. If Rajeshwari Kalyana Mandapam is free on any one of these dates, we can book it right away and then plan ahead. I hope it is available—Veena got married there and Rajan's wedding should also be held there.'

The marriage hall was fixed before the marriage date. Success was measured by the name of the marriage hall. Dates were variable. To have the wedding at Rajeshwari Kalyana Mandapam or Woodlands Hotel was crucial. Crucial for the success of the marriage, crucial for the social standing of the families in Chennai.

Sundaram promptly took his car out and went over to Rajeshwari Kalyana Mandapam armed with a notebook. He came back to be greeted by several expectant eyes. 'They are out for lunch,' he pronounced.

Except for a brief period in November–December when cyclones and storms lashed Chennai, whenever it rained during the other months, it was unseasonal. Just as Rajan set out for Gayathri's house to pick her up for the much-awaited dinner— and dinner it was at Rajan's insistence—it started raining.

Water, or the lack of it, was yet another leveller of Chennai society. Rich and poor thirsted alike. They drank the same salty water. And, now, a bone-dry Chennai welcomed the rain. The Red Hills were dry. The tanks were dry, the wells had run dry, borewells had to be dug deeper and deeper to get a drop of the salty water. It was the season for the neighbouring states to fight over the release of waters to save the crops in Thanjavur. Not that they had anything against Thanjavurians. And when the water was finally released, it was always too little. Over the last four decades no government had bothered to make a permanent arrangement for a regular supply of water for the Chennai*vasis*. 'Water for Chennai' was a popular slogan used to win votes but little else. In due course, it stopped being an election issue because the Chennai*vasi* voting public were not fools. So Chennai remained dry. When the problem became acute, water tankers rolled down the streets filling up overhead tanks of the affluent and lining pockets to help keep Chennai in a perpetual state of thirst. When clouds gathered and the heavens opened up, Chennai*vasis* breathed a sigh of relief.

Rajan cursed his luck. The one day he had chosen to take Gayathri out, the weather tried to screw it up. He took her to Park Sheraton in Sundaram's Maruti Esteem in the pouring rain. He realized that it didn't affect Gayathri one bit. She watched cheerfully the raindrops strafing the windshield. She seemed to enjoy the rain. He didn't care much for it. The wipers struggled to clear the water and he concentrated on the road to avoid the potholes on Raja Annamalaipuram and Chamiers Road.

'It's strange that whenever something significant happens in my life, it rains cats and dogs,' Gayathri smiled, raising her voice to make herself audible above the downpour. 'When I went to get my final school results, it rained like there was no tomorrow. When I got my admission into college, I couldn't go to pay my fees because the roads were flooded with rainwater. The day the results were declared, I sat at home watching the rain lash at my window. My mom tells me that the day I was born, she almost didn't make it to the hospital on time! And now this.'

'I hope you are not superstitious about these things.'

'No, not at all. My father is. Maybe not superstitious, but he is very particular about good days, Tuesdays, *Rahukalam*, *Yamagandam*, things like that.'

'My folks are no different,' said Rajan. 'If you are looking for something different, you are getting married into the wrong family.'

'I, however, try and respect my parents' wishes when it comes to these things. After all, there must have been something behind all this for our ancestors to lay down such rules. I am not sure whether we have evolved enough to start pooh-poohing what our ancestors have tried to put in place.'

'That's what everyone likes to believe. It's about time somebody actually tried to understand them and, where necessary, do away with outdated concepts and practices.'

A bus passed by and splashed water on the windshield.

Rajan stopped the car for a moment till the wipers cleared it. The rain had increased and was now pelting down. The headlights of the oncoming vehicles made it worse. They could hardly hear each other.

'You know, our family astrologer said that our horoscopes matched very well and that we were the ideal couple, but another, my uncle's, pronounced that our marriage should not take place! He said something about the seventh house coming under heavy afflictions, Saturn's association with Rahu,' she laughed out loud. 'Now tell me, whom do you believe? At the same time, you cannot dismiss these predictions outright or wait till one or the other is proved right.'

Rajan smiled. It sounded like their own Chandramouli.

The car sputtered and stopped. Rajan cursed under his breath fearing the worst. For a brief moment he had visions of Gayathri and himself standing out in the rain trying to clean a wet motor. He started the car and it revved back to life.

'Thank God I got the Maruti. With any other car, we would have ended up pushing it.'

It was a great relief when he stopped in front of Park Sheraton, handed over the keys to the bellboy and went inside.

They chatted. And they realized that it didn't look all that bad after all to have each other as life partners. They had almost come to like each other. She didn't mind that he didn't have a job and that he was not even looking for one. I hope you are planning to get one eventually, she asked. Yes, he was. She seemed satisfied.

What about herself? What were her plans? She had a galaxy of artist friends, she said. Right now she was in the middle of getting some exhibitions going for a few of them. Even Jatin Das had promised to participate in one. Her future—her professional future—she hadn't given it too much thought. Not having a clue about art and artists, Rajan changed the subject.

She ordered a plate of chicken tikka. Rajan was surprised but didn't show it. He was a strict vegetarian as was the rest of his family. But he was not fastidious like his parents. I'm a vegetarian by choice, he liked to draw a distinction, not vegetarian by birth like my parents. He was simply exercising his choice of not eating a living being. Gayathri had not bothered to ask Rajan if he had a problem with her being non-vegetarian. She assumed he had no objection. Non-vegetarianism was not an issue any more. He was getting married to a meat-eating Iyer girl.

She didn't want any dessert. She was on a diet—till marriage at least. He too refrained from his usual banana split in solidarity.

'Coffee? Tea?' he asked.

'I think I'll have a coffee. But before that, do you mind if I have a smoke?' she asked.

He almost missed it.

'A what?'

'A smoke. A cigarette.'

'You smoke?' he enquired, unable to keep the incredulity out of his voice and immediately felt silly.

'Why? You have a problem?'

'No, no . . . not at all. It's just that . . . well . . . you didn't look the smoking sort—'

'Why, Rajan, how do smoking sorts look?'

'Well . . . it's just that . . . with a family like yours, I thought that you would have been forbidden from smoking. An Iyer woman smoking? A father who has streaks of ash and vermilion on his forehead has a daughter who smokes? I can't believe it's happening in the middle of Chennai. I have lived in the US for two years but believe me, I have rarely seen anything weirder.'

'You are right. This must be a shock to you—'

'No, not a shock . . .'

'My father totally disapproves of my smoking. I picked up

this habit in college and I could have easily kept smoking on the sly without him knowing. But I wasn't comfortable with this Jekyll and Hyde personality. I told him one day that I smoke—not very much mind you—four or five cigarettes a day, that's it. There was much raving and ranting. We didn't speak for two months. My mother was most upset and thought that I was turning into some sort of a vamp. They consulted astrologers who told them not to make a great fuss over it and that I would give it up in due course. Anyway, after some time, my parents gave up and I swore to be discreet about it so as not to embarrass them. Of course I never smoke at home. Now an uneasy truce prevails even though my mother made me swear that I would not mention my smoking to my prospective suitors till after the marriage.' She laughed. 'How utterly short-sighted can one be? It would be a greater shock for you if you learnt of my vices after marriage.'

He was getting married to a meat-eating, cigarette-smoking Iyer girl. Rajan smiled at the irony. Arantxa had been a smoker too. She smoked Virginia Slims. He liked to watch the cigarette on her lips. She hardly took the smoke in though. But smoking had been her only indulgence. Rajan used to wonder why he had never taken to smoking himself. Practically all his friends were smokers. He even liked the smell of cigars. But Rajan was not tempted. The thought had never crossed his mind.

Rajan watched Gayathri as she started to light her cigarette. They, Arantxa and Gayathri, both sat cross-legged while smoking. She didn't take in too much smoke either. The only difference was that Arantxa used to put her face near his, puffed right into his face and laughed out, knowing full well that Rajan would start off on his lecture about passive smoking. Should he tell Gayathri about Arantxa? Dominique had advised him against it. Rajan was inclined to come clean. Rajan, if your Mexican really doesn't matter to you any more, then there is no point in talking about it to your future wife, you'll only make her suspicious of you for no rhyme or reason, Dom had said.

Hey Dom, where's transparency in marriage then? Rajan, do you tell your parents everything you do? Then why do you suddenly want to tell your fiancée everything you did, that too in the past? Look at the future, you dumbo. Looking at Gayathri as she sat cross-legged across the table, Rajan decided to keep quiet.

'Gayathri,' he said smiling. 'I have no problems about your smoking. I was just startled to find someone in Chennai smoking so openly in a restaurant like this where half your father's clients must be dining. They could very well go back and report to him.'

'Of course, that's the risk I run. It happened once and we stopped speaking for another month. But apart from smoking, I have no other vice. I promise you I'm not into drugs, smack, sleeping around with other men . . .'

'Well, that's a relief,' he laughed and signalled to the waiter. 'Gayathri, your smoking will not bother me and you can put it out of your mind. After our marriage you will have to suffer my sermon on a hundred reasons to stop smoking. But that's another story altogether.'

'Since it's our first outing together, I'm not going to ask you to dance,' she said suddenly looking at the dance floor. The man at the synthesizer was belting out slow tunes. A few couples were keeping pace on the floor, but not many. Couples who actually knew dancing went to racier joints, to proper discos, with bright lights and high decibel levels. It had not occurred to him to ask her for a dance.

'I was thinking of the same myself,' he lied.

In the first awkward sign of affection, he reached across the table, took her palm and held it in his. He was getting married to a meat-eating, cigarette-smoking, disco-loving, virgin Iyer girl.

Dominique sat on her bed cross-legged, a pillow across her lap, an open book on the pillow and a bookmark between the pages. She was trying to glean material for her next article in *Le Figaro*. But her mind was not on what she was doing. Over the last few days, she had been gripped by a bout of, for want of a better word, cheerlessness. She was neither cheerful nor sad, neither melancholic nor happy. She was just cheerless. And she wasn't sure why.

She had not heard from her fiancé for more than a fortnight. He had warned her that he would be incommunicado for some time, at least until he completed a project which would keep him occupied for several days. Whenever he found time, he managed to send her a routine Hi-there-I-love-you-Thinking-of-you message every other day till the messages had stopped altogether. She missed his messages. She missed his smile, his tender kisses, his warm body when he hugged her, his distaste for the Chennai dust and heat. He used to fill her in on what was happening in the world outside. And on what was happening to him. She missed that. But was it this that was making her cheerless?

It wasn't the untimely rainy weather either. Rain in Chennai rarely depressed people. There was a certain cheerfulness about the dark clouds and streaks of sunlight that appeared together. No, it wasn't the weather.

Was it something to do with Rajan, she wondered. She had rung him up that evening. Sorry Dom, I'm taking Gayathri out for dinner today, he had said. Sorry, I forgot to tell you. It was not as if Rajan was running away. He was just getting married. But she knew that he was not just getting married. A chapter was coming to an end. A chapter in their friendship. A childhood friendship, a friendship of the soul that crept upon one when one wasn't looking, one that lived on. One didn't need physical proximity to nourish it. It just existed. When Rajan was in the US they had hardly written to each other. But they knew that the other existed somewhere and this was enough to sustain their relationship. She felt a tingle down her spine but she could not quite explain it. It was different from what she felt for her fiancé. She was in love with Jacques. Deeply in love. And she waited for his messages which began with 'Ma cherie'. A childhood friendship was different. It was quiet, unobtrusive, deep-rooted, calm. A childhood friendship did not have a beginning or an end. Dominique buried her face into the pillow. She felt like crying but couldn't.

RAJAN DOTCOM

The first thing Rajan did after his return from the US was set up his laptop on his writing table upstairs and ask for a separate e-mail connection. It took a long time to get a separate line but Rajan was soon connected to the world outside.

When he decided to take off, he spent hours in front of his laptop every day. It became an extension of himself. He kept up a continuous stream of e-mails and peered into all possible information on the corporate world. He had time on his hands. He even read all the junk mail till a killer virus struck and washed out his entire address book and his software. He had no backup. Looking at the empty computer screen, he felt as though all his friends had deserted him. Rajan had to start from scratch.

He reconstructed his files one by one. His friends came back, initially, into his address book. Many of his enemies found their way in there too, but Rajan didn't mind. It was good to find familiar faces.

As he rebuilt his files, he became more confident. Chennai was not new any more. Faces were familiar. Their ways were familiar. Old friends in new folders. It was only a question of retuning. Like an unused veena. Initially one had to tune it every five minutes because the strings slipped back to their old rusty ways. When the veena player persisted, the strings lost their reluctance to tune up and they held. They held so tight that they cut the fingertips of the veena player.

Rajan was retuned. His people and files were back with changed addresses and new telephone and cellphone numbers. Almost everyone had an e-mail account, a Hotmail address. Rajan, however, never lost his US contacts. The addresses and numbers of his American friends, with a few Mexicans and Chinese thrown in. He kept them separately on a floppy.

As he was reconstructing one of his files, he noticed the buzz on the screen. An invitation for a chat on the net from John. John Carey was his classmate at Wharton and now an entrepreneur. Rajan was quick to respond.

HI, RAJAN. IT'S JOHN. WHERE HAVE YOU BEEN? I'VE BEEN LOOKING FOR YOU. OUR COMPANY CIRUS IS ON THE VERGE OF BIDDING FOR A HUGE ORDER AND PRETTY CONFIDENT WE WILL GET IT. WE WANT TO URGENTLY TIE UP WITH SOME IT PROFESSIONALS IN INDIA TO DO SOME BACK OFFICE JOB. YOU GUYS ARE SUPPOSED TO BE BLOODY GOOD AT THESE THINGS. COULD YOU ASSIST?

HOW?

I HAVE AN OFFER. YOU COULD START UP AN INDIAN SUBSIDIARY FOR US AND HEAD IT OR PUT US IN TOUCH WITH SOMEONE WHO CAN.

Rajan looked at his screen. He could not understand.

I DON'T UNDERSTAND. BE A LITTLE MORE SPECIFIC. WHAT'S ALL THIS ABOUT?

Slowly the words started taking shape.

WE NEED IT PROFESSIONALS FROM INDIA TO BACK US UP. IT INVOLVES BACK OFFICE WORK AND RESEARCH WORK FOR OUR CLIENTS. I HEAR CHENNAI IS THE BEST PLACE FOR THIS. SINCE YOU ARE THERE, WE THOUGHT YOU COULD START UP A SUBSIDIARY FOR US IN CHENNAI OR IN ANY PLACE IN INDIA YOU THINK IS CONDUCIVE. THE CAPITAL AVAILABLE IS A LITTLE OVER A MILLION DOLLARS, INCLUSIVE OF SALARIES FOR TOP GRADE IT PERSONNEL AND TEMPORARY OR PERMANENT STAFF, DEPENDING ON THE QUANTUM OF WORK. IF YOU HEAD THE FIRM, AND BELIEVE ME I WOULD VERY MUCH PREFER THAT, YOUR SHARE WILL BE A PERCENTAGE OF OUR STOCKS AND $60,000 PER ANNUM, APART FROM OTHER PERKS. WE

WANT A MANAGEMENT GUY TO HEAD IT, NOT A TECHNICAL GUY. THAT'S WHY YOU ARE OUR CHOICE. THE FOCUS IS ON PUTTING IN PLACE A NETWORK OF PROFESSIONALS AND STAFF TO MEET THE DEMAND FROM OUR CLIENTS. THE TIME FRAME FOR PUTTING THINGS TOGETHER IS FIVE TO SIX MONTHS FROM TODAY. ARE YOU INTERESTED?

Rajan reread what was on the screen. This was serious stuff. John Carey was a fine guy and he wasn't given to flights of fancy. If he was making him an offer, it was serious. Americans didn't fool around with business. Neither would John. And he needed an answer urgently. Maybe not immediately but certainly in the next few days. Rajan saw his days of taking off coming to an end anyway what with all the wedding plans afoot. He knew John well. John had a sound head for business. They had vibed well at Wharton and Rajan saw in John a right mix of caution and inventiveness. And Cirus had been doing well even before John joined it.

HEY, ARE YOU STILL THERE?

Rajan's fingers moved purposefully towards the keys.

YES.

It was easy to identify a thug in Chennai. Or a 'rowdy', as the Chennai*vasis* called them. They were well built to the point of being fat, had a fierce, serious expression and a striking moustache, wore a coloured lungi tied around the waist barely covering the navel, a towel over the shoulder, and walked with a swagger. Not all those who looked this way were rowdies but all rowdies looked this way. At least in Chennai.

Four such rowdies, in gaily coloured lungis, landed up at Clive Avenue on a Sunday evening. As soon as they asked 'Is Iyer there?', preferring to address Sundaram by his caste name rather than simply as 'Doctor', Sundaram realized that something was wrong. They stood just below the steps outside the verandah and waited.

'What is it? Is there anything I can do for you?' asked Sundaram, trying to sound casual, buttoning up his shirt and coming out to the verandah.

'Iyeray, what is this we hear about you getting angry with our man?' said the rowdy standing right in front, sporting a big belly and a white T-shirt to cover it.

'Your man?' Sundaram repeated.

'Yes, our man.'

'Who is your man?'

'That chap Devanathan, the Tax Man.'

'What do you mean your man?'

'We know him well, Iyeray. Why are you so angry with him?'

'I'm not angry with him at all. He will hopefully get what is due to him—a proper conviction and jail term. I have my doubts, however, that he will actually be convicted. In fact, he was—'

'I understand you perfectly. He is scum and deserves punishment. He has eaten other people's money like water. But why are you after him?'

'I have nothing personal against him. He has been duping me and a host of others and the time has come to reap—'

'If you have nothing personal against him, then why did you give a statement against him?' the rowdy interrupted again, with a voice straining to be patient and reasonable while his demeanour suggested otherwise.

'If I don't give it, who will give it? After having done what he has done, do you suggest that he go scot-free?'

'No, no, not at all. He is a bastard all right. But your statement will ensure a conviction for him. You didn't have to do that. He has a family and children just like you. Moreover, everyone in his department is scum. Why target him? All of them should be caught and hanged, not just him. You should not have targeted him, Iyeray.'

'I'm not targeting him, for heaven's sake. Let all of them be caught. I don't care. And anyway it's too late. I have already given the statement.'

'You can always withdraw it.'

'What? Withdraw it and prove to them that I'm a lunatic? This is not a game. Devanathan had it coming and I can't withdraw my statement now.'

'It's better you withdraw your statement voluntarily, Iyeray,' the rowdy said, his voice suddenly becoming stern. 'Why go for a fight? He will fight dirty and you will be forced to fight in the gutter like he does. It does not behove a respectable Brahmin family like yours to descend to his level. You are a peaceful sort. You leave it to us and go your way. We'll take care of him.'

'How?'

'That you leave to us. But for now, withdraw your statement. That's all we ask.'

'Is this the way you people shield criminals? You should stay out of all this and let the law take its course.'

'Law will take its course, don't worry,' the rowdy laughed so loud that his belly popped out of his white T-shirt. The other three fierce-looking rowdies grinned as well at the thought. 'If you don't withdraw your statement, someone else will ensure that the case does not see the light of day. So why are you wasting your time, Iyeray?'

'In which case, why do you people want me to withdraw my statement? Look here, thanks for your unsolicited advice. Let me see what can be done.'

'Whatever you do, withdraw the statement for your own good, Iyeray. There is no need to make this a big issue and involve others as well. You come from a respectable family, why do you want to get into the gutter like the others?'

Sundaram was not an idiot. He understood it was a veiled threat.

Beebee decided just at that moment to come out of the house and walk into the verandah. The rowdies got distracted.

Beebee was a full-grown golden retriever, a big girl. When she came out, strangers found adequate reason to be apprehensive. Beebee looked at the rowdies and stopped short. To those who knew her it was clear that she was contemplating whether to go any further and get beaten up by the rowdies or retreat quickly into the safe confines of the house. To the rowdies, Beebee looked as if she was wondering which of them to bite first.

The rowdies stepped back.

'Iyeray, call back your dog lest it bite us.'

'Don't worry, it bites only bad persons,' Sundaram soothed them, warming up to the idea. 'You look like good people to me. I think you shouldn't poke your nose into these small matters. Leave this Devanathan business to the taxwalas. They will decide what to do.'

'We are leaving now,' said the rowdy grimly clothing their retreat in a veneer of dignity. 'If you know what's good for you and your family, you will withdraw your statement. See you later, Iyeray.' And off they went.

CV was excited about the whole idea. Start a Subsidiary? Sounds great. You should grab it with both hands. I will put you in touch with the best guys.

Sitting in CV's stark office, Rajan and CV pored excitedly over the lengthy e-mail in which John set out his plans for India. Rajan was clearly excited. This seemed tailor-made for him.

'Draw the curtains, there's hardly any light inside. CV, you have an amazingly empty office.'

'That's how I make my money. Cut down on non-essentials.'

'At this rate, you will cut down on your customers as well.'

There was a knock and CV's secretary came in on high heels, draped in a bright blue salwar kameez with a plunging V-neck revealing a generous cleavage. She was holding a tray with coffee for two. With a self-conscious gait, she placed the tray on the table, clutched at the dupatta which was threatening to fall off her chest and carefully tossed back the lock of hair which had, as if on cue, fallen across her eyes. She was young and pretty enough—she tried anyway. A coy smile directed at Rajan and CV, and the apparition disappeared.

'Why don't you cut out a non-essential like her?' Rajan asked CV and they both burst out laughing.

'I can, but I won't save much, you idiot! I'll have to pay the same for the person who replaces her.'

'CV, you lech! I thought you had mended your ways since college! I didn't realize you still sleep around.'

'Shh! Barely . . . I barely manage, what with a wife prowling around and—'

'You sonovabitch! It's time you gave all that up, CV. You are married now . . .'

'Boss, a man needs diversions once in a while.'

'She seems more like a full-time diversion!'

CV laughed. 'She's quite a handful, I agree. Great in bed but no brains.'

'I didn't realize you were looking for brains. But don't be idiotic, CV. Stop all this nonsense. What will your wife say?'

'Rajan, don't worry. I keep both of them happy and satisfied. After marriage you will also realize that one needs variety. You can't get stuck with one partner—in personal life or in business—'

'CV, keep your philosophy to yourself. I still think you're being foolish. Anyway, that's your headache. What are you going to do about my headache? How do we go about making some sense of John Carey?'

'Let's ask Shiva. He's a consultant with Farid Hussein Associates. You can't get a better head to advise you. He will know exactly where to start.'

G.R. Shivaramakrishnan was contacted. For the sake of the Americans, Rajan wished he had had a shorter name. He couldn't imagine a passport with Gobichettypalayam

Ramasubramaniam Shivaramakrishnan on one page but that was probably what it had. The Americans would go berserk. They would end up calling him Gobi for short. The pity was that that was not even his father's name leave alone his. Gobichettypalayam was the place he came from. And Ramasubramaniam was his father's name. Chennai*vasis* traced their lineage from their name. Shivaramakrishnan was his first name, his middle name and surname.

Lineage and pedigree mattered to Chennai Brahmins. If it was Ramasubramaniam's son Shivaramakrishnan, he had to be good, of the right pedigree. It was not a surprise then, that he was doing well. He had inherited his grandfather's brains and his father's sharpness, they said. And the shrewdness of the Gobichettypalayam people. It was no wonder he was doing well. And he was unmarried. He was a good catch.

Shivaramakrishnan—Shiva for short—was one of the best around. Rajan and he had been classmates in school but Shiva had taken Science and Engineering and Rajan had opted for Commerce. They had lost touch. Once Shiva was roped in, Rajan realized that the matter was in safe hands. Shiva knew exactly what John was talking about and took charge. He called in his concept men, his friends Bashir Ahmad and P.V.R.N. Rao. The latter's initials were longer than his name but no one had ever had the courage to ask him what they stood for. The task on hand was to produce a project report in a week. John Carey was happy. Rajan was happier.

For a brief moment, Rajan had forgotten about Gayathri. She had called and he had not returned her call for a full twenty-four hours. He returned at two in the morning. It was well into the afternoon the next day when he woke up and called her.

'Don't you return calls?' Gayathri asked.

'Well, I had, for the first time since my return, something really worthwhile to do and turned in very late yesterday,' he explained and tried to tell her about the project. She seemed distracted.

'Why don't we do another dinner and you can tell me all about it?'

'Okay.'

'I will choose the place this time.'

'All right.'

'Bell Metal. Game?'

'Bell Metal? Isn't it terribly er . . . noisy?'

'Yes. That's the idea. Once more to Park Sheraton, those sentimental songs will make me cry. Let's go to a place where things really happen.'

'So you want me to tell you all about this new project of mine sitting in Bell Metal and shouting over the din? Over hard rock and heavy metal? I won't be able to speak or hear normally for a week after that.'

She chuckled. 'Then don't tell me. Tell me another time. Let's go to Bell Metal, it'll be fun.'

Rajan agreed reluctantly.

'And wear jeans and T-shirt. Nothing formal.'

'And you?'

'Jeans and T-shirt!' she laughed.

Rajan rang up Dominique to tell her that they would have to cancel their gym session. He was taking Gayathri to dinner at Bell Metal.

'Bell Metal!' Dom couldn't keep the surprise out of her voice. 'That's for guys who want their minds blown off.'

'That's already happened to me.'

The letter read: You have been warned once. You have ten days. If you don't agree, you will have to face the consequences. It had arrived by the evening post. Written in Tamil, the letters had been cut out of magazines and stuck on a piece of paper. Whoever stuck the pieces had been sloppy with the glue. There was even a spelling mistake.

Sundaram had opened the letter and sat staring at it. The postmark said Trichy. It didn't need a detective to know that the sender was in Chennai. He called Lakshmi and Rajan and all three grim faces stared at the letter almost expecting the words to suddenly come to life and start speaking.

'It's those rowdies, no doubt. Devanathan is not going to give up till I withdraw the statement and I am in no mood to do so,' Sundaram was clearly tense and belligerent. 'He can't blackmail me like this. I propose to get to the bottom of this nonsense.'

'I agree entirely,' Rajan endorsed. After a long time, God knows how long, the father and son had something they could agree entirely on.

'I don't know why you started this in the first place. Devanathan can go and hang himself. How the hell are we bothered? We have a wedding coming up now and all I need is to go around with Black Cats guarding me,' wailed Lakshmi, sounding totally exasperated.

'Okay, okay, don't start. Let's not go over the whole thing again. All I want you all to do is to be careful. Take some precautions like don't go out alone, don't open doors without knowing who it is. I am meeting Commissioner Kalimuthu tomorrow to ask for police protection for our house.'

'If those rowdies want to do something, no police can stop them. They are all in each other's pockets,' Lakshmi said.

'That's the hazard of standing up for one's convictions. You remember how your own father complained against the collector of his district and had him arrested for taking a bribe—'

'That was decades ago. That was a different era. Now everyone is a thug. Why should we get involved in a losing battle? And prove what? That you are a man of principles? And to whom? To other thugs?'

'Lakshmi, honest people are dwindling in numbers. And honest people who will stand up and defend their principles are practically non-existent. We can't keep on compromising throughout our lives merely because the world around us is changing for the worse. I have already committed the sin of giving in and bribing him all these years. And for what? Just to ensure he accepted my returns and didn't keep raising objections and harassing me. At least now, let me answer my own conscience by making sure he pays for his misdeeds.'

'This is going to affect Rajan's marriage preparations.'

'You are getting scared and worked up unnecessarily. This is not going to disrupt the marriage or its preparations. You shouldn't worry so much. Besides, they don't have the guts to try anything against me—'

'—and if they do try something, it's not as if they're going to ask for your permission first.'

Gayathri acknowledged Rajan's black jeans and light green T-shirt with an approving nod when he picked her up from her residence. She was in blue jeans as well, and had on a white round-neck T-shirt over which she wore a blue denim jacket, unbuttoned. She looked animated and pretty.

Bell Metal was teeming with people. Gayathri had booked in advance for a corner table by the window opposite the bar. A nice cosy place, or so Rajan thought. The light was dim and the bar brightly lit revealing gleaming rows of liquor and liqueurs. Cane chairs and wooden bar stools stood erect supporting bottoms in blue denim. Jeans seemed to be the uniform. No wonder Gayathri had been so particular. The place was alive with everyone moving around with the air of knowing everyone else. Madonna was trying to drown out the conversation.

'Hi Gaya, what's up?' shouted a tall, wiry guy with a pencil moustache in a black T-shirt and faded jeans, as he came over with a cocktail in his hand.

'Viren, meet Rajan. We are getting engaged soon.'

'Engaged? Hey cool, babe! You didn't breathe a word of it

to us. Hey guys!' he called out to a group a couple of tables away. 'Come over here. Meet Gaya's guy.'

They came over, jumping over the cane chairs. Rajan half got up from his chair, and with an embarrassed smile shook all the hands that came his way. Some bent to kiss Gayathri on both cheeks. She got up and called the waiter nearest their table. 'The next round of drinks is on me,' she shouted and there was clapping. The others in the place looked up briefly to see what the commotion was about and went back to doing whatever it was they were doing.

'Some of them are my classmates from school, some from college. Viren is from my college. He is an artist and paints, mainly oils. That guy in the blue T-shirt is Babu, from college. The girl in red is Madhavi, a classmate from school. Next to her is Geeta, another budding artist. The other—'

'Gaya, save your breath. They all look the same to me in this dim light and their uniforms.' Rajan ordered a Campari with 7-Up and she a Planter's Punch. The salted groundnuts came with the drinks.

The rhythm changed suddenly along with the decibel level. Daler Mehndi came on and, as if on cue, the crowd got off their chairs and moved onto the floor. The psychedelic lights came on. Gayathri got up, caught Rajan by the hand and pulled him up. The floor was large but the dancers jostled for space. Backsides rubbed against other backsides and shoulders brushed each other.

They began to move to the music as hips gyrated struggling to keep up with the beat. Rajan had no idea that Daler's Punjabi, which no one south of the Vindhyas understood, could evoke so much excitement.

The air conditioners worked in vain to prevent the dance floor from becoming hot and sweaty. Gayathri was enjoying it. She was a natural. She swayed, shook and kept pulling Rajan towards her. Trying to get a piece of him. Rajan was enjoying the attention. He was, however, becoming deaf. They stopped briefly, for a refill and some rest. Another Campari–7-Up and Planter's Punch, gulped down quickly. Gayathri took off her jacket revealing the white T-shirt underneath. She was sweating, glowing with happiness. She said something but Rajan had gone deaf. He laughed as if he understood. Then, they went back to Daler.

Rajan motioned to her that he had had enough. She pulled him towards her. He stayed on briefly but then slipped away to their table. She looked at him disapprovingly and stayed a while longer dancing with Viren. It was with an effort that she broke away and came back to the table flushed and smiling. Her white T-shirt had become translucent with sweat. Rajan realized, with a start, that it revealed more than it concealed.

'Gaya, your T-shirt has become transparent,' he pointed out. 'I think you should put on your jacket.'

'Why? You don't like my tits or what?'

'Your tits are fine,' he said without missing a beat. 'I'm not sure whether you want everyone here to see them in their pristine glory.' He was getting used to her sharp retorts.

'That is exactly what I want,' she laughed. She did have a lovely smile. 'Look at Deepa . . . I mean the one over there with Viren. Her top is not even big enough to cover hers. Look at Viju there. Look around you. You can see as many breasts through T-shirts as you want. That guy there even has his hands over one. It's sexy, these see-through shirts.'

'Being sexy does not mean showing off your you-know-whats. There are other ways of doing it. Your T-shirt and jacket look sexy on you as—'

'Thank You, Your Highness—'

'I don't think you should waste your time competing with Deepa or Asha—not on this account at least. The days of bra-burning are over. The Americans gave it up long ago.'

'Not in Bell Metal, they haven't. Rajan, get real. This is the way girls chill out in Chennai. It's their identity, their statement. What do the girls do in Wharton? I bet they do the same. And they probably have bigger and better-looking tits.'

'Maybe, but this is not Wharton, it's Chennai.'

'Yes, it is. So?'

'You don't have to show your you-know-whats to make a statement. The women in the West stopped baring their bodies to make a statement long ago. People who bare bodies do it for other reasons. In fact, the saree is widely regarded as the sexiest dress in the world.'

'So you want me to go around in a saree, is that it?'

Looking at her, he wasn't quite sure whether she was joking or serious. Signs of exasperation were creeping into her face.

'Gaya, sometimes I am not sure whether you are serious or arguing for the heck of it. I am suggesting no such thing. All I'm asking you to do is to put on your jacket because your T-shirt is fast losing its utility as a covering for your body.'

'All right, if that's what you want.' She got up, put on her jacket and sat down with a frown. 'Now what? Go home?'

'You are getting unnecessarily upset. Over nothing really.'

'I think it is you who are getting worked up over nothing. I'm not a whore. I will—'

'Of course not. All I was suggesting was that, now that we are sort of formally engaged, you could be a bit more circumspect about showing your you-know-whats to all and sundry. You know, there—'

'All you guys are the same. When you leer at girls, you want them to show their tits so that you can drool. But when you're engaged to them, then you suddenly ask them to cover themselves up like an Eskimo.' With this outburst, Gayathri fell silent.

Bell Metal was going deaf with the noise but at this table, silence reigned supreme. Rajan let the silence linger a little bit longer. Anything more would have only prolonged the argument.

'Why don't we have a sandwich? I'm quite hungry,' Rajan said trying to change the subject.

'I'm not,' Gayathri said, trying to be difficult.

'Well . . . what do you propose to do?' Rajan tried being nice.

'I don't know. You tell me.' Gayathri was still sulking.

'Okay. Let's go home,' said Rajan giving up.

She was a bit surprised that he had called her bluff. She thought he would try to coax her a bit longer. He paid the bill in silence, left a large tip, she noticed, and they left.

A SEMICOLON

When Rajan took his Maruti out early the next day to drive over to Shiva's consultancy firm, he wasn't even aware that his days of taking off had come to an abrupt end. His mind was working overtime with John, Shiva and Gayathri. The Maruti left the city and turned into the road connecting Velacheri and the old Mahabalipuram road.

Three centuries earlier, when Robert Clive rested his tired legs at this very place, fresh from his victories down south in Arcot and Tiruchirapalli, he looked north only to be greeted by unkempt green fields and a gentle sea breeze. Fort St George was still several miles ahead but well within the reach of the British. A string of hamlets dotted the countryside. Little did one know then that these hamlets would be swallowed into a city housing ten million. Three years ago, one could still see the green around this road, feel the pastoral laziness amidst the occasional three-storey buildings.

Today, a different vision greeted the uninitiated eye. The place was unrecognizable. It was bustling with buildings and cars, cables and wires. The Tidal Park was overflowing and e-Chennai had moved out onto this road. The place had been totally transformed.

Rajan parked near a cyber café, picked up a hot cup of coffee and went into Shiva's building. Rajan and his team were together again. They had work to do.

It was well into the evening when the boys broke up for lunch. The project was taking shape and they didn't want to waste a single moment.

Rajan drove back agreeing to meet again later. Driving back from Velacheri to Clive Avenue, he realized that his mind was not on the road. Changes were taking place in his life and he felt a certain uneasiness he couldn't explain. Wasn't he the one who, defying his father's wishes, decided to take Commerce? Didn't he choose to go to the US and take to the American life? Wasn't he the one who chose to return from the US, defying all conventional wisdom, to settle down and eke out a living? He had always been dead sure of everything he had done and was fully prepared to take on life's eventualities. But now he was uneasy. It was not anything in particular. Not yesterday's tiff at Bell Metal. He was just getting less and less certain of his own world.

He was on Royapettah High Road and the familiar Hanuman Temple flashed by on the right. Rajan, as a young boy, had religiously visited the temple with his father every Saturday. He asked God to give him good sense since Sundaram had told him that that was all that a youngster needed to pray for—the rest would follow automatically. There was the ritual offering of a garland of vadas, Hanuman vadas, after prayers. And back home to cut open the garland and devour it. It all seemed so long ago. He suddenly realized that it had been more than five years since he had last visited the temple or for that matter any temple. It wasn't that he didn't believe in God. He was just too engrossed in his own world.

Rajan had almost driven past the temple when he changed his mind, swerved to the left, almost colliding with a cyclist, and stopped near the kerb.

'Son of a whore!' shouted the cyclist loudly. 'Which bastard gave you a car to drive?'

He parked, took off his sandals, left them behind in the car, crossed the road barefoot and walked towards the temple.

He was in front of the powerful black granite Monkey God after five long years. Having been brought up by Paati on a rich diet of stories on Hanuman's prowess, Rajan had always looked at the Monkey God with awe. Today, he appeared no less majestic. Black and powerful. It was almost as if nothing had changed. He even remembered his shlokas. It all came back to him. The smell of camphor, vermilion and ash, butter and burning lamps. The dampness of the floor on his feet. He went around the deity till he emerged on the other side in front of the idol of the Monkey God's mentor, Lord Rama.

'Please do an *archanai* in my family's name,' he asked the priest.

'You have to get a token from there,' the priest pointed towards an emaciated, shirtless Brahmin sitting behind a low wooden counter, sweating, and fanning himself. 'If you want camphor, bananas, betel leaves, the basket can be bought outside.'

Rajan thought about it for a brief moment. He stretched out to take a *tulasi* leaf from the brass plate in the priest's hands, pressed it against his eyes, popped it into his mouth and walked away. He left, peaceful, happy. It was a Saturday.

Gayathri had rung up and wanted him to call back as soon as he came in.

Rajan had decided he wasn't going to take any shit from her. He had tried to be as nice as possible yesterday but she had not been reasonable. He wasn't even sure whether he should return her call. He could keep mum and send out a silent message that he wasn't one to take any nonsense. He had to convey this now at the very start, else, after marriage, it might be too late. He thought about it some more. If he didn't ring up, it would look churlish. After all, he was supposed to be the more sober of the two, wasn't he? If he appeared petty, then how was he to handle the marriage? He rang her up. It was Gayathri who picked up the phone.

'Rajan, before you say anything, you were right and I was wrong. Okay? I'm really sorry for the scene yesterday. Sorry. It won't happen again. I promise.'

'It must have been the Planter's Punch.'

'Next time I decide to bare my . . . er . . . soul, I will seek your permission, okay?'

Preparations for the marriage were picking up.

Sundaram had managed to get the Rajeshwari Kalyana Mandapam premises to conduct the marriage and was being congratulated by one and all on his good fortune. Sundaram's status went up a notch among the Chennai*vasis*. It was an auspicious start.

Lakshmi was always in a tearing hurry. There weren't too many days left and there was still a lot left to be done. Having been through Veena's wedding, she knew what she wanted and what to look for. She zeroed in right away on the saree houses. To begin with, Kancheepuram silks for the bride. One for the engagement, one for the *jaanavasam*. One to be worn during the tying of the *taali*, one for the reception. The list was endless. She went in and out of silk shops looking for traditional silk sarees. The Rasi Silk House, Nalli, Kumaran Silks.

Most sarees bought during a wedding remained unused during the girl's married life. For one, the sarees were nine yards, which had long gone out of vogue. The preference was six yards now. But tradition said it had to be nine yards and that was that. For another, Chennai was too hot for silk sarees. Cotton and light sarees were in. But the brides were not spared. Kancheepuram silk sarees were not just sarees—they were family heirlooms, to be treasured, put away. So the exquisite Kancheepuram silks lay quietly at the bottom of the steel almirahs, waiting to be bequeathed to a future daughter-in-law.

Veena accompanied her mother to help her make the selection and bring the sarees home 'on approval'. Paati,

Lakshmi and Veena were the Selection Committee. Dom was an informal adviser. When in doubt, they deferred to Paati. There were few who could match Paati when it came to choosing sarees and diamonds. From a mile away, she could identify whether someone was wearing American diamonds or the real thing.

'Rajan, which one do you like?' they asked.

He liked the light pink with the intricately woven zari and violet border and the bright green one with a broad zari border. His choices were immediately vetoed.

'I don't know where you get your Muslim taste,' Veena murmured. '*Mithai* pink and parrot green indeed!'

'Then why did you get them "on approval" if you didn't like the colours in the first place,' he asked.

His question was dismissed as frivolous and argumentative.

Veena was important in the decision-making machinery of the Sundaram family. Whether it was Sundaram, Lakshmi or even Paati, they liked to chat with her before taking a decision. Moreover, she, in their opinion, represented the modern point of view. They didn't want to be outdated. Veena enjoyed this role even after she married Jayaraman and moved away. Being the girl in the family didn't deter her one bit. Her parents had seen to it that she grew up to be a confident, self-assured woman, unlike many of her friends who played second fiddle to their brothers—the man in the family—the 'heir'. It was not as if Rajan didn't get attention. He got more than his share in any case. But she wasn't in his shadow. Of course, the fact that she was older helped. She was Rajan's buffer. Messages from Rajan to Sundaram and Lakshmi went through her and vice versa. When Rajan couldn't get something across, she did. When Veena married and left, she left a void in their lives.

'Rajan, don't become like our neighbour Arvind the Wife

Beater,' was the only piece of advice Veena gave him when she left.

The occupant of No. 5, Arvind the Wife Beater acquired his reputation overnight. Several years earlier, Arvind's wife Bhargavi had come running to Sabarmati one night in panic—Arvind had threatened to beat her up. He is threatening to beat me and kill me, she sobbed uncontrollably.

When the newly married couple had moved into Clive Avenue nearly a decade earlier, it was evident to one and all that there was a social disparity between the husband and wife. He had studied in Chennai right through, joined the elite Indian Institute of Technology and finally landed a plum job in Chennai. She, on the other hand, had just completed her schooling and was in the first year of college. That, too, in Nagerkoil, deep down south in Kanyakumari. She had barely travelled beyond Madras and was a novice to the ways of city dwellers. Her only exposure to Indians from other parts of India was through the North Indian tourists, camera in hand, heading for Kanyakumari to glimpse the confluence of the three seas. There were several white and yellow foreign tourists as well, but they rarely stopped in Nagerkoil. In a fit of misplaced nostalgia, Arvind's mother, who hailed from Nagerkoil, had forced him to marry a girl from her hometown. Arvind's father had died several years earlier and didn't have a say in the choice of bride. Arvind had accepted. She will be the ideal wife for you, his mother had advised him. She will be dutiful, obedient, keep the house running and serve you well. She is not only attractive but unaffected by the false values of city girls. City girls are untrustworthy and after a few years will demand this and that till you become a nervous wreck, she had warned. He had fallen for that, and her beauty, and had married her.

Bhargavi was attractive no doubt, but a total stranger to

the city. She was scared of practically everything and very self-conscious. She was embarrassed of her English (which in fact wasn't too bad), her Tamil (which was different from the Tamil spoken in Chennai), her lack of higher education (she wasn't that highly educated, it was true), and her overbearing husband made all of it much worse. She was shy, timid and withdrawn. Arvind couldn't persuade her to come out in front of strangers or even friends, particularly if they were men. Bhargavi, this is Madras, you have to meet men and converse with them freely, he said. But Bhargavi had been taught not to talk to men. How could she suddenly sit on the sofa with these men and chat cross-legged as if she had known them all her life?

Her hairstyle was all wrong—a long, well-oiled braid intertwined with jasmine. When she tried to bedazzle Arvind with her silks and diamonds, it increased his libido but not his regard for her. He craved her flesh at night and wished she were another person during the day. He cringed from her backwardness.

Arvind realized that he had made a mistake. Now he was saddled with her. He ignored her and barely sought her company. That made her isolation only worse. When she went to him after he returned from work, he shouted at her. She made a serious effort to read, English novels and magazines particularly, and build up her vocabulary and confidence. She succeeded far beyond her expectations but Arvind did not notice. She was just not good enough, he had made up his mind. Then one night, he came towards her with his fist clenched threatening to beat her and throw her out of the house.

Barely a year after that, things did take a turn for the better. Once, when she had gone out to the temple, Arvind chanced upon an e-mail lying on her table. It was from her cousin, Kamala Ganesh, who was a social scientist living in Bombay. Suspecting that she was a feminist as well, Arvind had always kept her at arm's length and discouraged Bhargavi from interacting with her. Now, out of curiosity, he read her letter.

Dear Bhargavi, I was thinking a lot about what you had told me about your marriage and decided to send you something I wrote last year. I have always found the dual personality of the Tam-Bram man very interesting.

Rustic, backward, ethnic, no style
That Tamil wife, that peerless pearl
That paragon of virtue with jasmined braids
In silks and diamonds in the dazzling heat
But she comes in a package, you ought to know
With a husband in tow, alter to her ego.
He is modern, with it, man-about-town
Yet scratch the surface and you'll find his nineteenth-century grandfather.

He is a stickler, this Tamil spouse,
For the highest standards of quality
Idlis soft and white (like jasmine)
The way Mother made it, nothing else will do.
Coffee twice, thrice even four times a day
Each time fresh decoction, fresh milk
Piping hot, frothing in a three-foot stream
Hissing between 'dabara' and 'tumbler'.

Wants a full meal at 8 before going to work
Sambhar, rasam, curry with coconut, the works
And a little tiffin dabba brimming with curd rice
With a tiny piece of mango pickle.

He reads the newspaper for an hour and a half
Then forgets to fold and put it back
He declaims on the state of the entire globe
But can't serve himself from the dish on the table
Someone needs to spoon it onto his plate
His favourite dress: white dhoti, soft and old
And a banian with a hole or two in the back
No matter which of your friends is visiting.

Takes pride in dissociating from everything rural
Is embarrassed to be with Bhargavi in public
Peppers his speech with three-letter words
IIT, IAS, IIM, MIT
MBA, USA, dot com
Technocrat, bureaucrat, corporate
Oh the trauma and chaos, hypocrisy and confusion,
The conflicts, the various stages of evolution
Of the Tamil male, no doubt her spouse,
Unresolved dilemmas, questions, tensions.

The fine print for this passage to 'modernity'—
Home would remain the bastion of 'tradition'
Bhargavi would remain as she always was,
The last refuge for his battered 'self'
His Tiger balm, his Iodex, his ego massage
To assuage colonial guilt and shame
So while saree remained saree with minor revisions
Dhoti changed to trousers (the quintessential turncoat).

Thank God for Bhargavi, that peerless pearl
That paragon of virtue in jasmined braids
In her 'backwardness' basks our man
She is a foil to his progressive, liberal mask
She lets him feel that he is in control
Of the complex modern world outside the door.

Hope he reads it!
Regards,
Kamala

Arvind the Wife Beater read it. And reread it. He was
angry at first, enraged. He stopped talking to her for several
days. Then, in a fleeting moment, he put himself in Bhargavi's
place. It wasn't easy. But he did. And he cried. It wasn't easy for
him to cry, but he did. It wasn't easy for him to apologize, but
he did. It wasn't easy for him to ask her forgiveness, but he did.

It wasn't easy to turn into a new man, but he did. Arvind was no longer the Wife Beater. But the name stuck.

The Chief Cook, specially hired for marriages, was summoned. Like in all Brahmin households, they had a 'family marriage cook'. Narasimhan was a short, stocky man, pot-bellied from eating his own elaborate meals for breakfast, lunch and dinner. Lakshmi went over the menu with Narasimhan and quickly realized that there was hardly anything they could add. Or subtract. *Avial, pachchadi, paal-payasam*, two types of curry and one *koottu, sambhar, rasam*, lemon rice, *thair*, not *moru* . . . the list went on. Very little could be dropped. It all had to be there. Otherwise the lunch would be less than traditional. People would say, 'Did you notice, there was no *thair vadai*, the *paruppusuli* wasn't too good and I couldn't get a second helping of *avial*. They must have been economizing.' It wasn't easy to please Tamil Brahmins. Or for that matter, any Tamil. Paati looked at the list and had nothing to add. 'Tell that Narasimhan to get good, big plantain leaves,' she said. 'I don't want small or torn ones on which you cannot serve *rasam* or *payasam* properly.' Narasimhan went away with, 'Don't worry, Amma. Leave it to me. I will do it like I did it for Veena's marriage.'

'Rajan, careful. Positively no dowry. Keep reminding your parents once in a while, since parents are prone to forget this in their excitement of finding a bride.' Paramesh thatha warned Rajan, recovering in their house after one of his drinking bouts.

'Don't you forget your causes even when you are drunk?'

'Rajan, you are too young and idealistic to realize. Even the best of human beings cannot resist the lure of money. Keep an eye on your parents.'

Rajan sat down to write out a list of classmates he wanted to invite and found that the list came to all of ten names. Many of his classmates were outside India, based mostly in the US. Even among the ten on his list, two were in Bangalore, two in Delhi, one in Bombay and two in Madurai. Is there no one to call for my wedding, he wondered.

Like the Palestinian Christians of Bethlehem migrating to the US in the face of Islamization of the West Bank, the Brahmins of Chennai found that the best way to beat the reservation system in Tamil Nadu was to migrate, to Delhi or to Bombay. Even better, to the US. The Chennai Brahmins became holding companies. They held on to their house, their land and their way of life, while their youngsters fled to the US. The oldies stayed behind to manage the holding company and felt happy in the knowledge that their children had escaped from Chennai. When the youngsters got married and had kids, they sent an SOS to the oldies which is when the oldies also fled to take care of their grandchildren. Since they hated the US, they had no company, there were no crowds, no one to talk to in Tamil, not much to see—they kept one foot in India and the other in the US.

One leg in the river and one leg on the marshy bank, went the Tamil saying.

Rajan crumpled up his list and threw it away. He would do another one later, in consultation with CV.

Rajan was getting to know Gaya. Barring her quirks—he was getting used to those too—she was delightful company. She seemed to be warming to him as well. They met again at Murukku Stop for snacks, and enjoyed themselves. Dosa and idli were great for bringing people together. They had put Bell Metal behind them, way behind.

Even though Bell Metal was forgotten, Rajan found Gayathri a little different. Perhaps he was the one who was different, still it amounted to the same. Opposites attract, he kept reminding himself. She is basically a lovable person. And most importantly, she is honest. He liked that. It's funny, he thought, how you select someone first and then start finding qualities in her to like. Why the hell couldn't I like someone first before selecting her? Anyway, it was too late to mull over such possibilities.

When Rajan asked her to accompany him to a book reading, she hesitated at first but accepted when she saw the frown on his face. When she finally turned up—fifteen minutes after it was over—she stood nervously, smoking a cigarette and glancing furtively at Rajan's face to see whether he was annoyed. He was, but didn't show it.

'He was good. You missed something,' he said. 'You know, some of these Indian authors in English are really good. If you are interested, I could lend you some of their books.'

She apologized profusely. It wasn't as if she was not interested in reading. It's just that other things took up her time.

Gayathri decided to make it up to him by inviting him to a dance recital by Suryakanti's troupe. Was this tit for tat, he wondered. He sat through the performance as though he had been forced to drink castor oil. When she dragged Rajan backstage to meet the dancers, he expressed his delight at their performance and said, truthfully, that what he witnessed was a unique show, since he had never been to one before.

On the way back, Rajan and Gayathri stopped by at Marina. They sat down on the sands and looked out at the boundless sea and watched the waves crashing onto the shore. They forgot how different they were. This was not the time for talk. It was a time to hold each other close. They waited for it to grow really dark before touching each other.

Opposites did attract.

Rajan had not exercised for a few days and felt a bit stiff. He was in the mood for the gym. A good workout always did wonders. He called up Dominique.

'Game for the gym?'

She paused for a brief moment.

'I already went there this morning.'

'So?'

'Would Gaya mind you going out with me so frequently?'

'Don't be idiotic.'

There was another pause. He could hear her mind working. Furiously. Was it all right for her to go with Rajan?

'Okay, hang on,' was the verdict. 'I was in the middle of my next article for *Le Figaro*. Give me ten minutes to wind up and get ready.'

Rajan told her about the progress they were making on the project as they drove towards Sterling Road, about Shiva and the boys, about Gayathri and Bell Metal. He skipped the part about their fight—it was too silly. Dom could be spared the lovers' tiffs.

'Why don't you make Gaya a member?' Dominique suggested. 'You can then take her to the gym instead.'

'Don't be silly. The thought never occurred to me. In any case she doesn't look the gym type.'

'I'm sure she will become a gym type if you ask her properly.'

Dominique was on the treadmill while Rajan sweated out on the weightlifting bench. He did a few laps in the pool. After his swim, they sat quietly by the poolside, enjoying their tiredness.

'Dom, you mentioned your next article. What's it about?'

'It's about the rise of Hindutva in Indian body politic. I then touch on the effect it has on the Christians in India,' she laughed. 'It'll tickle the French Christian senses all right.'

'I'd like to read it when it's finished. Must be interesting.'

'In fact, it's almost finished. I was editing it a bit. Why don't you see it on the way back home?'

He dropped her off, parked his car at Sabarmati and walked back to her house.

Rajan had always found Dominique's room too feminine. There was a rather ornate wooden dressing table with perfume bottles standing to attention. There were creams, cotton buds and lipsticks. An ornate wooden bed to match the dressing table. Carefully chosen photographs of her parents on the bedside table. It was elegant all right. The light green walls, the various hues of green on the curtains and bedspread and the crescent-moon paper lampshade that hung by the bedside reminded Rajan of the Pakistani flag. There were papers strewn about on her worktable in disarray, her jeans thrown casually over a chair. A few CDs lay on her bed. There was an exercise cycle in the balcony, out of the sight of inquisitive eyes. The room was feminine, but not overdone.

She handed him a sheaf of papers as he settled down in a chair.

'This is the English version,' she said, sitting on the bed.

It was well written. She was good at what she did, and with France's renewed interest in South Asia, it was no surprise that *Le Figaro* had chosen her. She watched Rajan while he stared at the paper. Rajan was always intense when it came to reading. Almost nothing distracted him and she marvelled at how much he was able to absorb in a short time. When asked, he said that he tried to focus on the 'catch' words and the sentence fell into place. She remembered how, when she was asked to read a full new chapter on the Indian Independence Movement a few hours before her history exam, Rajan had read up several reference books at lightning speed and had narrated the entire thing in a capsule. Now that he was opening a new chapter in his life, the old chapter was drawing to a close. She would miss him, she knew. She was almost sure he would miss her too.

'It's good,' he said finishing. 'Quite good—for a French woman who pretends to be an Indian.'

She ignored the remark.

'I don't quite agree with your spiel on Indian Christians towards the latter half of the article. It's as though other religions don't exist in India and the Christians were being targeted by the Hindus. By the way, Hindutva is not anathema to secularism. You are taking a typically Western view of—'

'No, I'm not. You will be surprised at how many Indians agree with me. There are several more Babri Masjid demolitions waiting to happen and several more Staineses waiting to be murdered. To whip up emotions and divisions in society is not in the Indian ethos. To absorb and assimilate is. You must—'

'Assimilation does not mean digesting all the shit that is thrown at you. Assimilation essentially means enriching one's own culture by cross-pollination without encouraging your own vitals to be eaten away. I think—'

'Stop that crap, Rajan. Your arguments are too theoretical and pseudo-intellectual.'

'India is essentially a multireligious society. It couldn't have come about in a day or happened by accident. It's multireligious because Hinduism assimilated other people, other religions. Some say that Buddhism was in danger of disappearing from India because Hinduism assimilated its teachings and made them a part of its own.'

Dominique kept quiet. Rajan turned the pages, rereading a few lines. And they argued. He provoked her but she could hold her own. She didn't write articles for the heck of it but because of her convictions. But now, she realized that she was not concentrating. Her mind was restless, preoccupied. She had never been like this before. The more Rajan argued with her, the more it disturbed her. It wasn't his arguments—she was quite used to his ways. It was something else. Something she couldn't quite put her finger on. As the discussion went on she fell silent. She didn't reply.

'You are not listening, are you? What happened?' Rajan enquired, looking up.

There was a sudden stillness in the air, the stillness of an injured soul.

'Dom, what's wrong?'

She just shook her head, burying her face in the palms of her hands.

'Dom?' he got up concerned.

'I don't know. Really. I'm just sort of upset. I've been feeling very low for some time,' she cried softly. 'You know, a feeling of helplessness, that life's going by without me being able to understand or influence anything that's happening?'

'Why? Has something happened?'

'I don't know,' she sobbed. 'I can't think of anything. I just don't know. I don't know what I'm feeling any more.'

Rajan sat next to her, took her right hand in his and put his left arm around her shoulder. She was crying softly. He had never seen her this vulnerable before.

TOTAL BANDH

The pint-sized Pillayar Temple under the banyan tree at the corner of Sterling Road was nothing to write home about. It looked like any other Pillayar Temple under a tree at an intersection.

There was no dearth of intersections in Chennai and Pillayar Temples had sprouted like mushrooms everywhere. A granite Ganesha was installed under a tree and before one could say 'Pillayar', a concrete structure had come over it and a temple was born. It obstructed the footpath and forced the pedestrians to walk on the road. Accidents and deaths increased when drivers stopped their vehicles suddenly in the middle of the road to get a glimpse of the Pillayar. But the temples remained and could not be removed. The people who built the temples put a hundi in front of the idol, collected money from the devout and became rich. Even trees whose barks remotely resembled an elephant's trunk—as did most tree trunks—were promptly smeared with vermilion and sandal paste, and turned into *swayambhu* Pillayars, gods created by nature.

But on that day, the luck of the Pillayar at the corner of Sterling Road ran out. Some miscreants had tied up the priest in the early hours of the morning and desecrated the idol with a garland of fish. That too, stale fish.

By breakfast time, the news had spread. The Muslims have struck again. To create communal tension. They never did accept Partition. This was their way of proving the two-nation theory. It was probably the Christians. Reacting to the attacks against them in Orissa. But then why in Chennai? Maybe it was neither of them. The Pakistani ISI? That was always possible. They could be relied upon to pursue single-mindedly their aim to dismember India. But why Chennai? Was it because it was a soft target? Or better still, Pak-based Lashkar-e-Toiba. That sounded plausible. They were against infidels, and what better way to start their jihad than to desecrate a temple. No, it might be some disgruntled elements in one of the numerous Dravidian political parties in Chennai after all. Or just a poor bankrupt fisherman wanting to vent his ire on God.

People picked the theory that appealed to them most. The ruling party blamed the Opposition, the Brahmins blamed the non-Brahmins, the Hindus the Muslims, the Muslims the Christians. Everyone was happy to have someone to blame. And by noon, mobs went out onto the streets, stoning shops, attacking pet suspects and burning buses. By evening, violence had broken out, the police were called in, and both the ruling party and the Opposition called a bandh the next day. Schoolchildren cheered in delight, college-goers seemed indifferent. Paramesh thatha considered it a legitimate protest of the downtrodden against the bourgeoisie.

Rajan was in Velacheri when his sister called. Jayaraman had warned her about the disturbances in the city. Rajan was to go home immediately and take safe routes. What the safe routes were, nobody knew.

'Go through Koturpuram and via Nandanam,' suggested Veena.

'And face the mob near the Raj Bhavan?' asked Rajan.

'Then try Mount Road.'

'You must be mad.'

'Adayar? At least you can stop at our place if the bridge is closed.'

'Veena, I'll find my way home. If I can't, I'll come to your place.'

'Okay, you decide, but be careful.'

Rajan called Gayathri. She was at home.

'Rajan, tomorrow's a holiday. You remember, I told you about those artist friends of mine? They are free tomorrow and I have called them over for a lazy evening and dinner, to meet you. Don't be intimidated.'

'Don't be silly, why should I be intimidated?'

'—they're not like the bunch at Bell Metal, that's what I mean. So don't say no. You must come.'

He agreed. He had nothing much to do in any case.

Gayathri was into the Chennai art scene and she knew her stuff. She could tell a Bhupen Khakhar from a Ganesh Pyne, an old M.F. Hussain from a new one. She could talk as intelligibly on the Impressionists as on Mughal miniatures. She was a good painter herself. She painted portraits and abstracts. Rajan understood the portraits but not the abstracts. He could learn a thing or two by mixing with her crowd, he thought.

The roads had become deathly quiet, it was like a calm before the storm. People hurried home suspicious of other human beings. Rajan drove down the fast emptying streets. In a way he was relieved that the traffic had thinned. He decided to take the Koturpuram road, go via Nandanam Extension into Chamiers Road and straight to Alwarpet. He rolled up the windows, turned on the AC and the Beatles. Nothing like the old favourites to savour the bandh. Enjoying the freedom of driving fast, he turned into the road leading to the bridge that connected to Nandanam. It was then that he saw the mob. In fact, he almost missed seeing it, engrossed as he was in the Beatles. They came into view suddenly and, since Rajan was confident that he wouldn't meet with any trouble, unexpectedly. They were several hundred metres ahead engaged in setting fire to a green and white Pallavan Transport city bus. He could see a few hundred—lungis, *veshtis*, khaki trousers—in the centre of

the road. It was the first time he saw a real mob in action. The
fervour with which they hunted for objects to destroy. Then
the police charged. The mob ran helter-skelter, jumping barriers,
onto the pavements, throwing stones in their retreat, at the
police, at the shop shutters and vehicles parked nearby. The
road was strewn with glass. The bus was by now engulfed in a
ball of fire. A thick black smoke rose up in the air.

He tried to reverse the car as swiftly as he could. A few
from the mob were heading in his direction and thumped on
his car as they ran by. A stone hit his car out of nowhere. Rajan
dodged the charging bodies and, without another glance, sped
away in the opposite direction. It was when he was a couple of
kilometres away that he realized his hands were trembling. He
stopped the music and rolled the windows down to catch his
breath and listen. No. He heard nothing. Towards Adayar he
drove, the bridge, down to Alwarpet, and, finally, home.

Rajan's heart was beating fast. But he had returned in one
piece. Dom was at home. A quiet evening with her would do
him good. He decided to go over.

'Rajan, I have to tell you something. Come inside for a
second.' Lakshmi called him when he returned from Dom's
house.

'What is it?' he enquired.

'Rajan,' Lakshmi spoke lowering her voice. 'This the
second day in a row you have spent at Dominique's house.'

'Third,' he corrected her.

'I want to tell you something,' she said, her voice dropping
lower. 'Don't get me wrong. It just occurred to me so I thought
I should tell you. You are soon going to be married to
Gayathri. The whole of Chennai now knows about it. Dom is
like a daughter to me and both of you have grown up like
brother and sister for two decades. But you must be a little bit
more circumspect from now on. All of us understand your

childhood friendship with Dom. But, you cannot expect the same understanding from Gayathri or her relatives or friends. For them, she is another girl—a French girl. If they see you too often with her, or they hear about it from a third person, they will get a very different impression of both of you. This is bound to create unnecessary complications. Rajan, you must realize that Dom is not a small girl anymore. She is a full-fledged, good-looking woman. While I am fully aware that she is engaged to a Frenchman, other people may not be willing to see reason. They will talk loosely, enough to ruin a fledgling relationship and, eventually, a marriage. Why should you put yourself in such a position? The best solution and, probably the only practical one, is for you to keep away from Dom for some time. It's not going to be easy. What you do after marriage is your headache, since Gayathri will then be a party to what you do, but what you do now is our responsibility. I request you to please stay away from the Leonards' place.'

Rajan was stunned. Looking into his mother's eyes, he knew that she was dead serious. Lakshmi had made up her mind some time ago. Rajan would have to tone down his relationship with Dom. Didn't Lakshmi herself do it when she married Sundaram? She had left behind her childhood friends in Tenkasi to join Sundaram. Anjana, Revati, Deepa and Venkat. All of them became dim memories. They had tried to keep in touch, but they too got married and the link was lost forever. Now, they knew where the others were and remained content with that thought. No more. In fairness to Sundaram, he had never asked Lakshmi to do what she did. That was the custom. The girl joined the boy and usually cut her links with her friends, in some cases, even with her own family. She visited her family during her pregnancy and, after that, whenever she could or was allowed to. The girl was a part and parcel of the husband's family and hardly had an existence outside his circle—his friends were hers, his lifestyle hers and her life's course followed his. It was not thrust upon the wife nor did she think of it as an imposition. That was how it was.

In this case, however, Lakshmi was trying to reverse the logic. She was asking Rajan to cut off his ties, sever the umbilical cord. She didn't want Rajan to derail her carefully laid-out plans. As it is, the flaw—the minor flaw—in the horoscopes had to be sorted out quickly and quietly. Lakshmi was prepared to be heartless when necessary. And it was necessary now.

'Amma, you are asking me to do the impossible. I know that you are thinking of my welfare. But the answer is no. I don't even want to get into this.' Rajan's curt reply laid to rest any further talk but not the issue itself. As he left the room, he realized that there was one thing he didn't have any control over. What if Lakshmi went to Dominique and asked her to stay away from him?—Would Dom agree? Rajan knew that the answer to both questions was yes.

After a long time, Rajan woke up late and had a leisurely morning cup of coffee. Then he read *The Hindu*. He could relax. Shiva and his men had indicated that the project would be ready in a couple of days. Things were going according to plan.

There was a strange stillness in the air. Something was missing. He tuned his ears to the stillness. Yes, it was clearly missing, the sound of morning traffic. While Clive Avenue was a cul-de-sac with no cross traffic, the sound of impatient horns, screeching brakes and revving-up engines wafted in from Kasturi Ranga Road and Cathedral Road. One could never escape it. Today, there wasn't a sound.

'Amma, there doesn't seem to be any water in the overhead tank,' announced Revati calmly as she made this sudden discovery in the kitchen while washing some vessels.

'Oh God! Of all days, why do we have to run short of water today,' lamented Lakshmi. 'We can't even call the water truck to fill up the tank. The municipality chaps must be off today thanks to the bandh.'

'Just when I thought that there would be enough water for a few days in Madras,' Sundaram added. 'Anyway, there is fortunately some water in the underground sump. It was good that we filled it up the day before yesterday even though we had to call for a water truck and give those rascals five hundred rupees. In any case, let's fill up the overhead tank with the water. Let's also try the handpump and see whether we can pump some water into the sump.'

Rajan, Lakshmi and Revati were rounded up to handle the pump. Each took turns till they got tired and gave way to the next. Water trickled into the underground sump and there was some water again. The overhead tank was also half full. That would see the Sundarams through the bandh. Sundaram promptly pulled out his neatly written 'DON'T FLUSH' sign and hung it over the flush. This was his contribution to conserving water. Pour water, don't flush. That was the motto.

CV called just before noon. The bowling alley near Stella Maris College was open, he had checked. Shiva was also free. Was Rajan game? It seemed a good idea.

As the three walked to Madison Bowling, the looming white building of Stella Maris College appeared on the left.

'How many days have I spent in the tea shop across the road ogling the girls going in and out! The good ol' days!' sighed CV, looking wistfully at the closed wrought-iron gates of the college. He half expected some girl to open the gate and drag him in. A lone watchman was slumped in his chair, deep in slumber, oblivious to the passion building up inside CV.

The steel shutters of Madison Bowling were half down. Murugesan, the young US-returned owner, didn't want to take too many chances with the bandh. As the three ducked into the bowling alley, they found a few more like them taking advantage of the bandh. 'Chilling out', as Gayathri would say, Rajan thought. They'd have a game of snooker and then do a bit of bowling.

Someone was calling out loudly from the street. The sound of running feet, the cry came nearer and a stout dark man draped in a blue lungi entered. He took a second to adjust to the dim light and spotted Murugesan at the counter.

'You son-of-a-whore!' he cried. 'Why the hell are you keeping the shop open today? You have your brains in your arse or what! A mob is coming down the main road.'

'Since the shop is in the side lane, I thought—'

'You idiot. Shut it right now. I came to warn you. Some of them know that you are open and will come any moment now.'

The man ran out. Rajan and CV rushed to assist Murugesan in bringing down the shutters. A big lock was quickly put in place. They were locked in. They hardly had a choice. There was little point in stepping out. They heard shouts, slogans and the sound of running feet.

'Bastard, shut the shop!' someone called.

'Or we will set the shop on fire, you son-of-a-whore.'

Running feet and more shouts. There was a babble of voices and loud cries. More and more seemed to be coming in from the main road. They heard the familiar voice of the dark stout man shouting over the commotion and din. 'Leave them alone, I say. They are shutting down. He is just foolish and has promised to leave.' There was a loud crashing on the steel shutters. The noise shook the inmates. Probably a stone. Another crash. And another. And a few more.

There was silence inside. Everyone looked at the steel shutters almost expecting them to be ripped down and the mob to come in. Rajan looked around quickly to see whether he could spot any sharp instrument. His eyes fell on the billiards cue. It didn't help.

'Come out, you arseholes.' Someone banged on the shutters and shook them violently. Another joined in.

'Okay guys, now leave them alone and disperse. He has learnt his lesson.' It was that same familiar voice.

'The bastards will do anything for money.'

'All these guys should be finished. Only then will Tamils prosper.'

'Down with casteism,' someone shouted. Rajan wondered what that had to do with a bowling alley. A crash and the sound of falling glass.

'There go my lights,' said Murugesan, emotionless, face ashen. Some more falling glass.

'My neon sign.'

'Enough, guys. Stop it. Let's keep moving.' They heard the sound of shuffling feet.

'Set it on fire.'

The smell of burning wood wafted in through the shutters. 'The chairs outside.'

'You people have burnt enough. Get moving. There are other places to go to.' There were murmurs of protest and then the footsteps receded.

The voices became fainter except for the odd shrill cry and a few misdirected stones hitting the concrete outside.

'*Dai* Murugesan, go home right away. They've left.' It was the dark man again.

No one moved. Murugesan didn't need any more incentive to wind up. His face was regaining colour. 'Why the fuck did I have to come back to Chennai? Fuck those guys. Fuck the Government. What's the use if they can't even protect the property of their citizens? Bloody hoodlums. Fucking thugs. I should have gone with my instincts and stayed back in the US.' The bowling alley was being put back in shape. The cues were returned to their proper place and the snooker balls kept in frames. Murugesan stepped out through the back door to see whether the mob had left. They had.

The entrance resembled a battlefield. There were stones strewn all over, broken glass pieces, a gaping hole where the neon lights had been. All that remained of Madison Bowling was MAD----- OWL-----. The charred remains of the chairs lay on the ground. The table had somehow survived.

'Fuck you guys! Bastards! Mother fuckers!' Murugesan's car had mercifully been parked behind. It remained unharmed.

The afternoon bandh celebrations ended as quickly as they had begun for the Three Musketeers.

Rajan was all set for the evening. The afternoon episode was put behind him. There was no point in alarming his parents, especially after the event was over. He drove over to Gayathri's place.

They sat on the balcony upstairs enjoying the sea breeze, the banyan tree arched over them. 'My friends are quite a handful, I'm warning you. Don't get put off.' Gayathri didn't want Rajan to be caught by surprise. She wore a dark blue flowing dress with white embroidery and tiny mirrors on it. She looked alive and pretty.

Before Jyotika came into the room with Mohan, Rajan could smell her Cool Water. She was a Kuchipudi dancer and he a film music composer. 'They are not married, but live together,' whispered Gayathri quickly into Rajan's ears. 'Congrats Gayathri, and you too Rajan,' both said in unison. Jyotika offered both her painted cheeks to Rajan and he pecked carefully trying to fight off the Cool Water. Mohan kissed Gayathri.

Viren, whom Rajan had briefly seen at Bell Metal, was next. He came alone. He had looked tall, wiry and seedy at Bell Metal in his black T-shirt and jeans but now looked his best in a full-sleeve shirt and grey corduroy pants. Even Gayathri seemed a bit surprised. 'Darling, meet Viren, the budding painter. You met him at Bell Metal. He is probably the only one to combine oils with watercolours. I will show you the one he gave me. It's exquisite.'

Soon, they all started trooping in. Ramanan came with his German boyfriend Karl. 'They live together as well. So be careful about the questions you ask.' Gayathri's timely warning again. Ramanan wore an earring and it was easy to tell who was who in the couple.

Madhavi, Gayathri's classmate, came in smelling of Dune. 'I'm not an artist,' she warned. 'I just happen to be Gayathri's classmate.'

The Sandeepans were a regular couple, married that is. That came as a surprise and a bit of a relief. They were dancers working on East–West fusion. They had trained with Ananda Shankar for a while and had even been invited for the Dusseldorf festival the previous year. The balcony was filling up. Ganesh, the well-known Tamil author, Guru and Devayani, the dancing couple, Palanivel the architect and others had all turned up.

The cool sea breeze stirred the treetops. Rajan surveyed the scene and liked it. The crowd was warm and friendly. They didn't bring any baggage. Some were pompous, but not without cause. Most were opinionated but then who wasn't. They were willing to listen to Rajan even when he didn't have a point of view. Rajan was getting into the flow of things. In fact, he was beginning to enjoy himself. Gayathri went about with gay abandon. It was obvious that she revelled in such a crowd. Looking at her, Rajan was a bit envious. She locked her hands in his and took him around. Rajan let himself be led. Since her parents were not in town, drinks were being served as well. Wine, beer and brandy flowed freely. Why brandy, Rajan had asked. Chennai*vasis* preferred that to anything else, even at the height of summer, Gayathri had explained.

After the first two rounds of drinks, the decibel level got louder. So did the laughter. Gayathri had a glass of claret in one hand, the stem clasped delicately between her fingers. There was a cigarette in the other. She had decided to smoke at home taking advantage of her parents' absence. She kept giggling and laughing. The wine is getting to her, Rajan thought. She must be drinking it too fast. Rajan had himself downed two beers and was feeling quite mellow. He gently disengaged from Gayathri and went over to the Sandeepans and joined in their lively debate. Ganesh, the Tamil author, was feeling a bit left out since the others were speaking to each other in English. Rajan, who knew his *Shilapadikaram* from his *Tirukkural*, tried to draw Ganesh into the conversation and put him at ease. Ganesh was pleasantly surprised that someone in this crowd knew Tamil literature. Rajan looked around. Gayathri was nowhere in sight. She must have gone to get the dinner ready, he thought, and decided to go look for her.

When he went downstairs, past the Ganesh Pyne and the study, he heard a familiar giggle. What was Gayathri giggling about? He stopped and peeped in. Mohan and Gayathri were locked in an embrace and Mohan was trying to kiss her. Mohan's back was to Rajan. Gayathri was not trying to get away. Suddenly, her arms went around his neck and they kissed. For a second, Rajan stood stunned. Then, almost instinctively, he ducked out of view. Rajan's mind went momentarily blank. He wasn't sure of what to do. What was he supposed to do? Was it really Gayathri he saw? Yes. Even if he had downed a couple of beers, there could be no doubt, it was Gayathri. He looked around and saw no one. No one had seen him either. It seemed as though he had done something wrong, snooping around like a burglar. Should he continue as though he hadn't seen anything? Should he confront them? He ruled out the second option almost immediately. That would be immature. He went back upstairs and quietly joined the crowd. This was the sensible thing to do. The party carried on.

The group Rajan joined was in the midst of an animated discussion. Rajan nodded his head but couldn't hear a thing. His mind was still reeling, trying to make some sense of what he had just seen. What the hell was Gayathri up to? Was it the claret or something else? With Mohan? When had Mohan come into the picture? In a few minutes, Gayathri and Mohan came upstairs. She was giggling her head off. He looked smug at having found such an ardent admirer. Rajan watched them from the corner of his eye and pretended not to notice.

Dinner was served, and Gayathri led Rajan downstairs. He let himself be led. He was feeling rotten, like an apple eaten away on the inside by a worm. The zest he had was suddenly gone. He stood there like a punctured balloon. He was dying to get hold of her and ask her for an explanation. But that would have been silly. His mind was about to explode. She was going around urging people to attack the food. She was unsteady on her feet. Rajan could barely concentrate. With hardly anything on his plate, he went and sat next to Jyotika. She kept up a lively monologue and he smiled and nodded encouragingly from time to time. Every minute the party dragged on, it was getting more and more painful. Not even the sight of the Sandeepans cheered him up. He made some small talk with Karl. Gayathri came across to them and took him away.

'You don't look too well. Is anything wrong?' Gayathri slurred over 'anything'. She was tipsy.

'I'm listening intently to everything, Gaya.'

Dessert had been laid out, rasgullas and ice cream. Then liqueur was served, Drambuie or Cointreau or both. Hot coffee and cigars ended the meal. It seemed the party would never come to an end. Gayathri had wanted the party to be big and lavish. And that's how it was. One by one, people started leaving. They kissed Gayathri and Rajan goodbye. Mohan merely pecked her cheeks, Rajan noticed. The bastard! When Mohan came to kiss him, Rajan fought the urge to punch him in the nose and offered to shake hand instead. Viren left last of all.

Gayathri was still at the doorway. Rajan turned around and walked towards her. He had to get it over with. He wanted to confront her and ask what the hell that was all about. It was becoming unbearable, the questions. She turned around and saw him standing directly behind her.

'How wash it, dahling?' she slurred. He saw her bloodshot eyes. 'You liked my fendsh?' She would remember. She had to remember. Rajan looked into those bloodshot eyes. She looked back, blank, vacant.

'I have something important to talk to you about, Gaya,' he paused. She looked into his eyes, glazed. He waited a moment. 'But not today, tomorrow,' he added. She kissed him goodbye.

It was way past eleven when Rajan drove back. He was so disturbed he was barely able to concentrate on the road. Fortunately, Clive Avenue was not far. As he turned into Kasturi Ranga Road, two men appeared right in front of his car out of nowhere, waving their hands. He reacted instinctively and pressed the brakes stopping inches from the men.

'Saar, saar . . . come out, there's a man lying on the road. Come out and see,' they came around to his window.

As Rajan got out, a strong hand covered his mouth from behind. He felt a sharp pain in his back. The man in front pulled out a knife and plunged it into him. A blunt object hit his head. He heard voices before he passed out.

THE THIRD UMPIRE

When Rajan came around, he woke up to darkness. There was a dull pain in his head. He tried to move but couldn't. He could hardly feel his arms and legs, he felt like a person with a head but no body. After lying like that for a while, he sank back into a stupor.

Lakshmi waited outside the ICU in the corridor. It was evident that she was in a state of shock. Gayathri sat next to her, very grim. The hospital smell made the situation seem grimmer than it actually was. Even a healthy person inhaling that air felt that they had only a few hours to live. The broken plastic bucket seats, rocking precariously on steel frames made the scenario even more depressing.

It was more than fifteen hours earlier that Rajan had been wheeled into the hospital in an unconscious state, bleeding profusely. It was sheer providence that a few minutes after he was stabbed another car had turned into the same road. The thugs had fled, leaving behind a bleeding Rajan. The occupants of the car that found him had searched Rajan's pockets and on finding Sundaram's visiting card, had promptly contacted him. Rajan was taken to the hospital in half an hour—the same hospital Sundaram worked in. But Sundaram refused to work on Rajan. He just couldn't. His second in command was woken up and asked to do the needful. Wearing a mask and the ghostly surgical cloak, Sundaram stood in the operation theatre watching his colleague attend to Rajan's wounds and cuts, and gave directions when necessary. The operation took all of two hours. By the time Rajan was wheeled into the ICU, Lakshmi, Veena and Jayaraman were waiting.

'He got away by the skin of his teeth,' Sundaram broke the news calmly. 'He will be fine.'

They silently waited for him to say more. Lakshmi's eyes were red and swollen. Veena had been crying too. Jayaraman had been left to handle both.

'I'm telling you, he will be fine. He was knifed—'

'No!' Lakshmi wailed loudly on hearing the word 'knife'. Veena held her as Lakshmi sobbed uncontrollably.

'Listen, Lakshmi, he is going to be all right. Believe me. By God's grace, none of the injuries are life threatening. All the wounds are in the sub-scapular region, below the shoulder blades and away from the spinal cord. Thank your gods that the lung was not pierced.' He took care not to use the word 'knife' again. 'Dr Cariappa operated on him under my supervision and everything went off well. He will be in the ICU under observation, and in a couple of days, he should be out.'

None of them quite believed Sundaram entirely. That was the price for being the father and the doctor. He was, however, their best source of information. For now, they had to take his word for it. They decided to ask Dr Cariappa later, when Sundaram was not around. When they spoke to the doctor, he confirmed that what Sundaram had said was indeed correct. They informed Gayathri in the morning. Dominique was given charge of taking care of Paati.

Jayaraman met Commissioner of Police Kalimuthu. Kalimuthu was aware of the incident. He promised to have Devanathan interrogated immediately, and the goondas rounded up.

'I will get to the bottom of this,' he assured. 'My men will get them to spit out the story in no time.'

Rajan was savouring every bit of the attention he was getting. Sitting upright on the bed, he was enjoying the soup and bread with his family all around him. He felt like a hero. Veena, Gayathri, Jayaraman, Lakshmi were all there. Arvind the Wife Beater and Bhargavi kept Lakshmi company throughout. Dom, the Leonards, Shiva, CV, Bashir, and P.V.R.N. Rao had dropped in twice. Even those who had never spoken to the Sundarams rang up making anxious enquiries about his health. 'It's only in such situations that one gets to know how many friends one actually has. There is still hope for Mankind,' Lakshmi philosophized. Paramesh thatha spent a whole day with Rajan, regaling him with stories of Communist exploits and talking about the current political scene. He then decided to spend another whole day with Paati to keep his sister company. Gayathri's parents had rushed back after hearing about this. Dominique dropped by often initially, but, subsequently, her brief was to keep Paati occupied—with chess and bridge. Paati was hardly in a mood for chess and cards. Dominique was also told to see to it that Paati took her medicines and that Revati served her her meals on time. Paati had been told about Rajan the day after the incident and she had worried herself sick. The fact that Paati's husband had also been a doctor made matters worse because Paati was convinced that her knowledge of ailments was as much as her husband's had been. Sundaram's answers to her queries on Rajan's condition had to be precise. She was quick to point out when he was ambivalent. He had to fill her in on all the technical details before she was satisfied.

Rajan had been in hospital for three days. He even had his laptop brought to him. The doctors promised to let him go in two days. Veena took Lakshmi home so that she could rest and relax. Lakshmi had been the worst affected. Jayaraman promised to return in the evening. Sundaram was on his rounds in the hospital. Rajan found himself alone with Gayathri.

Rajan hadn't forgotten that dinner. He had observed Gayathri closely over the last few days. Gayathri seemed to be

genuinely affected by the turn of events. Rajan tried to detect
any artificiality in her concern for him, but there was none.
Her actions appeared genuine. Then why had she behaved that
way the other evening? He couldn't get the incident out of his
mind. But this was hardly the time to broach the subject.

'There's something important I want to ask you, Rajan,'
Gayathri said quietly when they were alone. It caught Rajan
unawares.

'What?'

'There's something important I had wanted to ask you
since the day of the dinner.'

'Ask me?'

'Yes.' Rajan could see that she was extremely uneasy.
Gayathri looked up to find him staring at her.

'Did you really enjoy the dinner that day?' she asked.

Rajan looked confused. 'Why do you ask?'

'Because you appeared as if you didn't enjoy it at all. It
almost seemed as if I had dragged you into it. You looked like
a person who had been forced to come to the party . . . You
didn't enjoy my friends' company either. They are not the best
in the world; they may even be a weird bunch. But you were
totally ill at ease. Somehow I've always got the impression that
everything you are doing for my sake is pro forma. I'm not
talking about the Bell Metal incident, where I admit I behaved
atrociously. You just happen to give the impression of tolerating
me and my lifestyle rather than really loving me, let alone
involving yourself in my life. I am not asking you to change
overnight or even change at all. I don't even expect you to be
mushy or demonstrative. All I ask you is to tell me if there's
anything about me or my life you don't like. I am entitled to
know, Rajan. We have to understand our likes and dislikes
before we get married. If you don't tell me what you feel about
me, I won't know. I can only suspect but never really know.
You have to tell me. Even if what you say hurts, I have to
know.'

He looked at her. Tears were welling up in her eyes. She averted her eyes and looked away. Rajan kept quiet. The silence seemed to last forever.

'Rajan, I'm sorry,' she choked. 'I didn't want to bring this up now. Of all times and places, especially at a time you're fighting to regain your health. It's silly of me and I'm truly sorry. I just couldn't help it. However, I have wanted to ask since the moment you left that night. It has been preying on my mind. Every time I look at you, I think about it. I couldn't sleep without unburdening this on you. Sometimes I get the feeling that we are, without quite realizing it ourselves, making a mistake.'

'Mistake?' Rajan spoke for the first time.

A teardrop trickled down her left cheek. She wiped her eyes. She composed herself. 'Rajan, I dread to think this. But going by the way I see our relationship developing, I wonder whether we are making a mistake by getting married to each other. I don't know. This is just something that struck me. I want you to think about it. Give it serious thought. We are supposed to be mature people. Unlike our parents, we even have the luxury of judging our compatibility before tying the knot. I can't help feeling that somewhere we are two very different people with very different world views. Coming from the US, I thought you would be a party-going type, an extrovert. Not shallow, mind you, but still someone who likes to get into the swing of things. But your interests seem to be quite different. Even that doesn't bother me too much. But . . . my smoking, non-vegetarianism, drinking, even my talking . . . You don't seem to approve of any of it.'

'I never said any—'

'You don't have to *say* anything, Rajan. I know. You just don't approve of what I do. Full stop.'

They sat looking away from each other. He stared at the blanket and she at the mosaic floor. Rajan's first and instinctive reaction was to deny vehemently all that she was saying. He wanted to say it was not true at all and put the relationship back on track. He didn't want to hurt her. But he knew this was not a game. She was dead serious, and she was very disturbed. Her outburst had come after she had given the matter considerable thought. She spoke from her head, not just the heart. She obviously understood Rajan much better than he thought she did.

'I don't know what to say, Gaya.'

'Don't say anything now. Just think about what I have said. You don't have to tell me now.'

He could hear her breathing. There wasn't very much to say. Gayathri couldn't have been clearer. They were two very different people. Did that mean the end of the road? Not necessarily. After all, compatibility did not necessarily mean thinking and acting alike.

'When you put it that way Gaya, yes, maybe we are very different. Probably not meant for each other.' He meant it as a question, but it sounded like an answer.

Even before Commissioner Kalimuthu was approached, Balakrishna Shastrigal had been summoned and ordered to invoke the gods. And some goddesses.

Lakshmi and Sundaram wanted him to prepare for the *Mrityunjaya Homam* to ensure the victory over death. Not that Rajan was dying. But the Sundarams wanted to feel reassured that everything would be fine. To perform *Mrityunjaya Homam* even while Rajan lay in hospital enjoying his fresh tomato soup. While Balakrishna Shastrigal was at it, they also wanted him to perform the *Navagraha Homam* and the *Ganesha Pooja*. A three-in-one affair. After the three-in-one invocation, Yama, the God of Death, would find it near impossible to come near Sabarmati, what with all the gods and some goddesses guarding it.

Balakrishna Shastrigal was asked to organize the three-in-one *homams* the next day. He called in late that evening and confessed that he could get only two more Shastrigals. He couldn't get hold of a third. They needed a fourth—three was inauspicious. The Sundarams reluctantly agreed to postpone it by a day.

'All these Shastrigals are only after money,' Sundaram cursed them. 'You wave a hundred-rupee note and they will go after it wagging their tails. Someone must have tempted the third Shastrigal with money and he must have refused our Balakrishna.'

The four tufted Shastrigals, when they did actually turn up together, filled the house with the sound of invocations, *japams* and prayers. Pure ghee was poured into the fire and smoke filled the house. Since the Sundarams, Veena and Jayaraman had to participate, Paramesh thatha found an easy excuse—he had to keep Rajan company—and ran away, far from the opium of the masses. The tufted four were also paid handsomely in the end, a fitting finale. Balakrishna Shastrigal was paid a little more. Not for nothing was he the head Shastrigal.

Astrologer Chandramouli sat with an air of devotion throughout the four-and-a-half-hour ceremony. It was only after the four well-fed and satiated Shastrigals left that he approached Lakshmi.

'Amma, if you recollect, I had mentioned the flaw in the horoscope and the need to correct it urgently. It seems to have had its effect on Rajan earlier than I had thought.'

Lakshmi was silent. This had been the single issue weighing on her conscience. Her shock had been compounded by her conviction that she was somehow responsible for the attack on her son. She couldn't for a moment bear the thought that her silent manipulation of the two horoscopes had led to Rajan's misfortune. She had always meant to correct the flaw with the necessary pooja, but it had been too late. She was, somehow, directly responsible for the tragedy.

'I have no idea what to do. This has been most unexpected,' she said, groping for something to say. 'I'm now wondering what to do. Do we proceed? If so, we should have the *homam* very soon to get rid of the flaw.' She paused. 'However, some of the flaws are a bit too entrenched to go away that easily. If this is the case, should we go ahead with the alliance at all? Believe me, I don't know what to do. I still haven't spoken to my husband about this. I don't know how he will react to the news. Moreover, Gayathri's parents are also to be consulted. What will they think of all this? What about Rajan and Gayathri themselves? If they come to hear about this . . .'

'Amma, I think you are still in a state of shock,' concluded Chandramouli. 'Take your time, and decide after talking to Saar. Whatever happened has happened. Now it's time to look ahead and take the right decision. Rajan is getting better and he is going to be all right. Take heart from that Amma. This is not the time to despair. Rajan has a good, strong horoscope and things can only take a turn for the better whatever you decide.'

'I don't know.' Lakshmi was crushed. 'I just don't understand anything, any more.'

Balan the Milk Man was disturbed. He had gone—God knew how many months later—to the San Thome Church on Marina Beach. He had always turned to this church for solace. The towering spires of the Basilica built over Apostle San Thome were grand enough to humble any human soul. As a youngster, he had walked past the weather-beaten Basilica every other day doing a quick cross across his chest. He felt His presence whenever he felt the need for his parents whom he had never seen. He used to sit on the bench inside the church and wonder what it was like to have parents, real parents who would love him and pamper him. He felt a twinge of regret that he didn't have a home to go to. But then, how could he ever regret when the Lord Himself was his mother and father. He had been told that the poor were indeed rich in spirit. The church was his home. Now the church, more than a nineteen hundred years old, his home, had been spruced up and the whiteness of the spires was matched only by the purity of Heaven. The church was indeed special to him. An oasis of calm amidst the madness of the city and the beggars sitting outside the walls.

Balan prayed to the all-compassionate Lord Jesus for Rajan's health and to the tomb of the Apostle for his complete recovery. He then asked the all-forgiving Lord Jesus for forgiveness for acts not yet committed. He had not yet beaten up the rowdies who had stabbed Rajan. He had not yet broken their teeth. He had not yet pulverized their bones and broken their hands and legs. He had not yet sent them on a stretcher to the hospital. He asked forgiveness for all these acts, not yet committed, but planned for very soon.

When Balan came out, a row of beggars greeted him again. Beggars belonged to the category of people who knew no religion but were born with the awareness that all those going into places of worship were prone to a weakness, alms giving. While the devout may have cheated their clients of lakhs without batting an eyelid, they always threw a five-rupee note into a beggar's bowl, especially if the beggar sat outside temples, churches or mosques. The devout didn't want to openly displease the gods. Good deed for the day done, these people got the licence to do unspeakable things during the rest of the week. Balan took one look at the beggars and shook his head in disgust. 'If any one of you is prepared to come with me with cycle chains and sticks to beat up a bunch of rowdies, then you will earn your bread and I will pay you well,' he shouted to them. 'Otherwise, no god is going to help you.'

He went to Sundaram to plead that he be given a chance to 'set the rowdies right'. 'Ayyah, I know who these guys are. I will teach these sons-of-whores a lesson. The police will not do anything since they are powerful rowdies having the backing of ministers. Leave it to me, Ayyah. I will set them right. Rajan

is like my own son. I have seen him go in a pram on the same
street where these bastards stabbed him. I will set the mother
fuckers right. I have dealt with such third-rate sons-of-whores
earlier and I know how to deal with them.'

Sundaram dismissed him outright. 'You stay out of this,
Balan. This is not for you or, for that matter, for me. There are
people charged with the duty of finding the culprits and they
will do so. Don't get into this and buy trouble for yourself. You
people see such nonsense in Tamil films, come out believing
you are Robin Hood and take the law into your hands. You
attend to your work Balan and *stay right out of it.*'

Balan remained totally unconvinced. 'Okay Ayyah, I defer
to your wishes. You are a good man. But let me tell you that
you have no idea of what you are talking. Which world are you
in? Law will nail them? If they find even one of these mother
fuckers or do anything at all on this matter I will be surprised.
And Ayyah, one last thing,' Balan was not one to give up easily.
'Every morning, I have asked my boys to bring only Karuppayee
to your house from now on. She is the best cow I have. If our
boy Rajan drinks her milk, he will not only fully recover all his
health but any injury will vanish without a trace. You know
Ramalingam Saar in Poes Garden. His child had health problem
last month. I asked him to take Karuppayee's milk. The child
was cured in a week.'

Karuppayee, the Black One, was Balan's favourite cow. The
fact that the cow was as white as freshly fallen snow was only
of academic interest. Balan had called the snow-white cow the
Black One because he didn't want the evil eye to fall on it.
Karuppayee was special. She got the best cattle feed. She had
the luxury of a separate shed. Soon, Balan started attributing
medicinal properties to her milk. Every morning Karuppayee
was ordered to stand in front of the 'Beware of Dog' board at
Sabarmati, to cure Rajan with her miraculous milk. Sundaram
wanted to say that any milk not diluted with water had
curative properties but decided against it.

Lakshmi finally let out the truth about the horoscopes to Sundaram. It was the truth but not the whole truth. She got cold feet and shifted part of the blame onto Chandramouli. He was the one who indicated that the flaw could be corrected by a *homam*, she told Sundaram, and asked how they should proceed.

Sundaram had been taken aback. He listened patiently to Lakshmi like he would to a patient with high blood pressure. 'Lakshmi, you should have told me about this earlier. Haven't I told you several times that that damned computer of Chandramouli's was totally unreliable? This is what happens when we rely on computers and not human intuition. You did not care to listen to me. Now see where we have ended up. What if that damn Chandramouli was wrong about correcting the flaw as well? What if he can't correct the flaw? Then the marriage is doomed.' Sundaram was furious. Chandramouli's foolishness had placed Rajan's life in danger. And it caused considerable embarrassment. He told Lakshmi just as much and Lakshmi went into another bout of depression.

Lakshmi and Sundaram had to inform Gayathri's parents of the matter. It was only right to do so. Any decision had to be taken jointly by the two families. For the moment, the couple was not to be involved. They went across to Gayathri's house and called their astrologer there as well. Their astrologer agreed that there was a flaw. But it could be corrected. At least that's what he thought. He couldn't be sure. Couldn't be sure? How could there be a marriage if they couldn't be sure? The situation was becoming impossible. The parents' mood fluctuated wildly between despair and hope. They had got used to the idea of a Rajan–Gayathri wedding. The couple had met and liked each other. Both were Iyers and both families were more than well-to-do. In their own way, each one quietly prayed that an astrologer would come their way and tell them to go right ahead.

Rajan returned home to a hero's welcome. His room was transformed into a visitor's room. He was advised to go slow on physical activity but prescribed exercises. Paati was most relieved to see him in person.

'All this crime and killings convince me that your America is a safer place,' she said in disgust. 'Sometimes I wonder why you came back to this filth. In our time, our houses were never locked during the day and even in the night. Now look what's happening to Madras.'

Rajaram IAS presented him with G.V. Desani's *All About H. Hatterr* and a T.S. Eliot collection. Daulat Singh brought almost a whole shop of sweets and savouries. 'Beta, this is prasad from Vaishno Devi specially for you. My *maasi* was there three days ago.' The Leonards were there too. Arvind and Bhargavi brought some of Rajan's favourite dishes. Even Selvan the actor sent a bouquet of red roses.

Dominique was most amused. 'They never did this to you when you returned from the US.'

'They will if you return from the dead,' answered Rajan dramatically.

Dominique was careful not to get in the way whenever Gayathri came in, in spite of protests from both. 'Don't run away, Dom,' pleaded Gayathri. 'We don't need so much time together. We only end up fighting.'

But Gayathri and Rajan did need time together. They examined their relationship from all directions. Rajan had taken to Gayathri, with all her smoking, non-vegetarianism and friends. It was a package and he liked it. He was not hesitant to say so. To call Rajan conservative and an introvert was being foolish. He had done things in the US which no Tamil Brahmin would have dared to do—without being ostracized from the Tam-Bram community. But then, Gayathri did do odd things. Very odd things. And that he couldn't understand. She did not seem to be in full control of herself and that bothered him no end. Were artists supposed to be like that? No, she was just out of control and the liquor only added to the problem. He wasn't sure whether he wanted his wife to be that odd. It wasn't a nice feeling to be a reluctant bystander. She was just made differently and he, well, differently. While there did not seem to be any real need to decide now, especially when Rajan was recuperating, wasn't it better to take a decision sooner than later? Both stopped short of taking that decision. Like most people their age, they weren't sure. Rajan and Gayathri reluctantly faced the reality, or what they thought was reality. The marriage wouldn't work. They were too different. Why get into something when they knew that it may not work? Parting seemed to be the logical thing to do. They were still not too involved with each other to make the separation unbearable. When the decision to part was taken, they both seemed relieved. 'A sure sign that we have taken the right decision,' Rajan said. But, how were they going to break the news to their parents?

The parents were showing signs of desperation. A decision had to be taken soon, since if the marriage had to take place, preparations for the event had to be resumed. By mutual consent, they selected and consulted a third astrologer. A neutral third umpire.

The third umpire watched the replay in slow motion and decided that this was just not cricket. He upheld the decision of the two astrologers. If they couldn't be sure, then they just couldn't be sure. The players were both out and not out. The decision was now left to the parents.

There had to be a painless solution but there wasn't one. The chances of failure were too great. They couldn't let their children risk their lives and lead a life of pain. There were too many cases where the couple had been affected precisely because such ominous signs had been ignored. The parents reluctantly faced reality. The marriage would not work. Parting seemed to be the logical thing to do. But how were they going to break the news to the couple?

CUL-DE-SAC

Rajan was still in his teens when Rajiv Gandhi was assassinated. The assassination had taken place in Sriperumbudur, very close to Madras. Rajan's parents had gone into a shell and maintained a grim silence for the next few days. For many old timers it marked the end of the Nehru era. To all Tamils, Nehru was someone special, especially because he had been fair and handsome. This was important to the colour-conscious Tamil society. 'The Nehru family is completely finished. It must be a curse. They were destined to perish. Not even the spiritual merits accumulated by them over generations of selfless service to the nation could finally save them. This is destiny. There cannot be a greater example.'

After Rajan's stabbing, a similar grimness overtook the Sundaram household. His mother was worst affected. She could not get over the thought that she was somehow responsible for the attack on Rajan. The sparkle in her eyes had disappeared. She suddenly looked tired and she rarely smiled. Veena was by her side all the time and that had helped, but only marginally. Hearing that Lakshmi needed help, Lakshmi's younger sister Meenakshi flew in from Bangalore to keep her company and lend a hand at running Sabarmati. Lakshmi had someone to talk to and Meenakshi was a good listener. Lakshmi's condition improved. But Meenakshi couldn't stay on very long. She had her own husband and children to look after. Meenakshi had to go back. Lakshmi was alone again and soon slipped back into depression. She barely noticed when anyone walked into the house or stepped outside. She went about her household duties listlessly. Even Paati expressed her deep concern to Sundaram about Lakshmi's health.

Sundaram coped better, but just about. He had the appearance of being stoic and calm. This was the role assigned to him as a Tamil Brahmin husband and father—to be stoic and calm, emotionless, if possible. His hospital routine continued, not a day was missed. But something was gnawing inside him. Wasn't his statement against Devanathan the income tax crook that had started it all? There were crooks galore and corruption was rampant in every Chennai street corner and in every Indian bone. He could have let Devanathan's obnoxious act pass by without a murmur, and paid up like so many others did. Acts of omission were still not as serious as acts of commission. In India, the corruptee, and not the corrupt, lost and came to grief. If he had kept quiet and let the matter pass, his son might have been spared the ordeal and the family the tragedy. Sundaram could not get over the thought that he was responsible for the attack on Rajan. Lakshmi and Sundaram came to the same conclusion. They had failed their son.

Sitting in his pooja room, Sundaram prayed for Rajan's recovery. The rows of gods and goddesses stared back. They were willing to help Rajan recover even though They had not been able to stop the attack on him. They ought to have known but did nothing to stop it. Why Rajan? That was Sundaram's question. Why did You pick on Rajan? What has he done to incur Your wrath? You could have targeted me instead. Why the youngster? Sundaram thought long and deep about whether he should withdraw the statement he had given to the Income Tax Department. If something happened, none in the Income Tax Department would come to his assistance anyway. But then, the damage was already done. After all that had happened, if Devanathan went scot-free, it would be a shame. Rajan's attack should not go unpunished. Sundaram wasn't ready to give up the fight just yet.

Rajan's hospitalization had caused a temporary but brief setback for Shiva and his boys. But they were determined not to let the deadline slip by. Fortunately, much of the groundwork had been done and it was a matter of fleshing out the details. They carried on without Rajan. John Carey's deadline was met. The project was completed.

The boys celebrated by opening a bottle of champagne in Rajan's room upstairs.

In the US, deadlines were everything. And when the deadline was met, John knew that Rajan had indeed assembled a group of professionals for the job.

'Thanks a lot. Will get back to you as soon as I examine the package. Get well soon, Rajan,' John's e-mail said.

An important ingredient of the Tamil Brahmin code of social conduct was the Enquiry. On auspicious or inauspicious occasions, one enquired.

On Deepavali mornings, for instance, one had to ring up—sufficiently early—relatives and friends and enquire, 'Have you had your bath in the Ganga?' Even if one stayed two thousand kilometres away from the river, one had to ask 'Have you had your bath in the Ganga' on Deepavali. If one didn't, it was considered rude and impertinent. 'Last year he had rung up and enquired. Why has he not called this year? He ought to ring up elders and enquire.' Some grew concerned about the welfare of the non-enquirers. 'Hope all is well with him. He calls every year to enquire. Wonder why he hasn't called yet.'

If a wedding was finalized, one had to enquire. 'Congratulations! I believe there is a wedding in the family.' The enquiry had to be suo moto and there was no need to wait for formal intimation of the event. It was considered a sign of closeness.

Enquiries were also in order after weddings. 'So, a daughter-in-law has come into the family?' After return from the US, 'I believe you have returned from America?' On getting a job,

'Your son seems to have got a big job in a big company?' And so on. Enquiries could be made through phone or by a visit.

Some enquiries were especially reserved for the ladies of the Brahmin household. 'Are you still taking bath?' when addressed to another lady meant 'Are you still not pregnant?' Politer still was to address the enquiry to the mother, 'Is your daughter still taking bath?'

While friends could enquire after events or occasions both good and bad, enquiries from relatives fell into two categories. Relatives who were considered close and on talking terms, enquired, like friends, after both good and bad. But estranged relatives, with whom one never kept in touch, could enquire only during calamities or tragedies.

When weddings took place, estranged relatives maintained a stoic silence as if they had not heard about it. In any case, they were not invited. They never enquired during Deepavali or after an engagement. Nor did they enquire after an estranged returned from America. But when someone broke an arm, estranged relatives immediately rang up to enquire: 'I am sorry to hear that your son has broken an arm. We were shocked when we heard about it. He is such a wonderful boy. How did it happen?' When someone died, estranged relatives not only rang up but also visited. There were words of consolation and offers of help. After this brief show of solidarity, they went back to being estranged. The estranged usually made it a point to mention this to friends and other close relatives, ending the conversation with 'after all, blood is thicker than water.'

Sometimes, tragedies brought estranged relatives closer till they were no more estranged. This was rare. The Tamil Brahmins didn't favour this mode of rapprochment. More often than not, the formerly estranged relatives realized that they had been happier before and went back to being estranged once again.

When Rajan was hospitalized, Sundaram's estranged brother Pattabiraman called to enquire.

Pattabiraman was Sundaram's estranged elder brother. In fact their relationship oscillated between estranged and formerly estranged. More than three decades earlier, they had had a fight over their share of property after their father's death. The fight threatened to spill over into the courts. While trying to prevent that from happening, Sundaram got a raw deal, moved away and settled down in Clive Avenue, which in those days was a bit of a jungle. Like the Pandavas, he took Amma with him, while Pattabiraman, like the Kauravas, took the property. Unlike in the *Mahabharat* however, where there was a winning side, in this case, there didn't seem to be any. Both lost and both won. Over a period of time, both established name and fame for themselves—Sundaram as a renowned surgeon and Pattabiraman as a well-known banker and then financial consultant. They began wondering why they had ever fought with each other, and an uneasy truce was struck.

Blood was thicker than water but estrangement seemed to be thicker than blood. In a few months, Sundaram and Pattabiraman realized that the truce was not working. They decided to stop being nice to each other and went back to being estranged. They flip-flopped for several years between estrangement and tolerance as Paati was keen to keep the siblings together. But it didn't work. They now lived happily in a state of permanent estrangement, enquiring during tragedies and keeping a studied silence during celebrations.

The phone call was therefore of no surprise. Under the Tamil Brahmin code of social conduct, Rajan's health was a matter for a telephonic enquiry but not grave enough for a personal appearance.

'Sundaram, I'm sorry to hear about Rajan. Is it serious?'

'No, Pattabi. It isn't. They certainly tried to inflict serious injury. But by God's grace, the injuries are not life threatening and Rajan's recovering well. What was aimed at his head, has only knocked the turban off.'

'You are a doctor, fortunately. Rajan is in safe hands. If there is any help you want, please tell us.'

'Thanks, Pattabi. Here, please speak to Amma,' Sundaram hastily passed the telephone to Paati and there ended the conversation between the two brothers. Blood was thicker than water and solidarity was established. The Enquiry was completed.

The Commissioner's Office had earlier told Sundaram and Jayaraman that Inspector Gurunathan was dealing with the case and that they would hear from him soon. They had waited several days but there had been no news. They persisted till Gurunathan could procrastinate no longer.

'Saar, we think that Devanathan was not behind the attack on your son,' said Gurunathan with some finality.

'Why?' Jayaraman asked.

'He was not even in Chennai on that day.'

'When has the presence of the person on the scene of the crime become a sine qua non for planning and organizing it? For heaven's sake, we are not suggesting that Devanathan actually stabbed Rajan. He must have *hired* others to commit it—like that rowdy from our locality.'

'Saar, that may be possible. However . . . keeping everything in mind and the circumstances of the case, we think . . .' he used the plural 'we' again, '. . . that it was a bandh-related crime. It seems to have nothing to do with Devanathan. Or any rowdy in your area.'

Sundaram and Jayaraman were rendered speechless.

It was strange that Rajan never missed the US. He never gave it a second thought after his return. He was never nostalgic, never talked about how much better it was in the US. He never craved for Diet Coke or a Starbucks coffee, never missed the City Centre in Philadelphia or the Vance Hall or Locust Lane.

It was as though Rajan had wanted to close a chapter in his life, come back to India and move on.

It wasn't that he had been unhappy in the US. In fact, he had enjoyed every moment of his stay there—both in the campus and outside it.

The Indian American community had tried to entice him with Indian food and then with their daughters 'eligible for marriage'. It hadn't worked. They even tried job offers with big salaries. By then, he was familiar with Indian American eccentricities. Rajan stopped being irritated by them when they mentioned how much money they had sent back to India or how much they had contributed to some disaster relief or the other. He learnt to ignore their ceaseless criticism of the Indian Government, Indian bureaucracy, Indian this and Indian that. Like good Indian Americans, he learnt to give a gift of twenty-one dollars for the wedding of a mere acquaintance, thirty-one dollars for the wedding of someone he knew better and fifty-one for a good friend. If he didn't pay up, he drank a peg of whisky and left. Without dinner. Sometimes the wedding invitation helpfully indicated the supermarket from where their gifts could be picked up. If still in doubt, the lady at the counter advised 'Sir, don't buy a steam iron. Someone just picked one up. You could buy them a digital diary or contribute towards a microwave.'

In the US, human values were reduced to very simple, recognizable monetary units and human action into quantifiable parts. Indians were pragmatists and soon excelled at this.

While Rajan liked their lifestyle, he failed to be enamoured. He had other plans. He had had a great time in the US and had done excellently in his studies. He now wanted to return to India. When his flight took off from Dulles Airport to take him back home and flew in an arc over Washington, DC, Rajan barely looked out of the window. Not even for old times' sake. He sat in the window seat engrossed in Woody Allen's *Without Feathers*.

When Rajan heard the police say that it wasn't Devanathan who had masterminded the attack but that it had been a bandh-related crime, Rajan wished he were back in the US.

It wasn't as if these things never happened in the US. Blacks and whites still didn't make a good cocktail. Neither did the browns and the whites. But the US never outraged him. It never made his blood boil. Chennai had outraged him. Devanathan made his blood boil.

Rajan had to be told. It couldn't be delayed any further.

When Sundaram and Lakshmi chose an evening when Rajan was out and came in together to Paati's room, Paati realized that it was no casual visit.

'Amma, there's something we need your advice on. It concerns Rajan's marriage,' Sundaram broached the subject.

Paati nodded her head, turning towards Sundaram.

'Amma, you are aware how meticulously we had planned for the wedding. We had Chandramouli come in several times, compare the horoscopes, set the time for the wedding . . . Chandramouli even gave percentages of compatibility for the horoscopes and Rajan and Gayathri got 87 per cent! We had tried to take everything into consideration to see to it that the marriage has every chance of success. The Sethuramans had also gone through much of the same routine and had come to a similar conclusion—that Rajan and Gayathri would be an ideal couple.'

Paati nodded again.

'There was one thing that Chandramouli had pointed out to us, but had said that the matter could be resolved by a special pooja or *homam*. There was a flaw in her horoscope, a *dosham*. This was supposed to affect the health of the boy but it could be overcome with a *homam* performed before the wedding. We had assumed that this was a minor matter that could be rectified easily and had proceeded with the alliance.

But when the stabbing occurred, we realized that all wasn't well and consulted a few other astrologers. So did the Sethuramans. It soon dawned on us that the matter was not as easy as it had looked. The flaw was serious. While all claimed that we might remove it with the *homam*, they couldn't guarantee it. There is a reasonable chance that it may not be removed. If that is so, then the marriage is doomed. Their lives will be destroyed in front of our eyes.' Sundaram paused. It wasn't easy to say what he said. Lakshmi was sitting on the edge of Paati's bed, her eyes full of unshed tears. She dabbed her eyes with the corner of her saree and looked away. Paati had not said a word. She waited for Sundaram to finish.

'You know we had first thought the match was ideal. We thought that Gayathri, with her background and qualifications, would be a good life partner for our Rajan. Before her horoscope had come to us, I had performed poojas at all the big temples—Tirupati, Madurai, Thanjavur, Marudamalai, Guruvayur. Lakshmi had special *abhishekams* for the deity in Kapaleeshwarar Temple every Friday and *vadamalai* at the Mylapore Hanuman Temple every Saturday. When Gayathri's reference came along, we thought our prayers had been answered. And now this. It has really come as a rude shock. What can I say. Whichever way one looks at it, I feel it is certainly not worth risking Rajan's, indeed, both their lives. I just don't know what to say . . .

'At least now, we know the truth,' Sundaram continued. 'The marriage will affect Rajan's health and may even prove fatal. He has already had a close brush and he cannot be exposed to this all his life. Sethuraman has also examined this from all angles and he agrees. My head feels as if it will explode any moment. We just cannot take this any more.' Sundaram stopped, running out of words, and looked at Paati expectantly for her reaction. She remained silent. There was pin-drop silence. It was uncomfortable not getting a reaction from her.

'Why are you quiet?' Sundaram couldn't help asking.

'What do you want me to say?' Paati asked.

'I have been speaking to you all this while and all you have to say is what do you want me to say? We want you to break this news gently to Rajan. The marriage cannot work. He has to understand that. We know he will listen to you. If we tell him, he will throw a fit.'

Paati was quiet for a few minutes collecting her thoughts.

'You two have nearly ruined Rajan's life.' Paati's voice was even and emotionless. 'You should have thought through this whole matter of horoscopes and flaws before you put Rajan through this. You were the ones who saw the horoscopes. You were the ones who brought them together. Now you want to separate them. It is almost as if you both are choreographing a puppet show and Rajan and Gayathri don't matter at all. Sundaram, remember you are not dealing with inanimate objects. You are dealing with the lives of two youngsters, youngsters who have a future ahead of them. Many years ahead of them. Two youngsters who have minds of their own—just like you had when you were young. Now, you want me to tell him that you people have made a mistake. How do you expect me or anyone to do something like this? I have—'

'Amma, I fully understand what you're saying,' Sundaram interrupted. 'In fact, not for a single moment have we not prayed for forgiveness for what we have put Rajan through. Lakshmi and I have hardly slept since the day we realized all this. Still, we now cannot walk away with our eyes closed as if nothing has happened. The situation, whether created by us or not, needs to be remedied. You must understand that. There is no other course of action for us.'

'Look, Sundaram. After Rajan came back from the girl-seeing ceremony, I spent a full hour talking to him about my own marriage and convinced him about taking the big leap. Now you want me to confess to him that all that I had said was nonsense. Let me be very clear. I refuse to be dragged into breaking this marriage. Remember one thing. When your father came as a young man and asked my father for my hand, I had, in a bout of instant fancy, said yes. We never compared horoscopes. Maybe my parents secretly did, I don't know. If they had indeed done so and our horoscopes had not matched, would I have changed my mind about your father? I don't think so. We were both young and the last thing on our minds was whether our horoscopes matched or not. I am sure that Rajan feels the same way. He is not going to be moved by this horoscope-flaw-*homam* business. And why should he be?

'When I was barely in my teens, my grandfather, that is your great-grandfather Natesan Iyer, used to say, "If you don't fit into the grand astrological scheme then make the grand astrological scheme fit into yours." He was an astrology freak. He used to say that there were very few things in life that cannot be changed by human belief, strength and determination. Believe. That was his motto. Believe and it will come to pass. That was Natesan Iyer.'

She paused as old memories flooded her mind. She continued, 'I am not here to give you both a lecture on horoscopes and astrology. All I want you to do is not behave as if the last word on a man's life is a horoscope. Interpreting it is an important aspect of our lives for us Brahmins, but see it in perspective. Give latitude to human spiritual strength. The subconscious never sleeps and knows more than what the conscious knows . . . It can work miracles. Never underestimate it.

'Then again, don't take me wrong, both of you. It is not that I don't understand your dilemma. I fully understand it. The tension both of you must be undergoing. In your position, my head would have exploded long time back. But you are pushing this thing too far. It is neither wise nor prudent to make this a do-or-die issue. All I assure you is that I will talk to Rajan about what you have just said. Convey frankly the details of what the astrologers have said. But I will not try to talk him into breaking off the marriage. You have made a mistake once. You cannot set it right by making another. If Rajan is comfortable with the idea of going ahead, I am not going to stand in his way. Not at all. Please understand that.'

'It's for his own good if this is stopped,' Sundaram said.

'Sundaram, let's not start again. I've said all I have to say.'

SUMMER RETREAT

Hindi was yet another leveller in the Chennai social fabric. In fact, it was a leveller of all Tamils. Hindi united all Tamils but in their common hatred for it. Brahmins and non-Brahmins, Pillais and Mudaliars, Iyers and Iyengars, Nadars and Chettiars, Thevars and Vanniars, they were the educated and uneducated, industrialists and farmers, rich and poor alike, united in their common hatred of the Hindi language.

The language of the North Indians, they said. The language of the Aryans. Wasn't Tamil the language of the Dravidians, the original inhabitants of India? It was the oldest language. And weren't the Aryans, the invaders from the west, an alien race? Before the Tamil Brahmins were initiated into the mysteries of the *Gayathri japam* during the sacred thread ceremony, they were already aware of the marauding potential of Hindi. Before the Pillais joined the Indian Administrative Service, they were warned of the Hindiwalas. Before the Iyers and Iyengars migrated to Delhi to study in the IIT, they were suitably briefed about the horrific propensity of Hindi to eat away at the vitals of the mother-tongue-speaking Tamils. And before the Tamil politicians went to attend Parliament in Delhi, they were carefully tutored in the art of chanting 'Stop Hindi Imposition'. Hindi hating was a hobby, passion, religion, policy all in one.

In the early sixties, when the Tamils demanded secession in opposition to Hindi imposition and several lives were lost, buses burnt and trains stopped, the north agreed not to impose Hindi on the Tamils. It was imposed on everyone else but the Tamils, thereby isolating them. The three-language formula for schools, by the time it descended from the mountains of Uttar Pradesh in the far north, passed through the dacoit-infested ravines of Madhya Pradesh, crossed the old city of Hyderabad and came to the borders of Tamil Nadu deep south, had become a two-language one. Hindi had been dropped from the school curriculum and the future generation of Tamils stopped understanding the rest of India. The Tamils stood isolated. Within India. In trying to isolate the north, the Tamils isolated themselves.

Not even the Hindi film craze helped. Hindi films ran to full houses in Chennai. Hindi film songs caught the Tamil imagination, even without knowledge of what they meant. Tamil girls slept with photos of Shah Rukh Khan and Aamir Khan under their pillows, without understanding a word of what they said.

The youngsters of Tamil Nadu didn't want to go to north India since they couldn't understand Hindi, so they went to North America instead. English was after all inherited from the good old British and could be tolerated. It was, therefore, with a sense of trepidation that Clive Avenue had viewed the entry of Daulat Singh and his family into their fold, more than a decade earlier. The fact that Daulat Singh's mother tongue was Punjabi and not Hindi didn't help, since he was North Indian. And all North Indians spoke Hindi, didn't they?

Daulat Singh Sodhi was a first generation Punjabi Sikh to settle in Chennai. It was not as if he was the first Punjabi or the first Sikh to settle in Chennai. Chennai had had a small but visible community of Sikhs for several decades. The Tamils were not just tolerant of their hardworking Sikh brethren, they liked them and soon took them in as one of their own. When

Ram Singh or Satwender Singh went in to bat, there were very few Tamils who had not wanted them to score a century.

Daulat Singh Sodhi's forefathers hailed from Lahore, then in undivided British India. Daulat's grandfather Gurcharan Singh had owned several acres of land near Lahore. When his tribe increased by four sons—and they were all sons, mind you—they came into their own in Lahore. People knew them. That's Gurcharan, the father of four sons, they said. That's the wife, mother of four sons.

Then Partition happened. Gurcharan and his sons would ideally have liked to sit out Partition in Lahore. They had nowhere else to go. Lahore was their home—their only home. But Partition had been cruel to millions and to Gurcharan. One of his four sons was brutally murdered in broad daylight by the mob. Overnight, they left for the Indian border, drawn as it was in blood, carrying whatever they could in their hands and on their heads. A few pieces of jewellery, clothes and some money—whatever they could salvage. Scurrying like coolies on the railway platform with bulky loads on their heads, they left behind their house, their land, their sprawling fields—and the funeral pyre of their murdered son. They had no time to wait and collect the ashes. They started their lives anew in India.

Nehru had promised all uprooted families land and land they got near Hoshiarpur. It wasn't even a tenth of what they had had in Lahore, but it was enough to start a new life. This wasn't the time for nostalgia and they went about as if Lahore had never existed. Daulat's father Baljit was the youngest of the three surviving sons. Daulat was a post-Partition child, born into a free India.

As the Gurcharan clan increased, more and more lived out of less and less. It wasn't easy. Daulat graduated in Commerce and realized that he had to chart his own path if he was to survive. It made no sense to stooge on the same land. Ambitious and willing to take risks, Daulat Singh landed up in the deep south—Chennai. In Clive Avenue. He took the only house available on rent.

Daulat's father Baljit never understood what Daulat saw in Chennai. Daulat's 'That's the best place for textile business' didn't impress Baljit one bit. Sikhs were industrious and willing to leap across the seven seas to strike a deal. But to Tamil Nadu? Tamils and Sikhs didn't gel, he was convinced. If they had, they wouldn't have been 2,500 kilometres apart. God would have placed the two states next to each other. If only the Tamils had stayed next door, the Sikh brawn and the Tamil cunning could have worked wonders together.

'Daulat beta, I just can't figure out what you see in these Tamils. You can't understand a word of Tamil. Roti is unheard of amongst those rice eaters. Their milk is not a patch on ours. Hot jalebis and milk on a cold winter evening in Hoshiarpur— you can't beat the taste. Sikhs are a warrior clan all of six feet and a hundred kilos. Tamil giants are all of fifty kilos and resemble a neem twig in winter. Anyway, winter is non-existent down south. Beta, just to make a few bucks, and probably to eat some authentic masala dosa and sambhar, is it worth putting up with all of this?' he asked pained. The beta was at pains to allay Papaji's fears. 'Papaji, don't worry. After dealing with those Dilliwalas day in and day out, you don't realize how tensionless it is here to do business. These guys are easier to deal with. Moreover, there's money to be made here. That's the bottom line, Papaji. There's money to be made here.' This was something Papaji had to readily agree to. Anything to get away from the Dilliwalas. And there was good money to be made.

Daulat Singh was in good company. He came determined to do well. To succeed. To win over his Tamil neighbours and the solitary French family. He didn't have to try hard. He realized that once the Tamils knew him, they went out of the way to make him and his family feel comfortable. He was a warm and gregarious person as well and that helped. And of course Daulat succeeded. In a few years, he had bought the house he had rented. Papaji never asked him any more questions.

When Daulat Singh saw Rajan's episode unfolding before his eyes, he was the first one to come forward to help.

Rajan had listened intently to Paati. He had least expected it. Deliverance had come when least expected. There was a flaw in the horoscope. He wasn't sure whether he should be happy or sad. After all, wasn't he supposed to be sad since it was his marriage that they were breaking up?

He presented a serious face. Boy, what a big burden off his shoulders! He had only to agree with Paati and the marriage would be called off. A painless way out. If he and Gayathri took the news well, the others shouldn't have any problem.

Paati had not quite finished. 'Rajan, I have said what I have been asked to say,' she spoke gently in her rasping voice. 'Now, let me tell you what I really want to say. If you, after hearing me out, still decide to go ahead with the marriage, you can be sure that you will have my full blessings and Guruvayurappan himself will protect you and your wife from danger.' She looked at him. 'Rajan, do what you think is correct. We—your father, mother and myself—have failed you. Have faith in yourself and do what is correct and best for you.'

Rajan listened. 'This flaw in the horoscope, this is a bit of a surprise,' he said truthfully.

'You don't have to answer me now. Think about it. Take time over your decision. It's not easy.'

There wasn't much Rajan had to think about. He wanted to hug Paati, answer her immediately and tell her how much lighter he felt. But that would be unwise. He looked serious, nodded his head and agreed to consider what she had said.

Rajaram IAS was approached. Rajaram IAS was one of the most senior bureaucrats in the Tamil Nadu Government and one of the few Sundaram knew well. Rajaram IAS had the reputation of being thoroughly honest. Sundaram had never really asked him for any help. He had had no need to. Their paths never crossed professionally except when Rajaram IAS had swooned and fallen down one day due to too much pressure at work. They were neighbours and good friends. Particularly because their paths had never crossed professionally.

Sundaram chose a quiet moment to meet Rajaram IAS at his residence. 'Rajaram, Devanathan's guardian angel is obviously very powerful. Who the hell is it? The minister? The Secretary? Whoever it is, can't you tell him that this chap is a murderer? Devanathan will not stop till I withdraw the written statement against him. Withdraw the statement? Forget it. The chap deserves to be hanged. Right now, we have to stop him, before he does any more serious harm to my family. Rajan has suffered and enough is enough. Lakshmi and I are having a nervous breakdown just thinking about it. Devanathan simply cannot go scot-free.'

Rajaram IAS heard him out. Yes, he would see what he could do.

He got back to Sundaram within a week. 'Sundaram, I am not sure whether I can do anything in this matter. He has a direct line with the minister and I do not understand his hold over him. Obviously Devanathan is keeping the minister's palm well greased. You should try someone in the party or some informal channel. My channels are leading to a complete dead end. Nobody is willing to bell the cat. The minister is not a pushover, mind you. He is one of the critical money-making machines of the party.'

Sundaram couldn't believe his ears. 'What? Don't tell me you can't do anything in this matter? You are one of the seniormost bureaucrats in the Government. Does this mean I have to withdraw my statement and this bastard goes scot-free?'

Rajaram IAS had no answer.

One could feel the pall of gloom settling heavily over Sabarmati. It was summer. The walls were drying and the paint peeling. Hedges turned brown, the lawn was crisp and browning, patches of earth showed and the patches grew larger. Don't water the lawn with a hose, the Municipality warned. There is a severe water shortage in Chennai. Violators will be fined. Better still, jailed. One couldn't water the lawn with a mug. The cement patch in front of the house singed bare feet. Balan winced every time he stepped on it. The jasmine wilted at the first sight of the sun, even before Sundaram could pluck them for his pooja.

Sabarmati wore a look of despair. It was as though the vital organs of the house were being eaten from the inside.

Rajan and Gayathri agreeing to call off their engagement had been the final straw. Sundaram had gone back to his quiet inscrutable mood. Nothing was happening on any front. Lakshmi's condition had not improved. She listened to Carnatic music and received no visitors. It was difficult for Dominique to believe that this was the same Lakshmi who had wanted her to persuade Rajan to meet Gayathri, that it was the same Lakshmi who had gone to all the saree shops in Chennai and brought home a trunkload of sarees 'on approval'.

The sarees had to be returned. The Kancheepuram silks, the deep blues, the *mithai* pinks, the reds with the zari borders, they all went back. Dominique and Veena went to return them. The diamond pendant, pearl earrings and bracelets went back to the jewellers as well. But the *kaasumalai*, the garland of gold coins, couldn't be returned. Lakshmi had melted three of her own gold chains to make it. It went into their bank locker. The silver vessels were put back into the locker as well. The booking at Rajeshwari Kalyana Mandapam was cancelled.

The betel-nut man, the fruit seller, the garland-and-flower man, the lights-and-tent man, all retreated from the scene. Narasimhan, the chief cook, was contacted. He would have to hang on to his plantain leaves and use them elsewhere.

A delicately worked wooden *yali* lamp stood in the corner of the drawing room. One could smell old weather-beaten country wood when one sat too near. Too much *yali* stuff, Lakshmi had complained. Half lion, half dragon. Sundaram had gone all the way to Madurai to pick up a few *yali* pieces when the Temple Car was stripped and renovated. The Temple Car stood stripped of its antique wood carvings and new garish-coloured wood carvings had taken their place. The antique dealers were happy with their loot and the temple authorities had a brand new rainbow Temple Car.

Sitting next to the *yali* lamp after dinner, Rajan told Dominique about that dinner party at Gayathri's residence. In great detail. 'The horoscope fiasco was only incidental, Dominique. We just didn't get along very well together. Maybe you should tell my mother about this. Not all of it. Just that Rajan and Gayathri were not compatible and in any case wanted to split. She may feel better. I will tell her myself. Somehow she still seems to hold herself responsible for the attack on me. Now with the breaking up, she has gone into a shell. You must try and pull her out of it. Veena is trying but she needs your help.'

Lakshmi cursed herself not just for the attack on Rajan and not just for not bringing to immediate attention the flaw in the horoscope. After the marriage fiasco, she dreaded the prospect of facing the outside world. To fix a marriage and then to see it broken up after the engagement was a no-no, a social stigma. It didn't matter why the 'alliance' had broken or what had caused it or who was at fault. The fact that the 'alliance' broke was incontrovertible and was enough. 'There must have been something wrong with the girl. I have known the Sundaram family for several years. They are wonderful people. Rajan is a fine boy and very intelligent. It's unfortunate that it had to happen to them,' said the considerate and the charitable lot. 'Something is obviously wrong with the boy. First he does absolutely nothing for several months, suddenly he decides to get engaged, and now this. All these US-returned boys develop some kink or the other. Rajan was not like this before,' said the inconsiderate and uncharitable lot. How could Lakshmi go outside and be ridiculed? It wasn't easy for a mother. It wasn't easy for anyone.

So she stayed at home and even missed her Friday ritual of visiting Kapaleeshwarar Temple.

It was strange that for a family like the Sundarams which had a large network of relatives very few could actually spend time to provide them with emotional support. Except for a fortnight when Lakshmi's sister Meenakshi had flown in from Bangalore, the Sundarams hardly got any support. Even with the best of intentions, the Chennai relatives barely spent a few hours with them. Those outside enquired anxiously about the family's welfare but could hardly be of much assistance.

Sundaram recollected the early days when his brothers, his father's brothers and their families stayed under one roof in T. Nagar. A huge house it was, with more rooms than he could remember now. The house grew up around the large open quadrangle in the middle, open to the skies. Hot sun during the day, cool sea breeze in the evenings and millions of stars at night. When the retreating monsoons brought rain and cyclones to Chennai, the cool breeze wafted through the open quadrangle into the rooms and sent its inhabitants scurrying for their shawls.

Food had to be cooked in huge vessels and served with saucepan-like spoons. There was fresh food for lunch, tiffin and dinner. There were no refrigerators to freeze and stock up. Chips and *appalams* were fried and stored in large copper tins with lids and pickles pickled and stored in massive porcelain jars. Jars of pickles stood on the black Cudappah stone shelves— lime, mango, *mahali*, *vadumanga*, there was something for everyone. The Tamils liked it hot—not as hot as the Andhrites, but hotter than the rest of India. For haters of hot pickle, there was salt-lime, dried *narthangai*, green and black *molagu* and *thokku.* For hardcore pickle-haters, there were chutneys, tomato, coconut, onion and mint. Rows of beddings were rolled up every morning from the floor and stacked one on top of the other in one corner of the bedroom. Bathrooms were shared based on urgency—of time and on the bladder. Toys and chocolates had to be shared, a jar of peppermints disappeared in a day. One wondered who pitched in with what, but the house was always full of people, employed, unemployed, students, loafers, kids, mothers, aunts and, of course, there was Paati.

The family stayed together. They shared in the happiness, the pain and in the running of the house. No accounts were asked for and none were given. If a breadwinner lost his job, the house continued to run. Someone or the other chipped in. Children were closer to their aunts than they were to their own mothers. The unemployed had the luxury of trying to make a living out of writing, selling cars or painting before quietly giving them up and settling down to a steady job as an insurance agent or a bank manager or a doctor or a lawyer. Fathers going astray were quickly brought in line by the family. Sundaram was friendly with his now estranged brother Pattabiraman. It was when the families started charting their own paths after their father's death that the estrangement started. The family was now reduced to Paati, Sundaram, Lakshmi and Rajan and, even though she didn't live with them any more, Veena. Gone were the sisters, cousins, cousins' cousins, uncles, *periammas* and *chittis*. But there was also Dominique.

When Veena was busy with Jayaraman and Aditya, Dominique managed to spend every morning and evening with Lakshmi. When she finished her work, she came over to chat with Lakshmi over tiffin. For a morning cup of coffee, after breakfast. Lakshmi couldn't but be amazed at how much time Dominique gave her. When Lakshmi listened to music, so did she. When Lakshmi saw *Mahabharat* reruns on TV with

Paati, so did she. The only time Dominique didn't turn up was during the occasional spells when she was out of town doing a story for *Le Figaro* when she was out for her gym session or when she went out with friends to watch a new English movie.

It was Dominique and Veena who persuaded Lakshmi to accompany them to Venus Colony to hear a Kathakaalakshebam. In one of her weaker moments, Lakshmi had agreed.

Kathakaalakshebam, the religious discourse, was mythology, epics, music, prayer and religion all in one. The narrator was portly, as they usually were from hours of sitting cross-legged on the dais. Soon the audience was transported into a world of great battles where good triumphed over evil; a world of gods propounding the ultimate truth, the world of the *Bhagavad Gita* revealing the mysteries of life and death and a world of ethics and morality. The Chennai Brahmins flocked to Kathakaalakshebams to reinforce their moral fibre and enhance their philosophical understanding of life. With the passage of time, the discourse came to be performed in English. Quotations from cinema dialogues and stories from popular movies competed for space with quotations from the *Gita* and the Upanishads and snippets from the *Mahabharat* and *Ramayana*. Slimmer narrators were in vogue and women narrators vied for space on the male dais. The Brahmins converged at these sessions in greater numbers, to see and be seen.

Dominique and Veena ruled out 'The Death of Abhimanyu' that was on Day One. In Lakshmi's present state, it was the last thing she needed. They opted for 'Lessons from the *Gita*' on Day Two instead.

When a nervous Lakshmi walked into the large hall filled with people that evening, she felt as if every eye had turned towards her. As if silent questions were being asked. It was as if they were coming to get her. She kept her eyes fixed downwards and sat down quietly. She wished she could disappear. The Mylapore crowd had turned up in great numbers. The who's who of Chennai society. Swami Sampoornananda was very popular and highly renowned. After an invocation to Ganesha, he started his discourse in fluent and well enunciated English. His resonant voice cut through the silence.

As the evening wore on, Lakshmi realized it wasn't difficult to come out, to face the outside world. She heard the Swamiji and felt better. After he finished, some familiar faces came over to Lakshmi to speak to her. To meet her, chat with her, laugh and enquire. The ice was broken.

AVIAL

'*Je ne le supporte plus. Dis-moi qu'est qu' on fait*,' Dominique shouted into the phone exasperated.

'*Mon amour, je viens, je viens. Attend un peu. Peut-être . . .*' came the feeble answer from the other end.

'*Dis-moi maintenant . . .* it's about time you gave me a clear answer. Here I am, waiting for a response and all you can mumble is maybe. Maybe. What does it mean?'

'Of course, I'm planning to come to India soon. But it's difficult to leave right now since I can't take time off just yet. In fact, you should be the one coming here, Dom. The Parisians are all out sunning themselves on the southern coast. I'm not sure whether coming to Chennai now—in that scorching heat—is the best thing to do. Why can't you come here?' the other voice pleaded in French.

'So what if it's summer here. You are not going to die in the Chennai heat.'

'It's not the heat. I just can't come, Dom. I have this job to do.'

'You think I am sitting idle, Jacques? You are not the only one who has work to do. The last time you came here, the whole damn time you were cooped up in my room cribbing about the heat. Now you want me to go to the south of France with you.'

'Dom, don't be silly! This has nothing to do with the south of France. You know very well that I'm just starting my career and I can't keep asking for leave.'

'Have you ever asked for leave?'

'Of course, I asked . . .'

'No, you didn't. They would have said yes if you asked. I'm sure they are off themselves to wander topless and bottomless in Nice and Cannes. I don't see why they should say no to you.'

'Let them go wherever they want, I'm not bothered. I'm only bothered about where I am going. And for now, the only place I want to go is up.'

'Fine. Do your career climbing and bang your head against the ceiling.' She slammed the phone down.

Jacques was a good guy, but a bit too practical sometimes. So practical that he couldn't understand that Dominique needed him now. She had been feeling rudderless for some time. He felt that she was being silly and childish. All she needed to do was take a break and come to Paris, where the ambience was far more hospitable and the sun less strong and all she wanted him to do was to sit cooped up in her room in Chennai, away from the hell-ish Indian sun.

Dom sat in her room resigned and exasperated. Jacques was frustrating. She felt like wringing his neck and knocking some sense into him. Damn it Jacques! I want to talk to you and all you can think of is how far up the career ladder you can climb. I wish you were here. She looked forlorn and cheerless.

Dominique had never felt rudderless before. She had always had close friends through her school and college days. She had that quality which made people seek her out. It wasn't the white skin—even though that was a vital factor in a colour-conscious Chennai Brahmin society. But it was Dominique the person they sought out. And being a non-Tamil, they told her things they wouldn't trust their parents with.

She retained her close circle of friends. They went in and out of each other's homes. Nivedita got married and moved out of their charmed circle, but Geeta, Chitra, Savitri and Isabelle, who was of French extract as well, hung on to each other as though college had never finished. They never missed a new English film release and went to most Tamil ones. It was a pity that very few colleges in Chennai were co-ed. The boys from the all-male colleges were desperate to meet girls from the all-female colleges. They came from all over—Loyola College, Pachayappa, D.B. Jain, Vivekananda—and camped outside Stella Maris, Ethiraj, SIET to ogle, whistle and make a spectacle of themselves. Dom was in Stella Maris and could hardly remain inconspicuous. Not with her white skin and blonde hair. Every Tamil boy wanted to marry her, suitors who knew full well that in the end they could never marry her. Their parents would collapse with shock and rage. So the boys were content to admire her from a distance, speaking to her awkwardly, making asses of themselves and fantasizing about her going to bed with them. How they wished she were a Tamil Brahmin. Alas, she was white, blonde, blue-eyed, Tamil-speaking and French.

Daulat Singh had had enough. Every time he saw Rajan wincing, he had the urge to catch Devanathan by the throat and sort him out for good. And every time he asked Sundaram whether he needed help, he was told to hold on. They were pushing the inspector in charge to show some results. Sundaram still had faith in the law-enforcing agencies. Daulat had none. Daulat's faith had evaporated the day his father had been beaten up in Delhi by an irate mob protesting the assassination of Indira Gandhi by her Sikh bodyguards. The law enforcers stood by the wayside watching the fun and let the thugs and looters trash Sikh homes and torch them. It was sheer providence that a few Hindu friends had taken charge of Baljit and his family and hidden them in their homes till the hours of madness passed. The old man Gurcharan had mercifully been in Hoshiarpur at the time. 'The marks on my back are there to remind me of Partition and my murdered brother in Karachi,' Baljit remarked philosophically. 'Just in case I ever forget.'

Balan the Milk Man had had enough as well. He couldn't bear to see Devanathan strutting around confidently up and down Clive Avenue. He didn't dare enter the houses but hovered outside. Collecting taxes. To think that the Income Tax Department couldn't even suspend him during the investigation spoke volumes about his clout. Devanathan would die of old age before the investigation was actually concluded. But Sundaram had shooed Balan off. He would have none of Balan's 'setting the rowdies right' talk. 'Stay out of this Balan. You are a good man and you must stay that way. Don't dirty your hands by doing foolish things. Leave it to the police to do their work.'

Daulat and Balan were dying to actually do something. But they didn't want to make the situation worse for Sundaram.

To make an *avial* of things is to create a total mess. That didn't actually happen when *avial* was cooked. It was a delicacy and made on special occasions.

Aditya's fifth birthday was a special occasion, an auspicious one. While Aditya was entitled to vegetable burgers from McDonald's on his birthdays, on his star birthday he had to put up with *avial*. The adults were keen on a traditional lunch after the pooja and it couldn't get more traditional than *avial*.

Even before the pooja began, Lakshmi was back in the kitchen. Her days of seclusion were coming to an end. The Kathakaalakshebam had done her a world of good. She was back to giving orders to Revati. 'Revati, let me show you how to make the *avial*,' she asserted, taking the ladle in her hand and hitching up an edge of her green cotton saree and tucking it into the fold around her hips. Vegetables had been cut into thin strips—the trademark for a good *avial*—and kept ready.

A large, shining stainless steel vessel stood at attention. Yam, French beans, non-French beans, drumsticks, raw plantain waited, warm and boiled. The ground mixture of cumin seeds, green chillies and coconut scrapings mixed in the thick sour buttermilk was added to the boiled vegetables. The vegetables simmered for some time, bobbing up and down. An odd carrot was sliced and thrown in for colour. Turmeric powder turned the landscape yellow. The salt had to be just right, Paati was very particular. The spices soaked in and a delightful aroma went up into the air. The *avial* was close to being done. Making *avial* was an art. It was Tamil culture. It was education, at least for Revati.

'Making *avial* is also high philosophy,' Paati explained, as she and Rajan watched. 'As Ramakrishna Paramahamsa said, the various vegetables in the cooking pot move and leap till the children start thinking that they are living beings. But they are not moving of their own volition; if the fire is taken away they will soon cease to stir. Similarly, it's ignorance to think and pride ourselves that "I did this", "I did that" and that "I am the doer". All our strength is the strength of God. All is silent if the fire is removed.'

Rajan had had enough of philosophy for one day and hastily removed himself from the kitchen.

Sakilivangi involved far less philosophy but far more effort. *Sakilivangi* was eggplants at their best. It was Paati's favourite. Even Lakshmi had a tough time getting it right. *Sakilivangi* was not for faint-hearted cooks. None but the best got it right. Paati had to pick up a plastic chair, sit and supervise its preparation. It took an inordinately long time before a dark gooey substance emerged steaming from the gas stove. The aroma wafted through the house till everyone knew that the *sakilivangi* was done.

'I wonder why today's generation doesn't have the time or the inclination to try out such rare and delicious recipes,' Paati mused, her eyes glowing at the *sakilivangi* successfully done.

'The fast food culture is ruining good traditional food. One day, people will not know what *sakilivangi* is.'

Revati couldn't understand what all the fuss was about. Why Paati and Lakshmi spent hours preparing only two dishes was beyond her. She kept quiet.

The priest finished the pooja and left soon after filling his belly. It was not every day that he got to eat *sakilivangi*. In fact, it was the first time he was eating it but pretended that he had had it before. He couldn't afford to appear too ignorant. The family members ate after the priest left. *Avial* was consumed generously and *sakilivangi* in small quantities and the rest went into the fridge.

'The fridge is the best invention of this century,' Paati agreed. 'You people have no idea of how, when we were young, we used to keep cooking round the clock, without a fridge, without gas cylinders. We had only wood stoves and numerous mouths to feed. Breakfast, lunch, tiffin, snacks and dinner. Looking back, it must have been a nightmare, but we survived, sometimes even happily.'

Avial with *sakilivangi* was a potent combination, even for a Brahmin stomach. Sabarmati soon went into a deep afternoon slumber. When they awoke, the aroma had vanished but another strange smell had taken its place. It was a smell alien to Sabarmati. It was the smell of stale fish.

A packet of stale fish had been thrown into the verandah with an accompanying message in Tamil: Don't you understand a warning? This time, we will not brook any delay. Call the police at your own peril.

Five-year-old Aditya's birthday began with the aroma of *avial* and *sakilivangi* and ended with the smell of stale fish.

Sundaram and Jayaraman had been frequent visitors to this red sandstone building. They gave up their vigil when they realized that nothing moved in the ongoing investigation.

Inspector Gurunathan had a stock answer for them—we are seriously pursuing all the leads we have. Now, they were forced back into the precincts of Inspector Gurunathan's lair.

'Saar, I am sorry. You cannot go in now to see Inspector Sir,' stopped the constable on duty, standing authoritatively outside the Inspector's office. His dark waxed handlebar moustache was big enough to deter all but the stout-hearted. His khaki uniform was smartly starched and his legs, fuzzy and thinnish, emerged out of the enormous pair of outsized khaki shorts. 'He is just leaving for the court.'

'We will wait here outside till he comes out. If he wants to speak, we will. If not, we will come back later,' said the determined Jayaraman.

'No, no, Saar. Inspector Sir is going to the court and he does not like anyone to accost him on his way.'

'We will not accost him, I assure you,' Jayaraman argued. 'If he walks past us, we will come back later. If he stops to talk to us, we have something very urgent to convey.'

'Of course, Saar, it must be urgent. But you are not to stand in his way.'

'We are not in his way, we will stand on this side of the corridor.'

'Saar, you don't understand,' the constable was impatient. 'Inspector Sir is very particular that no good character should stand in the way when he goes to a court hearing. You know, Saar, if he sees a bad character on his way out, he is sure to have the case decided in his favour and the culprits convicted. Call it superstition, but it happens. Please Saar, you are good characters. Stand away from the Inspector's path. And please, Saar, please don't tell him that I told you this. He may not like it. But it is the truth.'

'Whatever gave you the impression that we are good characters?' asked Jayaraman seriously. 'We have come here with hatred in our hearts and murder on our minds.'

'Saar, don't joke with me,' the constable squirmed. His severe countenance had given way and his handlebar moustache kept bobbing up and down at awkward angles. Jayaraman was quite fascinated by it. Does he wax them every day or once a week, he wondered. He realized that the constable was speaking to him. 'Saar, meet him later. What can I do? I am only following orders. Inspector Sir will come out any moment.'

'Don't worry,' consoled Jayaraman. 'We will go now. Just one question. Where are these bad characters you are talking about, the Inspector's good luck charm?'

'They are standing there,' he pointed his baton towards the corner of the compound. Sure enough, a seedy-looking man in a colourful lungi and a portly, squat lady chewing paan stood nonchalantly next to another khaki-clad constable with a moustache bigger than this one's.

'Who are they?'

'Saar, they are both bad characters. The man and the woman run a brothel. He pimps around for customers and she supplies the women.'

While they looked at the two, the constable was getting increasingly agitated. 'Saar, please go now.'

Sundaram and Jayaraman left. Though Jayaraman didn't quite care for the Inspector's superstitions, he deferred to the entreaties of the constable. It wasn't worth getting the Inspector upset at this juncture. He wanted some action and wanted the Inspector to be in a better mood. They walked away past the compound wall. Dark red blotches were splattered all over the white wall. Some red stains resembled creepy caterpillars, some smashed cockroaches. Paan spit. Generations of Tamils had passed by and spat chewed paan onto this wall. Bad characters, good characters, Brahmins, non-Brahmins, criminals, petty thieves, Inspectors and upright citizens. All passed by spitting paan. It was another leveller that held the Tamil society together.

When they came back several hours later, Inspector Gurunathan was beaming. He had got the conviction after all. The bad characters had worked their charm.

'The judge sentenced the rowdies to two years,' he bellowed buoyantly. 'They had tried to assault an old widow in Annanagar.' He was full of his latest victory. Sundaram added his insincere praises to puff up the Inspector.

After he had calmed down a bit, Sundaram and Jayaraman got the opportunity to narrate their new stale-fish story. 'We will catch the culprits in a few days, don't worry,' he assured them with new confidence, his vision coloured by his success that morning. He would have caught and jailed just about anyone now.

'At the very least, we need some police protection. It's about time you people focussed on this matter seriously. How long can this go on? Till he kills one of us?'

'No, no, saar. Don't worry. I am going to post a constable outside your house every night, don't worry.'

'And this Devanathan . . .' Sundaram was not one to give up. 'Please take another look into the whole matter and the leads in your investigation.'

'Yes, yes . . . we will catch the culprits, don't worry.'

'Any new leads so far?'

'Yes, yes . . . don't worry, I've told you, we will catch the bastards.' The long-playing record seemed to have got stuck.

They made little headway with Inspector Gurunathan. It was obvious that he, in turn, had made little headway in the case. Sundaram and Jayaraman went home with 'don't worry, we will catch the bastards' ringing in their heads.

THE AUTUMN

'I think the worst of summer is over,' declared Lakshmi leaving everyone to wonder how the hell she could come to such a conclusion.

The days were no different. The sun continued to beat down mercilessly and the Chennai*vasis* sweated it out. The leaves continued to dry up and crumble. The fans whirred furiously and the power cuts continued. There was still no water for the lawns. How then was it different?

But it was August and one had to assume that the summer was over. Chennai*vasis* started talking about how bad the summer had been and thanked God that it was now over. This summer was worse than the earlier one, they said. Global warming, too many factories and too few trees. They blamed the arrogant Americans, the European colonizers, fat-cat industrialists, corrupt bureaucrats. Now that they hoped summer was over, there would be rain. Gone were the days when Chennai*vasis* got excited about seeding the clouds for rain. The seeded clouds poured all their rain into the Bay of Bengal and went away. Chennai remained dry and sweaty. All that was left for the Chennai*vasis* to do was pray. And pray they did. Big *homams* took place. Huge amounts of *ghee* and oil were poured into the raging, sacred fires. Several Brahmin priests and Shastrigals took home the loot. But the rains failed. The gods failed.

The end of summer brought Navarathri and Deepavali

that much closer, even if they were still a couple of months away. That in itself was a comforting thought. Navarathri and Deepavali always brought rain.

Autumn in Chennai was a state of mind. Lakshmi was sure that the summer had finally ended when she came out of her self-imposed exile. She started meeting friends and laughing with them. For Beebee it was perpetually autumn in the cosy confines of the Sundarams' air-conditioned bedroom. Dominique's summer looked like it was ending when she made up her mind to spend a few days with Jacques in Paris. She could visit her employers as well and the fact that *Le Figaro* was paying for her ticket was great.

Rajan's summer ended the day John Carey called up to offer him a job. John's bosses had approved the project proposals and were keen to start the Subsidiary in India right away. Rajan was asked to head it. It was not entirely unexpected. Rajan had almost given up, what with the stabbing and break-up and the air of gloom around the house. He even wondered whether his decision to come back to Chennai had been the correct one. If all he had to show for coming back was a knife scar and a broken engagement, it wasn't too impressive. But he had made a conscious decision to come back. There had been no woolly-headed sentimentality and he didn't have any regrets.

The e-mail was brief. 'Get the team organized. You have a free hand. Send me a green signal and we will start sending the work from here. All the best.'

Rajan was delighted. Sundaram as well. His son a CEO! It was unimaginable. A CEO at twenty-five! He was happy but apprehensive. 'Son, I hope you know what you're getting into. Rajan's 'so if it bombs it bombs! I'll declare bankruptcy and do something else' did not reassure him one bit.

But then, Sundaram had already started looking at his son with new-found respect. A son rediscovered. His son had far more character and steel than he had given him credit for. He had behaved with dignity under pressure and Sundaram was moved. Sundaram regretted that he had been upset with Rajan for taking a break when he had. He was tempted to ask him to take a break for a few more months. Sundaram was a proud father and feeling prouder by the day. He decided that his son needed his full support in the new venture.

Rajan had been pleasantly surprised at Sundaram's behaviour towards him. He was no longer the father who had thrown his weight around. But it was also an uncomfortable feeling. He wondered whether everything was all right or whether there was a bigger gameplan hidden behind his father's sudden fondness. He was happier when his father passed unsolicited critical comments. He was more comfortable with his sarcastic remarks. But praise? It unnerved him. He wished his father would be normal again.

Rajan and his gang got down to their jobs right away. They had planned carefully for it and were ready to slog it out. Rajan resumed his daily commute to Velacheri. While Shiva continued as a consultant, P.V.R.N. Rao left his regular job and joined Rajan as his deputy. The registration, the renting of office premises, the recruitment, the paperwork, everywhere they went, they had to grease palms. The bureaucracy had to be bribed and 'contributions' to political parties made. It dawned quickly on Rajan that Chennai was full of Devanathans.

'Welcome to the real world, Rajan,' said Sundaram.

The company was well on its way. There was just some paperwork left to be completed in Delhi.

'I thought the laws were liberal, at least decentralized.'

'Not while bureaucrats live.'

As Air-India took off from the Anna International Airport in Meenambakkam, Dominique looked out of the window at the treetops below. Chennai looked lush and green. The familiar landmarks stood out and got smaller and smaller. St Thomas Mount. Old buildings, crowded streets criss-crossing, Tambaram and the electric train now resembling a worm. Finally the beach, the tiny catamarans and boats on the shore and the sandy beach stretching miles and miles down the coastline, and then the dark blue waters of the Bay of Bengal. It was amazing how small Chennai looked from here. She was overwhelmed with emotion. She was leaving home.

'Why the hell are you writing about mundane stuff?' he enquired. 'Why can't you write about the snake charmers, the cow worship, the naked fakirs, bride burning along with the Hindu–Muslim clashes. All this about Indian philosophy, culture, politics etc. and your intellectual analysis and opinion bore the French to death.'

Dom tolerated her cousin Mercier. For one thing, she had to stay with him and her uncle in Paris. Her uncle was divorced and lived in a spacious apartment with his son. The apartment was right below the Eiffel Tower and couldn't be better located. Mercier was like a younger brother and they fought like only young siblings could. Mercier had left his car at her disposal. He was a good friend, but just a wee bit full of himself.

When she landed at de Gaulle, the good feeling was back. Dominique got out of the airport, took the metro and then a taxi to her uncle's house right below the Eiffel Tower amidst the hustle-bustle of tourists jostling for photo ops. There once again were the familiar bridges, the river, the gendarmerie busy with their sirens and ripping down Quai d'Orsay. There was a sudden dip in temperature. Dominique felt jet-lagged.

She had almost forgotten how to speak French—not without

mixing English and Tamil in it. Her *Le Figaro* job saved her from forgetting altogether.

Paris in early September had more tourists than French people. They went around with their tourist books trying to distinguish between the Opera House, and the Louvre, Musée d'Orsay from another musée and the jardin of something from the jardin of something else. The only landmarks they could identify with certainty and without hesitation were the Eiffel Tower and the Arc de Triomphe. And the Moulin Rouge. They couldn't miss the Moulin Rouge and Pigalle for the world. It was almost a pilgrimage.

Dominique did none of this. She slept during the day and woke up at night. Jacques was coming in the next day from Toulouse and she could afford to take some time off, meet her friends, maybe even her employers. She could get that out of her way before Jacques arrived.

Mercier was still at it.

'Then why is *Le Figaro* still keeping me on their payroll?' she retorted, sitting cross-legged on the sofa.

'How the hell do I know? If I were them, I would ask you to send news on naked fakirs . . .'

'Sadhus,' she corrected.

'. . . the snake charmers of Kashmir . . .'

'There are no snakes let alone snake charmers in Kashmir.'

'. . . or the maneaters of Kumaon.'

'There are no maneaters in Kumaon, you idiot. The book was written decades ago.' Dominique was beginning to show signs of impatience.

'Or the cow-worshipping Hindus,' he didn't give up. 'There is far more interesting stuff to write about on India than the crap you dish out. You could give us the recipe for roasted "sheikh" kababs for example, or at least the recipe for the roasted and burnt brides of Delhi.'

'Oh shut up.'

'Then there's this prophet somewhere who believes that the earth is flat . . .'

'He is a British, you moron. He lives somewhere in England.'

'Okay, maybe I got that one wrong. But there are enough astrologers in India for whom the earth is still the centre of the universe. By the way, aren't there flesh eaters somewhere in the north-east of India?'

'If Idi Amin lives in north-east India, then he's the only flesh eater there. Mercier, you have no fucking idea what's happening in India and the more you speak the more of your ignorance you expose.'

'Oh yeah?' he shouted, waving his hand. 'What about the hundreds of naked fakirs who come once every twelve years, riding horses and jump into that holy river Ganges? The things they do in the name of the Hindu religion can put the Kama Sutra to shame! In fact, if they—'

'To come naked on horseback once in twelve years is better than flocking nude every year to Côte d'Azure, my dear. South of France is full of suntanned flesh. And pray, how the hell are you so familiar with the love life of Indian sadhus?'

'Dom, let me tell you a story to convince you that you live in a country of weirdos,' he continued. 'There was this grand fakir from India or swamiji, that's what he was called I think, who had come to Paris earlier this year. Sitting in the Hilton, he screwed around with hundreds of French women till the police had to lift him by the crotch and send him packing to Switzerland—that's where he lives now. Even your good friend Penelope had wanted to visit him here and sought a private appointment. She was saved by a whisker when he was arrested the same day. That's your fakir for you. He hired a penthouse at the Hilton, had his bills and libido paid for by his followers. Women flocked to him for salvation and he got his salivation in return. All in the name of meditation and eternal bliss. Bliss indeed! It lasted all of ten seconds and they were discarded after the act. That's your great sage for you, the great screwball of the earth!' Mercier was angry. He had reason to be. His fiancée had left him to join this swamiji's ashram in Interlaken. They had got engaged a few months earlier. And then, a perfectly rational girl became a devotee and left her life in Paris behind for a promise of a better life. Mercier had been shattered. He had seen his mom and dad separate. Now, his fiancée had left. He cursed the swamiji, cursed the fakirs, cursed the Indians, and concluded that all Indians were conmen and screwballs.

Life in Sabarmati came back to an uneasy routine. One wasn't quite sure when the next stale fish would arrive with some fresh threat. Sundaram had asked a private security firm to post round-the-clock security guards.

Sitting in the verandah, Sundaram was having his early morning coffee when he heard the familiar click of the gate opening. It was Balan. Sundaram waited for the familiar steps to walk across to the other side. Instead, the footsteps stopped. Sundaram looked up from *The Hindu*. Balan rarely came into the verandah, unless of course it was to collect the monthly dues. It was not the end of the month and all the dues had been paid. Each one waited for the other to speak.

'Ayyah, how long are you going to wait before you conclude that the police will not do anything on this matter?' asked Balan taking the initiative. Balan's patience had run out and he had decided not to wait any longer. The recent threat had had no impact on the police. Contrary to assurances, Inspector Gurunathan viewed the case as an irritant. A lone policeman came on his beat to Clive Avenue around eleven every night, blowing his shrill whistle. Like the 'toot-toot' of a steam engine, he 'pee-peed' from his whistle and left. As far as he was concerned, his job was done. And all residents of Clive Avenue were supposed to feel safe in the knowledge that the policeman was around.

Sundaram contemplated Balan's question seriously for the first time and confessed that he didn't have a clear answer after all. His faith in the system was slowly eroding. He was reminded, strangely enough, of his college days when he used to go cinema-hopping with his friends to watch Tamil films. The hero almost always took the law into his hands and thrashed the villain, and all his co-conspiratorial goons as well, for effect. Single-handedly, the forces of evil were smashed into pulp. The police came in a few minutes later to pick up the remains and take the bad guys to jail—if they survived the thrashing of the hero. And so it had been in Tamil movies for generations. Sundaram had always maintained that the movies were far removed from reality. Taking the law into one's hands? Nobody did this in a civilized society, not in south India at least. When he met the matinee idol and politician Chief Minister MGR later in life, he couldn't resist popping the question. 'Why do the police not arrive on time in your movies? They always let you handle the villain all by yourself.' MGR had laughed but his answer was carefully considered. 'Sundaram,' he said, 'I portray on screen the power of the awakened masses. The message I convey is simple. Power flows from the people. This message is not for people like you but those voiceless masses, those who have lost their voice through centuries of servility and subjugation and are mere mute bystanders of our history. The message is for them, to galvanize them to come out and voice their grievances. It is not to provoke them to violence but to seek justice.'

In Chennai, life imitated art. Balan the Milk Man stood there waiting for an answer.

'I don't know, Balan,' Sundaram sighed. He was tired. He felt ten years older.

'Ayyah, you can never get justice from these people unless you play their game. And you can't play their game and stoop to their level. I will help you in whatever way I can. I owe you both a lot. How can I ever forget the day you and Amma gave me twenty thousand rupees without a second's hesitation to start my life afresh? Now, it's my turn to help you.'

Sundaram was silent. Previously he had ruled it out completely and had warned Balan to keep out of it. But Balan was making some sense.

'When the police cannot make much headway, how can you?' Sundaram asked.

'You leave it to me, ayyah. We will see what happens.'

'How?'

'Just leave it to me, ayyah.'

Sundaram couldn't make up his mind. Balan waited for an answer. Finally, he went back to *The Hindu* and said quietly, 'Balan, don't make me say things I can't say.'

Balan called his most trusted lieutenant, Karim Mohammed Khan. They drew out a simple gameplan. They zeroed in on George Town in north Chennai. George Town lay beyond Fort St George and was so congested that if a mustard seed was dropped, it didn't fall on the ground. All things moveable and immoveable, high and low, fought for space. It hadn't always been like this. A couple of centuries earlier, the area was divided roughly into two, Muthialpet on the east and Peddanaickenpet on the west. While Muthialpet had been home to the Left Hand Castes, where those on the lower end of the social ladder lived, Peddanaickenpet was home to the Right Hand Castes, where the elites and brown sahibs lounged in luxury in the lush surroundings. And so the divisions remained for years. And, like everything else, got blurred with time. Now, within the confines of George Town lay a congealed mass of human beings and inanimate objects—a sweaty mass of indifferent pedigree. Not that it mattered or that anyone cared anymore. There was much more to do than waste time and money on caste or pelf in this crowded area. The only distinction still zealously guarded was the parcelling out of streets according to trade. Even smugglers had their own street in this area. Thieves came in stealthily at night to sell their loot, and people came in the morning to buy it. Balan and Karim, however, eyed Sembudoss Street, Rasappa Chetty Street, Mooker Nallamuthu Street and Broadway for hardware and steel. Don't shop in the same road for two different things was Balan's advice. There were enough streets for them not to have to.

Dominique's first day with Jacques was wonderful. He was great company. He took her to places she wanted to see, stopped at places she wanted to stop at. They walked from one end of the Louvre to the Arc de Triomphe past the Tuileries, Place de la Concorde, the hotels and onwards to Champs-Elysées. They walked around Hotel Elysées Star, down Avenue George 'Saank' and ended up at the Buddha Bar. It was teeming with people. She wasn't particularly hungry and they went upstairs to the first floor. It was arranged just the way she remembered it. She asked for a Pinot Noir 1991 and he followed suit. It was wonderful to be back in Paris again. She was feeling lighter after meeting Jacques and freer after having made her obligatory trip to *Le Figaro*.

Jacques was amusing and filled her in on his job, his colleagues, his new-found passion for French literature and his old passion for jazz. What a contrast it was between the Jacques she saw in Chennai the previous year and the Jacques now, amidst a Parisian late summer evening. Not to be outdone, Dom told him all about her job, her intention to complete a Ph.D on comparative developments in contemporary French and American writings and her tryst with Chennai boys who lusted after her from a distance. As she watched the colourful array of pedestrians swaying by—they only swayed in Paris, not walked—she realized she had missed Paris.

Then, Jacques had something to say. He had had affairs earlier, during his days in college, he told her. Dom was more amused than upset. Not many she hoped. It was good to know that he was normal. Were any of the affairs still carrying on, she enquired. No, no, not at all, came the emphatic answer. They had taken place several years ago and had been few and far between. But then Dom, he continued, not all these affairs had been with women. She didn't understand. Girls then? No. Some were with men, he said. Men? What do you mean, men? You must be joking, she replied laughingly. Surely he was not suggesting that he had affairs with men? But that was what Jacques meant. 'Dom, I used to be a bisexual. Not any more, believe me, but briefly, yes,' he spoke slowly. There was sadness in his eyes. 'In those days, those early days in college several years back—it seems like decades ago—when we wanted to discover life for ourselves and social mores and norms were meant only to be broken, those were the years when I went out with both sexes. It's not that I was gay. Far from it. In fact, I couldn't dream of myself as being gay. It was this urge, which comes only from the freshness of adolescence, to explore sex which made me do it. At that age, one could do no wrong and one went around with supreme confidence, free and unrestrained, believing, criticizing, breaking away, changing and discovering. Very soon I realized that I wasn't born to be with men. And that chapter ended as abruptly as it had begun. I had been a bisexual. And not liked it.' He stopped. He took a sip of the Pinot Noir. She looked away at the pedestrians, hardly seeing them. She felt as if she had been hit by a whiplash.

'Dom, it was important that I tell you the truth. It would have been a disaster if you had found out later from someone else. When I did what I did, it didn't even occur to me that I was doing something unnatural if not different. It was accepted like we accept day and night. Sometimes I keep awake in the night thinking how foolish we were and wondering what made us do what we did.' Jacques was calm and his voice sad. 'I can't get back my college days again and make different choices, can I?'

Dominique wasn't sure what to make of it. She prided herself on being liberal about these things. Her parents weren't. But she was, she knew. Times had changed. She had friends who were gay or lesbian and she hadn't given it a second thought. She respected the choices of her friends and took them for what they were. She tried not to judge or change them. Who was she to judge or lay down social and moral codes? It wasn't her problem either as long as it didn't affect her relationship with them. She herself would not walk that path, that she was clear. Her second cousin Françoise was gay and it had made little difference to their relationship. But when she heard what Jacques had to say, she was not sure how to react.

A host of unanswered questions churned inside her. Jacques could see that she was deeply disturbed. Her eyes said it all. She had so far not been called upon to make choices. Now, she had to. She had to decide for herself, for her life ahead. Was she comfortable with the thought that her life partner was a former bisexual? Where was the emphasis—on bisexual or former? Jacques looked eminently male and behaved like one. He was a great guy. And a former bisexual.

'Jacques, you have taken me by surprise,' she spoke for the first time. 'Well, I have no idea what to make of it, frankly. Personally I don't think that it should make any difference. I never thought that these things mattered. It was after all your personal choice and, most importantly, you are now out of it. Why should it matter? We all make mistakes. In fact, if I call it a mistake, I contradict myself. I am not here to judge. I have always considered myself liberal in thought if not upbringing. But Jacques, I don't know how to put it. I feel confused, for the first time since I got to know you. I was and am sure of you. I wouldn't have come this far if I did not feel good about you. Good about the way you are when you are with me. All this has just confused me . . . I can't find another word to describe my feelings at this point. It's just all too confusing, Jacques.'

'I'm glad you look at this differently, Dom,' he shifted uneasily in his chair. He wasn't quite sure of what she was saying. Was it okay with her or not? He wasn't sure. 'I know you will understand and forgive me. Understand that this was just a passing fancy. My mistakes are mine and I wish they had not happened. I made those choices consciously and I regret them. Not because they were bad or good. But because I was not created a bisexual or gay. God made me a heterosexual male and so I will remain. I know that now. It has not been easy for me to tell you all this, believe me. I don't want your response right now. It's not easy for you either—or anyone else for that matter—to digest what I have just told you. But I do want you to know that I love you. Very deeply. Dom, none of what I have just told you makes or will make any difference to what I feel for you.' He reached out and kissed her lightly on her hair. Dom smiled weakly and fought back the tears. Her eyes were averted and her right hand played nervously with the stem of the wine glass. She wanted to hug him then and there and tell him how much she loved him. Something stopped her. She sat silent, twirling the wine glass between her fingers. The sun had gone down and clouds were gathering. A light drizzle had started.

'Drop me back, Jacques,' she asked. 'I need some time on my own.'

Seventy-two hours after her arrival, Paris looked different. The fourth day was dreary, with no sparkle in the eyes of the Parisians. Dom had wanted time. To think. She wondered what to think. Wondered what to do. She had no one to talk to. Whom could she ask? Not Mercier. Not her divorced uncle. Not her parents. She knew what their answer would be. It didn't need a genius to guess. Isabelle? She called her in Chennai. Isabelle was out for the day and would return only the next day. Chitra? But Chitra was predictable. Get out of this, she would say. Monique? Monique wasn't sure. She knew Jacques all right, but not well enough. 'Dom, follow your heart,' she concluded. 'Take him for his word if you feel that he is being honest with you.'

Dominique called Rajan. He was in Delhi she was told. She didn't want to bother him there. He would have been ideal. He would have mulled over it and given her an honest answer, one she would have listened to. What if Jacques had kept this from her? She would have been devastated if she had discovered later. There were virtues to being honest and upfront. Her respect for Jacques went up all the more. Dom sat on the bed, eyes closed, listless, going over the same question a thousand times.

Even after liberalization of the economy, Rajan had to make an obligatory pilgrimage to Delhi to have a darshan of the bureaucrats of India's capital. It's strictly not required to make a *parikrama* of Delhi gods, Rajan's lawyer had advised, but Rajan decided to go anyway. He would spend a couple of days and pay his obeisance. It would be useful to establish contacts in Delhi. South Indians felt that Delhi was too far away and too far away it remained. They were cloutless in the capital. They ended up wringing their hands in despair, cursing the North Indian. Rajan didn't want that to happen to him. He wanted to start his career on the right foot. He had not seen Delhi in more than a decade. The moment Rajan stepped out of the airport, he knew that he had stepped into a different world.

Delhi was in many ways the antithesis of Chennai. New Delhi was huge in scale, spacious, with sprawling bungalows, broad roads planned carefully, and impersonal in execution. The city was absolutely impersonal and impassive. Chennai resembled a mufassal town in comparison. Chennai grew wherever there was space, like a money plant. What saved it was its people. While Chennai*vasis* were warm, helpful, informal nay casual and unruffled, Delhiites were impersonal, lacking warmth, almost crude and oblivious to each other's needs. In a way this wasn't too bad, since each one minded his or her own business. For Chennai*vasis*, the private life of their interlocutors came first. They couldn't proceed with any conversation till they knew all about their interlocutor's children, grandchildren, aunt's name and birthday, uncle's profession and monthly salary, father's place of origin and reasons for change of venue, sister-in-law's brother's marital status and, if unmarried, the horoscope and the reasons for his staying unmarried. Some boldly ventured further, but most were satisfied with the information given. Still, Chennai was a warm place to be in. Delhi was cold. Even in summer.

Rajan had originally planned to stay in Delhi for a couple of days, finish all his meetings, meet two of his classmates and, if possible, a few of his father's distant relatives, before flying back. The first bureaucrat to give him an appointment gave him time two days later. Rajan's schedule went out of the window. He quickly reconciled to the ethos of Delhi and its powers that be, and went to Gulati's at Pandara Park for dinner with Paul and Sharat, his two school buddies. 'What, Rajan! You continue to be veg?!' Karhai paneer, moong dal, palak paneer, naan and lachha paratha with onions and chillies. He was well and truly in the heart of north India. If he had to waste time, he decided to enjoy himself while he did. They ended the meal with meetha paan—Banarasi *pattha* and *geeli* supari. He planned to meet his father's relatives the next day. He had no excuse now not to meet them. 'This is the only way to maintain family ties. Otherwise your generation will have no idea of our family tree,' Sundaram had said. The next morning, having no appointments to bother about, Rajan woke up late, only to the sound of Shiva's frantic telephone call.

'Rajan, our office has been broken into and ransacked.'

By the time Rajan took the evening flight home, the police had come and gone. Some rowdies had broken into the building after tying up the watchman and turned their office upside down. Chairs were broken, glass table tops cracked, papers strewn around and the two computers smashed. No item was taken. In fact, the violent intruders had left behind something for Rajan, wrapped in a Tamil newspaper along with a fish, dead but fresh this time. The note said 'You are not going to be safe from us anywhere. You know what to do. Do it immediately before harm befalls you and your family.'

THE WOUNDED TIGER

'Saar, the rowdies have surrendered,' Inspector Gurunathan proudly announced. 'They have confessed to stabbing your son and ransacking his office in Velacheri.'

When Inspector Gurunathan came to Clive Avenue that morning, a posse of policemen preceded him and waited outside Sabarmati. A crowd had already gathered to witness the spectacle. A group of tourists who had just been offloaded to pay obeisance to Selvan, almost forgot their matinee idol and gaped excitedly at the police jeeps and the collection of policemen. Their day was made. There was actually something to see. They were quite sure that either someone was being arrested or the house raided. Must be laundering black money and stashing it up in the house by filling up their pillows, they thought.

Sundaram had just finished his pooja. Sporting a generous streak of white ash across his forehead to reinforce his faith in Shaivism, he stood bare-chested with the sacred thread across his chest and a silk *veshti* around his waist when the Inspector walked in. It was an unexpected but pleasant visit and both sat in the verandah. The morning was still young and cool. Lakshmi went in quickly to get some coffee. Revati looked excited that policemen had come calling.

'Saar, not only have they confessed to stabbing your son, but they have also confessed that it was Devanathan who paid them to do so. They are willing to cooperate and testify against Devanathan. What more do you want?'

'Why did they do that—particularly after all these days of keeping quiet? And just two days after ransacking Rajan's office?' Sundaram queried. 'There must be some reason.'

'You are right. The reason was my boys. My policemen have their own ways of getting them, Saar. You must not underestimate our resolve,' he laughed loudly, throwing his head back and opening his mouth wide revealing a set of blackish paan-stained teeth badly in need of repair.

Sundaram smiled back. That was one thing Sundaram never did—he never underestimated the police. He had always overestimated them.

'No . . . I never underestimated them,' he said truthfully. 'They deserve accolades for their determination, even though sometimes their lack of response may have annoyed the public like us.'

Hot coffee had arrived and the Inspector had by now warmed up. Revati had made coffee for the rest of the policemen as well. Lakshmi, typically, sat inside in the drawing room but was listening to every word.

'Saar, we are only doing our duty to the public,' he spoke with as much false humility as he could muster. 'We don't expect anything in return.'

I'll be damned, thought Sundaram. 'You people are truly selfless—'

'Don't mention it, Saar. We will never let you down. Your son can now go about in peace.'

'What next? When are you catching the big fish in the net?'

'We are preparing the case against Devanathan and will press charges. His days are numbered. These rowdies will give us all the information we want, Saar—source of funds, transfer of cash to them, time, place, etc. In return for slightly reduced sentences—which I will arrange with the judge—they will testify against Devanathan. They will tell the judge whatever we want them to.'

This was music to Sundaram's ears. Lakshmi began crying softly, with relief and joy.

There was another exchange of praises and thank-yous. Then, it was time to leave.

'Saar, I'm sure you will show your appreciation to my boys' efforts in an appropriate manner,' the Inspector hinted subtly, getting up from the cane chair. 'You can visit me in the police station or my residence any time you want,' he hinted not so subtly.

Sundaram agreed to visit the Inspector in his paan-painted lair to thank him appropriately.

Lakshmi couldn't stop crying. 'We have to do *abhishegam* at Kapaleeshwarar Temple today,' she sobbed, thanking all the gods she could immediately remember. 'May this Devanathan be wiped out from the face of the earth,' Paati cursed on being told the news. Rajan was in his office trying to get things back in order. They rang him up to tell him. Veena and Jayaraman were also informed. By this time the word was out. Clive Avenue was agog. Rajaram IAS, Bhuvana, Daulat Singh, Michelle, Arvind the Wife Beater and the watchman outside Selvan's house all came in to share in the good news. They congratulated Sundaram as if he had just won the Nobel Prize. In some ways, his achievement was no less. 'You may not have heard the last of Devanathan yet,' warned Rajaram IAS with his characteristic caution.

'Where is Balan?' Sundaram suddenly enquired. 'I haven't seen him the last couple of days.'

'Balan? He said he was off to visit a friend in Madurai for a few days,' Lakshmi said.

Rajan was as stunned as Dominique had been when she first heard about Jacques. A bisexual for a husband?

It was late when he returned but he gulped some food and went over to Dom's on receiving her message on his voicemail.

As they sat in her room, she told him all that had happened in Paris.

'I couldn't decide, Rajan. I just couldn't decide. I thought I would give him a yes or a no before my return. I turned the whole thing over in my mind a million times but just couldn't make up my mind. I couldn't say it was all right. It was such a shock. Do you know the worst part? I realized that I didn't feel the same way for him as I did before. I kept telling myself that I was overreacting and sat out the problem for a couple of days more. It didn't get any better. I couldn't get around to saying yes to him. I didn't want to lose him. But I believe him when he says that it was a flash in the pan. But things have changed. I feel differently now. What would you do in my place? I need your advice.' Dom's eyes were swollen. She sat on the bed, her back against the pillow and her chin resting on her palm. She seemed to have grown paler.

'Dom, if I were you, I would bid him goodbye.' He was blunt. 'It's better to live with someone about whom you have no regrets and are sure about. At least you now have the option of getting out. It would have been worse later. If there is some voice within you which says "hold back", then follow it. I can say that from personal experience. Gayathri was indeed a good person—actually, a very good person. But we still decided to split. Some voice in each of us said "hold back". And that was that. If you don't feel the same way for him, then leave him. There are other Blanchemaisons in this world. Believe me, you will marry someone one day who will actually treat you like a White House inhabitant.'

She smiled through her tears. Rajan insisted on calling Jacques by his surname. Rajan's words were the confirmation she was looking for. She was not brave enough to take the decision on her own. She agreed with him. She would talk to Jacques the next day. The very thought of speaking to him upset her and she wept. Rajan felt miserable too. All he could do was sit beside her and put his arms around her.

Rajan knew how it felt. He had gone through it himself. He, however, didn't want to be the spoiler. He insisted that she didn't have to go by what he said. She should ask Isabelle. Dom had. Isabelle had also discouraged her but not as categorically as he had. And the news had to be broken gently to her parents. They had guessed that something was wrong. But when she showed a lack of enthusiasm for the topic, they put it down to jet lag. Or a lovers' tiff.

When the smile disappeared from Dominique's face, Paati and Lakshmi were worried. She had grown up like a daughter in Sabarmati and they treated her break-up almost as an extension of Rajan's. Since Dominique never divulged the real reason to her parents, they assumed that Jacques had been having another affair and had dumped her. Lakshmi heard the story from Dom's mother Michelle and there was gloom again in the Sundaram household. Dom was such a lovely girl. How could he do this to her?

There was an instant outpouring of sympathy from Clive Avenue.

'Saala kuttha! If he were here, I would have had him lynched,' Daulat burst out.

Michelle was the most upset. It wasn't easy finding a French husband sitting in Chennai. She had half a mind to ask Dom to take a transfer to Paris, to go and find a suitable husband for herself.

As Balan walked up the drive, Sundaram walked down the verandah. They met at the steps.

'Balan, where have you been?' Sundaram asked.

'Ayyah, I had gone to Madurai to meet my friend Nallamuthu. He has been asking me to come for a long time and I took some time off to see him. But leave all that alone, ayyah, you don't know how happy I was to hear from Daulat ayyah that the rowdies have been caught. Now these bastards will spill the beans. Our police are capable of breaking their legs and getting the truth out of them. I hope Devanathan rots in hell.'

'I hope so too even though it is still not going to be easy to nail him.'

'You don't worry, ayyah. It's a matter of time. Our police may not be adept at catching culprits, but once caught, they are good at extracting confessions from them.'

Sundaram looked at the burly Balan closely. 'Balan, did you by any chance have a hand in this?'

Balan looked up surprised. 'Hand in what? The rowdies? How could I? Much as I would have liked to break every bone in their bodies, I wasn't even here. Moreover, you kept telling me to stay away from all this and I didn't want to disobey you. I am glad that your faith in the system paid off in the end.'

'I'm not sure whether this really is the end. Tell me frankly, Balan. I don't want you to get into trouble because of this.'

'Ayyah, how can there be anything between the rowdies and me?' he laughed.

Sundaram observed Balan's expression. He knew Balan was lying. 'Balan, I spoke to Daulat and he told me that he had not seen you since your return from Madurai. It couldn't have been Daulat who told you about this.'

Balan looked at Sundaram. His expression was dead serious. 'Ayyah, the last time I asked you a question, you gave me an answer. I will give you the same answer now. "Don't make me say things I can't say."' Holding a can of milk, mixed with water or not one didn't know, Balan walked away towards the rear end of the house.

Sundaram stood there for several seconds watching Balan's figure disappear round the corner. He had wanted to say something, but didn't. He looked around quickly to see whether their conversation had been overheard. There was no one. He turned and walked back to the verandah. For the first time in his life, Sundaram had been a co-conspirator.

Arvind the Wife Beater and Bhargavi came in after dinner and found Paati, Sundaram and Lakshmi engrossed in *Aadhi Paraashakti* on TV. Tamil classics on prime time. The youngsters hated black and white films and the oldies loved them.

'Mami, Mama, we have good news for you,' Arvind the Wife Beater said when the movie concluded and the TV was switched off. 'We have just decided to have Suresh's *poonal* ceremony early next month. We thought you should be the first to know.'

There were congratulations all around. Suresh was nearly nine years old and just the right age for the *poonal*.

'We were wondering whether we should wait for another year or two but thought it's better done sooner than later.'

'I agree entirely, Arvind,' Paati observed. 'Eight years is a good age for the *poonal*. The child will be eager to learn the rituals and is not too young not to understand them either. You are doing the right thing.'

'I am glad there is going to be some festivity in Clive Avenue,' Sundaram smiled. 'All we have been hearing this year is depressing news and I'm sure this *poonal* is a harbinger of things to come. Any such auspicious event is likely to bring divine blessings all around and will definitely have a cumulative effect on the welfare of all those living here, believe me.'

'Both Bhargavi and I want you and Mami to not only come and bless Suresh but be in the forefront and conduct his *poonal*. Our parents are not alive and you have both been like a father and mother to us. We want you to conduct his *poonal* and I want to print the invitation in your name.'

One couldn't ask for greater honour and Sundaram and Lakshmi agreed immediately.

The auspicious day, a Friday, was barely two weeks away

and there wasn't too much time left. The ceremony was to be at home which was as good a place as any. Arvind's house was spacious with a lovely lawn in front. In fact, the lawn was even bigger than the one at Sabarmati. The *homam* and the rituals could be arranged there. The lawn was to be covered with a *pandal* which could cover part of the road as well. Sundaram offered to have his lawn covered with another *pandal* and the lunch would be held there. At a single sitting, there was enough space for more than a hundred and fifty. They decided on two shifts for lunch—the first one for office-goers. Maybe a late third one too, if necessary. Invitation cards had to be printed and sent, Shastrigals for the ceremony to be arranged. None of the rituals could be ignored. Chief Cook had to be contacted and the menu finalized. Daulat offered to leave all his cars at Arvind's disposal for a week. Life returned to Clive Avenue. Almost every resident became an event manager. They were determined to make Suresh's *poonal* a success.

They heard soon enough. The witnesses had turned hostile. The rowdies had gone back on their confession citing duress and torture by the police. The value of their confessions stood but was diminished considerably. It was said that money had changed hands. In lakhs. Devanathan had won even before the battle had begun. This time, no policeman came to Sabarmati to make the announcement of defeat. Inspector Gurunathan stayed back at the police station. He didn't ask Sundaram to come and show his appreciation to his 'boys'.

Gloom settled over Clive Avenue yet again. Fear returned to Sabarmati. Devanathan was bound to be even more vengeful, now that the tiger had been wounded. Another watchman had been posted outside the office in Velacheri.

Rajan was up to his neck with work when he heard about the witnesses turning hostile.

Rajan had been thinking. About his tryst with Gayathri, his loss of friends, barring Dom and CV, because of migration, his father's compromise with Devanathan and his subsequent change of heart, the plunder of his office by the rowdies and, of course, the stabbing. It had been a rough welcome back to Chennai. Chennai had not been like this when he left it. It had been a carefree life. He had come back to resume his place in the matrix. But the matrix had changed. Chennai had become almost unrecognizable. His mother and father were less in charge of their own lives than before. It had been easy to flow with the tide before but when one decided not to do so, one entered an entirely different world. The fact that Gayathri turned out to be a non-vegetarian who smoked and that Rajaram IAS was more of a spineless bureaucrat than a littérateur was purely incidental. Chennai couldn't have changed so much so soon. He hadn't. In fact, nothing had changed. All that was there had always been there. It was just that Rajan had not noticed. Now he did. And Rajan didn't like what he saw. Rajan wondered whether he had made the right decision in coming back. He sought out his father.

Sundaram had returned late after a surgery. Lakshmi, as always, was waiting for him to come home. She never had her dinner before Sundaram did. It was another one of those customs imposed on Brahmin wives, but it soon became a habit. In the early years of their marriage, Sundaram found her starving whenever he was held up at the hospital. He shouted at her for not eating. This custom was a silly one and it was time she stopped waiting for him. But she kept quiet and continued to wait. She was exerting moral pressure on him to come back early. That was unfair, he charged. She promised that it was not so and continued to wait. He threatened to eat at the hospital if she waited for him. She asked him to go ahead and waited for him anyway. Sure enough, he always came back to dine at home. He couldn't stand food from outside. After several years of shouting, threatening and cajoling, he gave up. Lakshmi would never change.

Sundaram had just finished his dinner and moved into his bedroom, when Rajan decided to have a chat with him. Since Rajan–Sundaram relations were now at an all-time high, it was easy to. Lakshmi was still in the kitchen with Revati putting away the vessels. The nights were still warm and the air conditioner was on, drowning out the world outside. Sundaram had just stripped to his white banian and white *veshti*.

'Appa, over the last few days, I have been thinking about my return here, my life since my return and many other things. I'm increasingly veering towards the view that maybe it was a mistake after all.' Rajan had wanted to broach the topic gently, beat around the bush a little and soften his father up. He found himself doing quite the opposite.

'When I came here, I didn't come back out of sentiment or nostalgia. It was because I wanted to live here. With you, with my friends and with all the other things which had made my earlier life here so livable and, most important of all, comfortably predictable. But since coming here, I realize that I am seeing an aspect of Chennai I had never seen before. Maybe it was always like this—I hadn't had the opportunity to notice it. Still, it's all so new to me. Maybe I notice the change all the more because I've had a two-year break in between. But I'm sure, if you observe closely, much of it will be strange to you too. It's no more the comfortable, familiar Chennai it used to be. It isn't the Chennai of five years ago.'

They were interrupted by Lakshmi who came in wiping her hands and face on the pallu of her saree. 'What are you both discussing without me?'

'Amma, good you've come. I was just mentioning to Appa that after my return, I find Chennai quite unrecognizable. Things are different and not necessarily for the better. They have—'

'You have had a particularly difficult time, Rajan. It's not—'

'Amma, what I say has no direct bearing on the stabbing or anything else that might have happened to me. It's to do with a change in the basic character of Chennai itself. Have you ever seen this kind of money power at work? That too this openly? Politicians who are certified corrupt are voted back to power over and over again. Corruption is now a virtue. Criminals have started behaving with impunity and they get away with it. There is no one to check them. Appa, there is no use pretending that the police are the guardians of our freedom. Have you noticed the large-scale migration, not just to the US, but also to other parts of the country? It cannot just be that they are fascinated by things foreign. All of us—you, me and others, all of us—supported reservation since we genuinely felt that it was the only way out to create an egalitarian Tamil society. We even tolerated ridiculous levels of reservation like, 78 per cent, 87 per cent, but I never imagined that this would soon become a tool to drive us away from Tamil Nadu forever. There was a time when MGR tried to get a few things right for us, but that ended in a flash. It is almost a rule here that if you are a Brahmin, you will be given short shrift. Unless of course you can play the game of the day—money, bribery, corruption, muscle power . . . Then you end up like Devanathan. When I think of my own personal experiences over the last few months, I cannot think of a time when our society has been this crude and crass. And to top it all, it's a city without water. Why the hell should you two be pumping water from the handpump every morning? Like the great civilizations that ended because of lack of water or like the waterless capital Fatehpur Sikri was abandoned by Shah Jahan, I hope Chennai is too! It's not worth living here one moment. I don't see why we have to sit here and take all this nonsense.'

Sundaram agreed with every word Rajan had said. He could add his own list of woes.

'Rajan, there is nothing I can disagree with,' confessed Sundaram. 'But what option do I have? I have lived here all my life and all my friends are here. Chennai is still, after all that you say, the best place we have. You yourself are a product of Chennai. This is the environment you know best.'

'Appa, the more I think of my life here and the daily struggles both of you go through, the more I am convinced that it may not be such a bad idea to return to the US. It just isn't worth my time to start another uphill battle against all the visible and invisible obstacles I will have to face before I can actually start doing something productive.

'I agree you may not have a choice,' Rajan continued, 'but I have. It's not too late. In fact, before my return, John Carey and many others had wanted me to stay back and work with them. But I had had this vision of coming back and I refused. It will not be difficult for me to go back.'

Sundaram had listened patiently. He had been surprised himself when Rajan had decided to return. He was half expecting him not to. Now that Rajan was here, he accepted that he was going to be in Chennai for good. Rajan had had a tough time in Chennai, there was no doubt. His landing had not been smooth. But this quick turnaround was not quite what Sundaram expected. He was clearly disturbed. The thought of his only son settling permanently in the US upset him. With Veena moving out, Paati, Lakshmi and he would live their last years alone. There was a sense of security in the thought that Rajan would finally live with them some day. That he would take care of them. It wasn't as though they were young any more. They were getting on. Paati certainly. The thought that it was they who should be staying with Rajan never crossed their minds. The thought of leaving Chennai was unthinkable.

When Sundaram was young, he had stepped into his father's study one morning and found him poring over stacks of paper.

Peering over his father's shoulder, Sundaram realized that they were answer sheets of second year medical students who had taken their annual exams. The lot had been sent to his father for evaluation. Without disturbing him, Sundaram had picked up a few corrected ones and flipped through them. In one of the sheets, he noticed that against one of the answers, his father had written '0'. Intrigued, Sundaram read through the answer. Except for one solitary step which was circled in red and marked wrong, all the other steps had been tick-marked and were right. That didn't look too fair. Gathering courage, he had asked his father, 'Appa, sorry to disturb you. In this answer, I notice that you have ticked practically all the steps right but for one small mistake. You have still given this chap a zero. Didn't the answer deserve at least some marks?' Sundaram expected his father to shoo him off telling him not to disturb him. His father had looked at him and, surprisingly, without any trace of annoyance at being interrupted, had answered Sundaram seriously. 'Sundaram, most of the steps are correct. But if he had committed that—what you call, a small mistake—on the operating table, he would have killed the patient. I can't award him any marks for killing the patient, can I?'

Sundaram never forgot this exchange. It left an indelible impression on him. High standards were set and demanded. There was no compromise. That was what had kept the Tamils from staying ahead in the race. Exacting standards.

And Sundaram had seen their gradual—in fact rapid—decline. If anyone now did what Sundaram's father had done years ago, he would have been accused of being anti-Brahmin or anti-non-Brahmin depending on the student's caste. None dared to impose any stringent restrictions. They stood tyrannized by the students and the state. And not necessarily in that order. And why not? When students had paid lakhs of rupees as bribes or capitation fees, they demanded at least a passing grade.

Sundaram saw perfect logic in what Rajan was saying and

couldn't agree more about where Chennai was headed. Towards disaster. And Sundaram was powerless to stop it. He had learnt to adapt and move on. But the thought of Rajan leaving and them staying back, these were difficult thoughts and both Sundaram and Lakshmi knew that they had to confront the possibility some day. The day had arrived. By the time Veena left after marriage, they had already prepared themselves mentally. Weren't daughters born to leave the house? But sons. Sons were born to stay. And take care of their parents.

'Rajan, there is much I agree with. But think about it again. Think calmly. Don't decide in a hurry. We will discuss this again.'

POONAL

With Rajan so adamant, Sundaram had to give in. But on one condition. Rajan would have to get married before he left. Paati and Lakshmi were insistent. There was no question of Rajan going back to the US single. And before one could say 'Chandra', astrologer Chandramouli made a triumphant comeback in Sabarmati. Lakshmi was waiting for him with a bunch of new horoscopes. This time, Chandramouli noticed, the bunch contained some Iyengar girls as well. The Sabarmati household was obviously desperate. Between the horoscopes and the preparation for the *poonal*, Sabarmati was back in business.

The *poonal* preparations were on. The tables and chairs for the lunch were dumped at Sabarmati. The other chairs in No. 5. The kitchen was taken over by the Chief Cook and a temporary shamiana erected behind the house to store the huge vessels. A large *pandal* had come up in No. 5 and looked imposing. Arvind the Wife Beater and Bhargavi were running around like headless chickens seeing to the last-minute arrangements. Daulat's cars were dispatched all over Chennai, delivering, collecting and ferrying. Bhargavi's relatives from Nagerkoil had arrived and the Leonards had organized one of their company guest houses for their stay. The division of work in Clive Avenue was clear. For the guest house, one went to the Leonards. For cars, Daulat was tapped. Anything from common cold to the rare heart attack, Sundaram was there. All

bureaucratic matters were referred to Rajaram IAS. Even actor
Selvan chipped in now and then for glamour. Everyone had
their defined roles in Clive Avenue.

When the last of the chairs was removed the day after the
ceremony, No. 5 resembled the battleground of Trafalgar.
Burnt bricks, ash from the *homam*, drying plantain trees tied
to the *pandal* at the entrance, plastic bags and pooja flowers
crushed by human feet. After the lunch, the large banana leaves
on which the lunch had been served were unceremoniously
dumped in the huge waste dump at the corner of the road.
Stray dogs materialized from nowhere and dug into the dump.
Cows and crows ganged up to chase the dogs away and claim
some of the booty. Not to be outdone, the municipal lorry
came to pick up the banana leaves from the dump promptly,
not because the leaves attracted stray animals, but because they
realized that there was a one hundred-rupee note at stake. They
demanded fifty more and got it.

The *poonal* had gone off well. Sundaram and Lakshmi had
gone around with an air of importance. And rightly so. After
all, they were the seniors conducting the *poonal*. As the guests
streamed in, Mahesh, the three-year-old son of Arvind the
Wife Beater and Bhargavi, Aditya, Veena's son, and Sonia,
Daulat's daughter, were right at the entrance. While Sonia
sprinkled rose water on the guests with the silver sprinkler,
Aditya offered sandalwood paste from a silver bowl and Mahesh
held out a silver tray of crystallized sugar cubes and powder. By
the time all the guests were in, Mahesh had himself consumed
half the tray of sugar cubes. The smoke from the *homam* had
engulfed them. That was always a hazard in a religious ceremony
and the guests had come mentally prepared to cough through
the function. The smoke is good for health, many consoled
themselves without conviction. If this amount of smoke had
come in any other country, the fire alarm would have gone off

automatically and they would have been issued a warning and fined. But not here in India. Holy smoke was welcome. It cleansed the house of evil spirits and thoughts and, like a good disinfectant, kept it that way for several months. Whenever the inhabitants felt that the effect was wearing off, they performed another pooja or *homam*, and the house was disinfected once more.

As always, there were more invitees than chairs so they played musical chairs. Fortunately, the office-goers ate and left early and the others spread themselves out to enjoy a leisurely morning. Since there wasn't enough room to inflict a full complement of musicians—the *nadaswaram vidwan* and the *thavil* maestro and their paraphernalia—on the invitees, Arvind the Wife Beater settled for a cassette of Chinna Moulana's *nadaswaram* played on the tape recorder.

The climax of the morning came when a large silk *veshti* was spread over the heads of the Chief Shastrigal, Sundaram, Arvind the Wife Beater and Suresh and under this impromptu tent, Suresh was initiated into the sacred Gayathri mantra. *Om bhoorbhuvasvaha tatsavitur* . . . Suresh entered the second phase of his life as a Brahmin. He didn't feel any different, but he officially became a 'bachelor'.

Paati was there too—one of the rare occasions she came out. She walked across to No. 5 and sat right in front observing the proceedings with an eagle eye. The smoke didn't deter her. Gone were the days when she would sit with a cane in her hands and make her sons repeat prayers with the right intonation and pronunciation, but even now her presence was enough to deter the Brahmin priests from finding shortcuts to the religious ceremony.

Dominique had worn a Kancheepuram silk saree, an orange one, and she looked quite irresistible. There was not a soul who looked at her and didn't wish that she were a Tamil. Alas, she was white and French.

As the invitees left, they collected a plastic bag of coconut and betel leaves. Coconut? They were impressed. These days, people substituted cheaper oranges for coconuts. Coconuts spelt class. They were taken home to be made into chutneys or barfis or *thohayal*.

Actor Selvan came briefly and caused a near stampede. He came carrying a large gift which they later discovered was a suitcase. For a brief moment Devanathan ceased to exist. It was almost like the good old days. Clive Avenue had come together again.

Four horoscopes had matched well. Chandramouli was there to discuss the pros and cons. The choice narrowed down to two—one a doctor from AIIMS and the other an electrical engineer from Guindy. Within a few days, both options fell through. Rajan didn't want a doctor and the family of the electrical engineer didn't want their son-in-law to be stationed abroad. Lakshmi had to start all over again.

John Carey had been told of Rajan's change in plans. Rajan had offered to put P.V.R.N. Rao in charge and John was okay with that. Then, John offered Rajan a job. His own.

It was not entirely unexpected, but the swiftness of it was. John had always wanted to shift to a different line and now saw an opportunity. He had talked it over with his boss. If Rajan accepted, he could move, he was told. Rajan would be doing him a favour by accepting it. That was indeed a pretty position to be in. Rajan didn't have to think. He agreed, readily.

Things were falling in place, much sooner than expected. He only had to get married soon. God, get me a wife, Rajan prayed.

Navarathri was nearly upon them and Lakshmi had still not thought of a theme for the *kolu*. She had been obsessed with collecting horoscopes and Chandramouli was seen leaving with several every other day.

When word went around that Rajan was returning to the US and was back in the marriage market, there arrived at least a dozen horoscopes of girls studying in the US. Lakshmi had always been wary of US-returned girls even earlier. US-returned was a misnomer since many never returned. They stayed on. And on. Till they had kids of their own. Then they suddenly realized that all along they had wanted to come back and give their children an Indian upbringing. But their children refused. Some rebelled, violently, that too. They never did manage to return.

Only four passed Chandramouli's test and only one of the four passed Lakshmi's muster. The girl had gone to the US a year earlier to do her MBA. Her parents were in Chennai and brother, a financial consultant, in Mumbai. She came from a good family too. 'She plans to come back for the winter break to visit us,' assured the parents, 'we could have the girl-seeing ceremony then.'

Rajan can't have any objection to an MBA, Lakshmi was sure. Rajan had a careful look at the photo and a less careful look at the bioprofile of the girl and shrugged. 'She looks fine to me from this distance. Okay, I will see her when she comes here in December. I only wish she would come earlier since I am already going full steam with my preparations for leaving India.'

'I think she is worth waiting for, Rajan,' Lakshmi said unconvincingly. 'She is intelligent, from a good, well-known family, and looks attractive. Who knows? With an MBA from the US, she may well be the perfect match for you. Maybe that's the divine plan.'

A week later the girl's parents called up. The girl had decided not to come back to India during the holidays after all. She felt that instead of making a dash in December, she would come for a proper holiday in June when her course was completed. 'The Americans may just decide to cancel her visa or do something silly and ruin her career. She doesn't want to take any chances now.' The girl's parents asked Lakshmi, 'Can't you wait till next July?' The horoscope was trashed.

Navarathri arrived. Lakshmi was too tired to do a full-fledged *kolu*. She just had enough energy to do the usual nine steps and fill them up with all shapes and sizes of gods and goddesses and their steed. Aditya had wanted to display his electric train set and that was laid out on the floor. She had just enough energy to decorate the *kalasam* by converting the coconut and silver pitcher into a goddess. She then had some more energy to rip off the clothes of a big doll, tie a mini-*veshti* around it, paint three streaks of white across its forehead and, lo and behold, it became the philosopher Aadi Shankara. With a bowl, he was placed in front of the Kalasam Goddess. To sing his devotional songs. Lakshmi finally had just that bit of bonus energy to print cards and invite all friends and relatives for the *kolu*. Please come and take some betel leaves and nuts, she invited all those she managed to speak to on phone. And she had just a final burst of energy to buy plastic bags and put in coconut, betel leaves and nuts along with a piece of silk cloth for the women. Lakshmi was now ready for the nine days ahead. She was exhausted but ready.

The nine days went by. Friends dropped in, admired the *kolu*, ate sweets, sang a song if capable, took the plastic bags and moved on to the next house. I have finished four houses and have six more to go, one complained. I have just two more left since I started early, another said relieved. While the ladies went in to admire the *kolu*, the men folk sat out in the verandah looking anxiously at their watches. They were given *shundal* and sweets wherever they went.

The Brahmins were on their best behaviour. The kids studied on Vijayadashami and abstained gleefully on Saraswati Pooja. The men crushed lemon under their car tyres and drove around. The non-vegetarians among the Brahmins abstained from meat. As if the gods bothered. They even stopped consuming liquor. Their wives wished Navarathri came every day.

A few amongst them slipped in a horoscope or two into Lakshmi's hands and her eyes immediately lit up. Some even brought their daughters along. Most came reluctantly since they were always bullied by their mothers to sing. Lakshmi liked one of them instantly till she realized that the girl's *gothram* was the same as Rajan's, and the star incompatible. Rajan's rotten luck with horoscopes continued.

Sundaram was engrossed in a black-and-white movie on TV and Rajan lay on the sofa browsing through Richard Armour's *It All Started with Columbus* when Paramesh thatha waked in. Lakshmi had gone to the temple and Paati was reading in her room. A pall of inactivity and boredom hung in the air.

'Sundaram, the price for Devanathan's head is ten lakhs,' he announced.

'What do you mean?'

'You know the Finance Minister? He told me that if we cough up ten lakhs, he would at least get Devanathan to the courts,' his voice cracked with unspent laughter.

When Sundaram and Rajan looked perplexed, Paramesh thatha held his white *veshti* by one corner, picked up the cane chair from the verandah—he preferred it to the soft sofas which sank in uncomfortably—dragged it to the middle of the drawing room and settled down under the furiously circling fan.

'The Finance Minister and I are old buddies,' he explained. 'I thought you knew that. In fact, both of us started off in the Communist Party. He was much younger than I but we got close since he was basically a decent chap. But like all rascals, he also left the party and joined another—all because he felt that he had to taste power some day and that the Communist

Party had no chance against all the Dravidian parties. While he stood compromised, his judgement was vindicated after all. He is a minister now. Interestingly, he was fond of me and we never let go our friendship even though he is now on the other side of the fence. After all these years, we still meet once a month or so to play bridge. He loves bridge. And I play quite well—'

'Particularly if there is a peg of whisky to go with it,' interrupted Sundaram.

'Shut up and listen, I say, instead of passing wisecracks. I met the minister yesterday for another round of bridge. I brought up Devanathan. Surprisingly, he knew him well. As a thorough rogue. He, however, brought some money for the party and they kept bailing him out of tight spots. When I told him what happened to you, he was appalled. Genuinely appalled. He was categorical that he didn't want to be associated with any murder or crime. This Devanathan is getting to be a liability, he said, and was willing to cut him loose. I can fix him for you but for a price, he indicated. Ten lakhs. I need the money to get the others into the act as well. I am not taking a pie mind you, he explained. There are many guys to be paid off. If you manage ten lakhs, your nephew needn't have sleepless nights.'

Paramesh thatha paused and found Rajan and Sundaram all eyes.

'So there you are. This crook wants ten lakhs. I'm quite sure he's going to pocket most of it. That turncoat Communist has no compunctions about it. I told him that there was no way one could produce ten lakhs out of thin air. That rascal even said that there was no need to produce it out of thin air but only from the bank. The—'

'This is nothing but blackmail,' Sundaram observed.

'Of course it is,' Paramesh thatha was in full agreement. 'They all want money. I told him to go jump. I could say so to him and he laughed. I don't think you should do any such thing in any case. I just wanted you to know that Devanathan finally has a price on his head.'

'I'm almost tempted to bribe that bastard and be done with this whole thing. But then, I will only get deeper and deeper into all this muck and become accomplice to a bribery. I tell you, in this country, there is no salvation for any soul.'

As Chennai moved into Navarathri mode, Dom and Rajan got closer. They were two wounded souls. Dom in particular, had been deeply affected. A certain innocence of youth had vanished for good. A new understanding grew between them. Rajan became acutely aware of her vulnerability and was instinctively protective and gentle towards her. He discovered a whole new range of feelings for her when he thought that they couldn't possibly be closer than they already were. Dominique found a new comfort and warmth in his presence.

The Leonards had been worried about Dominique. They had caught her more than once sitting and staring at the ceiling vacantly. They tried to pep her up. She brushed their attempts aside with 'I'm fine.' But she wasn't fine. She was no longer the cheerful, carefree soul she used to be. She was no longer brimming with confidence. She wasn't sure about anything any more.

Rajan provided the rudder. She held onto Rajan for the moment while she tried to make sense of the future. It was not their childhood friendship that sustained them any more. The Blanchemaison episode helped redefine it. There was now a new depth and warmth in their relationship. They needed each other, they realized.

PAATI

Paati called Sundaram and Lakshmi to her room late one evening, long after the last doll of Navarathri had been put away. Dinner was over and the streets had gone quiet.

The lights had been switched off after the night watchman had spread his bedding out on the verandah floor. The night watchman wasn't supposed to sleep but he did. In fact, he slept soundly and even snored. Since he slept next to the door, the thieves had to step over him to get in. This was not a deterrent but was of some consolation to the inhabitants. In any case, his snoring kept them awake and alert to any thieves that might have been lurking about.

'*Yenna* Amma,' asked Sundaram, walking in.

Lakshmi followed him. They pulled the chairs closer to the bed where Paati was half sitting, half lying down. She preferred this posture since she could, without having to move, watch TV when she wanted and sleep if she didn't want to.

'You know, there is something I have been going over in my mind for the last few days,' Paati started in her familiar rasping voice. 'The more I think about it, the more I feel that I should share it with both of you. Now that Rajan has decided to leave for America, Lakshmi has been going hither and thither trying to get a horoscope to match. I keep seeing our Chandramouli making his rounds almost every other day.

'In this ordeal, one thing has stood out. Rajan is an extraordinary boy. He has handled everything with tremendous poise. Even when you asked him to break off his engagement, he never lost his composure. He deserves a girl who matches all his qualities.

'I remember how he looked quietly at me when I asked him to break off with Gayathri. But he did it without resentment or rancour. He deserves a good girl. Not just because he is my grandson, but because he has matured into a thoughtful and wonderful boy. Have you made any headway on the horoscopes?'

'No . . . not much,' answered Lakshmi, shaking her head. 'We just have to wait for more references to come in. My cousin Shyamala has written to me from Delhi, but I haven't got any details yet . . .'

'It's going to be difficult to decide in a hurry,' Sundaram added. 'While Rajan is in a hurry to leave, he is also worked up about this Devanathan. Rajan, the fool that he is, wants to sort that out before his departure. I hope he doesn't do something rash. Anyway, that's where matters rest now.'

'You must try harder,' Paati commented. 'At this rate you may not find it easy to get a suitable girl before Rajan leaves. He is not going to stay on endlessly waiting for us to do something. We had our chance earlier. We just have one more chance before he decides enough is enough and leaves for America. And once he's there, God knows what's going to happen. These foreign girls are waiting to pounce on him.' Paati shifted to a more comfortable position and continued. Her arthritis had got worse.

'That's why I wanted to speak to both of you. Day before yesterday, I was playing chess with Dom—after a very long time. She was chatting about her work, her split with her fiancé among other things. When the subject of her break-up came up, she naturally got upset. I told her to take it in her stride. Good riddance, I said. Don't lose heart over these things. They are ephemeral. You were born to be a cheerful girl and should remain that way. When I mentioned Rajan's impending departure, her eyes became moist and she began crying. Like a child. She cried saying that one by one everyone was leaving her—some of her friends had drifted away to other places, then her fiancé and now Rajan. She said she was feeling a big void. Even Isabelle was threatening to go back to Paris. With Rajan gone, she said she didn't quite know what to do. "Paati, I don't know what to do," she cried, the poor child. She wondered whether she should move out of Madras—to Paris or somewhere. Don't do anything drastic, I told her. All these separations are temporary, I consoled her. But she was quite clearly very upset. And this set me thinking. What I saw in those eyes was not just a sense of sadness and loss but genuine fondness and affection for Rajan. After all, they have literally grown up together. I realized then and there that what we require for Rajan is a girl who is fond of him the way Dom is. It was certainly love that I saw in her eyes. It was then that I started wondering about Dom. A girl who has practically all the qualities we are looking for, a girl we know well, a girl who can blend in with our family—'

'Dom? For Rajan? You must be joking!' Sundaram's voice was incredulous.

'Now . . . now, don't jump before I finish. Listen to me first before you comment. Dom is a fine girl. Frankly, I haven't seen many like her amongst our own girls. She is almost a part of our family. She was born and brought up right here in our street. For two decades, she has run around in this house as much as Veena or Rajan. She knows Tamil, knows our background and culture, even if she is French. Rajan and Dom are so close themselves and—'

'—surely Amma,' interrupted Sundaram again. 'Surely you cannot suggest that Rajan and Dom get married. What's happened that we have to suddenly get a French girl for him?'

'Sundaram, don't get excited. Obviously, at the end of the day, if you don't like my suggestion, you don't have to take it. What I'm saying is not a knee-jerk reaction, mind you. It has crossed my mind earlier. I have indeed given this a lot of thought. It's of course totally unorthodox. People will talk. But then they always talk, whatever the decision. They will always find something or the other wrong. You are not answerable to them in any case. The only people you have to answer to are yourselves. Your conscience. And Rajan's of course. Mind you, there are a lot more virtues in such a match than you think. All you—'

'Amma, I think you have gone totally senile.'

'Sundaram, don't close your mind to what I am saying. Just listen with some patience. You yourself saw what a great help Dom was in the aftermath of Rajan's break-up and stabbing. Lakshmi knows how well she stood by her and supported her when she went into a depression. Even otherwise, Dom has grown up here like a sister to Veena. If not for the fact that she is French, you would accept her with your eyes closed, horoscope or no horoscope.'

'Amma, I'm fully aware of all that you have said. But she is, at the end of the day, very different from us. She just won't fit in. She is still French. Her culture is different. Her religion is different. Their way of life is different. They are indeed different people. They are foreigners, for heaven's sake. That's not to say that they are not wonderful people. Dom has all the qualities you have just mentioned and more. But she cannot become our daughter-in-law, however close she may be to us.'

'Then how was she able to fit in all these years?' challenged Paati aggressively. 'People are not chameleons to keep changing their colours. We know Dom well. Rajan knows her as well as anyone else, probably better. In fact, after his return, he seems to be even fonder of her than before. I noticed that he sometimes goes out of his way to spend time with her. I'm not trying to imply anything. It's just an observation.'

'That's right,' agreed Lakshmi. 'I have noticed that too and had warned Rajan to stay away from Dom when we were finalizing Gayathri's horoscope. My words didn't have too much of an effect on him. I, however, don't think he is in love with Dom or anything, since he would not have agreed to marry Gayathri if he had been.'

'I don't think we should get deterred merely because Dom is French and, of course, Christian. We should be—'

'Even for argument's sake, if we did agree to what you are suggesting, the Leonards and even Dom herself may be totally against the whole idea,' Sundaram counteracted.

'Exactly. Conversely, for all you know, Rajan himself may not agree to our suggestion. Then, that will be the end of it. Dom and Rajan are not kids and they know where they stand on matters like these. All I'm suggesting is that we need not rule out Dom merely because she is French and has white skin.'

'Amma,' Sundaram interrupted, 'Did Dom or Rajan ever raise this thing with you? Tell me frankly. If so, then that's an entirely different matter altogether. If not, then I'm surprised that you are suggesting something so preposterous on your own.'

'For once, I'm my own mouthpiece. Neither Dom nor Rajan has instigated me. Just as you both feel, I agree that it may be for the best if Rajan marries an Iyer girl. That would solve all problems. At least relieve some of our tension. Or would it? The world is changing quite rapidly. It is not as if all our forefathers did all things acceptable to society or that we were all paragons of virtue. Your granduncle Swaminathan had two wives, what was popularly referred to in those days as the Big House and the Small House. Such behaviour was in fact tolerated in those days. To top it all, his Small House was a Christian! Your grandfather's cousin Cheenu was perpetually found in the company of prostitutes and pimps. The saving grace was that his wife died young. My mother's sister-in-law— I think she was called Nirmala—ran away with a Muslim, in those days when even looking at Muslim boys was taboo. And you know what? They lived happily ever after. Rashid Ahmad, who shifted to Perambur a few years back, is her grandson. Sundaram, it takes all sorts to make the world go round. The world has changed and keeps changing. Gone are the days when girls got married and carried on with their lives unquestioningly. Girls don't take any nonsense these days. The number of alliances which don't work out have increased drastically. Lakshmi's own cousin's niece. What's her name? Yes, Padma—had a terrible marriage to a foreign-returned boy and had to split just a year and a half later with a three-month-old daughter to look after. In my days we remained wives irrespective of what our husbands did or didn't do. Nowadays, the tolerance level is low. You need to give priority to compatibility and what better than to consider a girl whom we know to be so perfectly compatible?'

Paati stopped.

Lakshmi got up to get some hot milk for her.

'Amma, yes, our forefathers did things which would not be tolerated by any spouse now. But they were able to preserve their family life because they married girls from our own community. Compatibility came from marriage within the community. That was the insurance. What you have done is to turn the argument on its head. It doesn't work like that,' Sundaram said firmly.

'Sundaram, Dom cannot be much more different than the Muslim boy Nirmala ran away with. Just because the boy or girl is from our Brahmin community does not make it easier or more difficult these days. Anyway, I'm just thinking aloud, that's all. Rajan himself may have other ideas about his future.'

'No . . . no . . .' Lakshmi hastened to add, walking in with a tumbler of hot milk. 'I don't think he has anyone in mind. I certainly don't think he is in love with Dom or by now he would have told us. All he keeps telling me whenever I show him some photo or the other is, "Ma, get me a good girl soon because I want to leave Chennai as soon as I can and get on with my life."'

'Poor boy, he must have had enough of all this! But he will certainly be better off with Dom than with an American wife.'

The room went quiet. Each one was lost in his or her own thoughts. Paati had indeed sprung a surprise. Sundaram believed that it was her way of goading them into action.

'Amma, I'm still somewhat perplexed at what made you suggest something like this. If you think we are not doing enough about finding suitable horoscopes, then believe me, we are doing all we can. All said and done, I am not at all inclined to look at Dom as our future daughter-in-law. Our cultures are just too different.'

'I'm hardly the person to force you. Not a day passes without me praying for his good health and a beautiful bride. All we can do is search and pray I suppose,' Paati replied.

'Lakshmi has given herself another month. We have contacted several relatives and close friends. Obviously we don't want people to think that we are desperate. However, we can't force things. It's not in our hands. It's all in His hands. We have performed *abhishegam* in the Anjeneyar Temple at Mylapore, Kapaleeshwarar and Madurai Meenakshi Temples. All we can do now is search and wait for the right time to come. Whatever is written in Rajan's stars will happen,' Sundaram concluded.

CYCLONE

Come November, Chennai came under the threat of cyclones. Every year, the story was the same.

Chennai was probably the city most threatened by cyclones but the least affected by them. Every time a cyclonic storm formed over the Bay of Bengal, Chennai was threatened. Wherever they formed, they always seemed to move in the direction of Chennai. Panic gripped the city. Storm warnings were sounded. And at the last minute, the cyclone changed its mind, veered away and hit the Andhra coast. Or, at least, the southern coast of Tamil Nadu instead.

When the cyclone approached, the Chennai*vasis* could feel it. The wind picked up velocity. Rain started coming down in sheets; it was not just a heavy downpour. Palm trees swayed like people possessed. Most withstood the wind. Those that couldn't cracked and fell across roads and gardens. Streetlights swayed. Crows could hardly fly. The clogged drains quickly filled up and overflowed onto the streets. Large puddles stopped all but the most stubborn cars. Particularly pathetic was the fate of old Fiats and Heralds—the rare Chennai*vasi* still drove the ancient Herald—stalled due to water flooding the engine. The drivers of newer foreign models drove arrogantly through knee-deep water. Umbrellas were of no use. The only thought of the Chennai*vasi* was to reach home.

This year was no different. Since the wind had picked up overnight, many decided to stay home when morning came.

The cyclone warning was out. Fishermen were advised not to venture out into the sea. The sea was rough and choppy. Some fishermen felt that the sea was safer than their homes—their thatch roofs caved in in any case—but they stayed back nevertheless.

Rajan remembered the last time he had ventured out in such weather. He had been in school then. His teacher, a man of many moods but above all a lover of nature, had announced to a handful of them that if they wanted to see a real tidal wave, he was willing to take them to the beach just before a cyclone to watch the huge waves rising and falling and lashing onto the beach. Rajan was a sucker for these things, and had biked to the beach, his raincoat barely a match for the rain. The teacher was there already. One by one they cycled in, struggling. One was dropped off by car, and was frowned upon by the others. Not committed enough, they felt. A small band of die-hards stood on the empty beach—the fishermen had long gone into their homes—and watched the sea rise and fall. It was a spectacular exhibition of raw energy all right. But there was no tidal wave. The waves lashed the beach with ferocity and the wind carried the spray a little more inland than normal, but no sign of any tidal wave. No tidal wave tried to engulf them. Rajan, who had anticipated that the Beach Road would disappear in front of his eyes, returned disappointed.

The wind and rain continued to lash Chennai. The only indication that it was high noon was the occasional patches of lighter clouds hiding behind the dark, heavy ones. Rajan chose to walk across to Daulat's house. He was sure to find him home. Daulat's factory and godown were closed. As Rajan and Daulat sat warming themselves with a hot cup of coffee, Rajan told him about the latest on Devanathan. The price to enmesh Devanathan was ten lakhs. Rajan came straight to the point.

Rajan could mobilize seven lakhs from his own resources. He had that much in the bank. It was not for nothing that he was working with John Carey. Jayaraman could chip in with three more and that made ten. He wanted Daulat's advice on how to go about it. Rajan had never bribed a minister before. Daulat heard him out before asking him some questions. 'Don't you need the money before your departure? Don't rush things. How do you know that the minister will do the job for you?' Rajan was taking a chance, he knew. But he was sure it was worth the try. He didn't want his father involved directly since Paramesh thatha would be devastated that his nephew and his son had compromised Communist principles. Moreover, Rajan wasn't sure how his father would react to the whole matter. Daulat did not hesitate. He readily agreed to do the job. He even offered to put in the ten lakhs and Rajan could pay him back later. Rajan would have none of it. This had become a personal crusade. And Rajan had wanted to end the chapter before he left. Rajan and Jayaraman would put in the money. He just wanted Daulat's help to have the amount sent across to the minister.

Sundaram settled down in the chair in his consulting room at the hospital. He had just finished a rather long and complicated operation. It had gone off well and, as always after every successful surgery, he had the feeling that came from having saved a life. He had asked not to be disturbed. He had switched off the lights and lowered the back of the chair to a reclining position. That was his way of easing tension. He didn't sleep but merely closed his eyes and meditated.

His mind wandered. Over the events of the last few days. More precisely, over the latest girl-seeing ceremony. The horoscopes of businessman Sanjeevi's daughter Radhika and Rajan had matched. Lakshmi and Sundaram had taken the first opportunity to arrange a girl-seeing ceremony. It had been a disappointment. The girl was good-looking, no doubt. She was even well qualified—an MBA from University of Chennai. But somehow, things didn't seem to have gone off well. The girl's father had spent most of his time asking Sundaram about his financial position. In such situations, questions like these were natural and even compulsory. But all that the man seemed to be interested in was Sundaram's earnings, the market value of their house in Clive Avenue, the market value of their other house in R.A. Puram, the rent he was getting for it, Rajan's possible salary in the US, his stock options and what Sundaram planned to leave Veena and Rajan in his will. The father started each one of his sentences with the three words 'Don't mistake me' and asked a terribly probing question about Sundaram's finances. Sundaram had cooperatively tried to answer all and hung in there for Rajan's sake. Lakshmi had been lukewarm as well. And most importantly, Rajan himself had not been particularly enthused. He had not yet said no but was clearly veering towards it. His luck was running out.

Sundaram remembered Paati. He had almost forgotten their chat. Paati's sudden burst of insanity regarding Dom had surprised Sundaram. While Sundaram had dismissed the idea earlier, the fact that Paati had raised the issue in the first place bothered him. Paati was not known to be irrational. There must have been something behind it. There was of course the possibility that she was going completely senile.

Sundaram knew that the Hindu Bad-Time Clock had started ticking. There could be no girl-seeing ceremony after mid-December for a whole month and Rajan wouldn't wait that long.

Lakshmi came out of Kapaleeshwarar Temple, waded through the teeming crowd, emptied the flowers, ash, vermilion and a half-broken coconut from the wicker basket into a plastic bag, returned the basket to the shopkeeper, passed the rows of cows obstructing the pedestrians, stepped gingerly over the squashed banana skins and leaves and jumped into her Maruti parked near Rasi Silks. She always left her slippers in the car, since it was silly to walk a few hundred feet and leave the slippers at the counter at the entrance to the temple. But without slippers, she realized that to get in and out of the temple was a nightmare.

The drive back took longer than expected due to a bad traffic jam near Luz corner. Selvaraj shouted expletives in every direction but that didn't help move the traffic one bit. Lakshmi resigned herself to a long wait and closed her eyes. Her mind went back to the girl-seeing ceremony of a few days ago.

It had been a disappointment. Even though the photos showed that the girl wasn't particularly fair—and colour was indeed important—Lakshmi had been delighted that the horoscopes had matched well. The girl was pretty and the family was well known. Sanjeevi was a big industrialist and owned several companies. There was no dearth of money. They were also Iyers even though they were from Ramanathapuram. At least they weren't from Thanjavur. Chandramouli had given high marks for compatibility. But the actual meeting had been disappointing.

The girl's mother—a sizeable woman she was—spent most of the time telling Lakshmi what she planned to give her daughter. Several diamond necklaces, a pair of obligatory traditional eight-stone diamond earrings, a traditional gold and diamond *neli*, several emeralds including one from Vienna, a gold *kasumalai* and the traditional gold belt, the *udyaanam*. She had described each one in great detail till Lakshmi had had diamonds coming out of her ears. She was about to launch full scale on how they planned to celebrate the wedding when Rajan and Radhika mercifully emerged and saved the day for Lakshmi. Lakshmi had hung in there for Rajan's sake.

Sundaram had not been enthused. Neither was Rajan and, left to herself, Lakshmi would have normally vetoed this alliance. But time was running out. This was the last shot at marriage before Rajan's departure. After great difficulty they had zeroed in on Radhika. If this didn't click, Rajan was sure to leave without getting married. She hoped against hope that it would. The rest was secondary. She could always suffer the mother and her obsession with jewellery.

Lakshmi opened her eyes. They were still inching down Royapettah High Road. She shut her eyes again. How she wished Dom had been Tamil. Paati's rambling had been just that—rambling. Lakshmi had been less surprised than Sundaram when Paati raised the subject because Lakshmi herself had wished several times that Dom had been an Iyer girl. Now, all the more so. She knew neither Dom nor Rajan was the type who would do something reckless or rash. When Radhika's horoscope matched Rajan's, Lakshmi had quickly forgotten Paati's outburst. Lakshmi prayed that this one would come through. She had visited Kapaleeshwarar Temple that Friday and performed a special *archanai* to Goddess Karpagambal. The peacocks watched a devout Lakshmi go mumbling round the temple thrice and drop a hundred-rupee note into the hundi. She knew that this was Rajan's last chance.

When Lakshmi opened her eyes again, the car was on Radhakrishnan Salai, out of the terrible traffic jam. There was some hope yet.

Rajan lay on the bed with a Ludlum in his hand. Radhika had been a pleasant-looking girl. When she smiled, he noticed that she had nice teeth. When she spoke, she impressed him with her management jargon. She looked confident and self-assured—her MBA had contributed to that no doubt. She was keen to impress Rajan and spent much of the time talking about her interests, her ambitions and her outlook. He listened attentively—he had always been a good listener. And he didn't miss out on the fact that whatever she spoke about, she ended it with a clear-cut estimation of the financial outlay. If she discussed her education, she made it a point to mention the exact amount spent towards her MBA. She tried to give him an

idea of what she planned for her future. Rajan realized that
they all centred on a zero-based budgeting approach. Rajan
clearly became uneasy at the turn the conversation was taking.
While he himself was vague about his future plans, Radhika
wanted to pin Rajan down to figures of salary, monthly
expenditure, cost of living in the US, possibility of raise. By the
end of the meeting, Rajan felt much married already.

His parents had left him to decide. It was evident that they
didn't want to repeat the earlier fiasco and show undue interest.
Even Paati was quite categorical. 'Rajan, you should make up
your own mind.' And he had an open mind about Radhika.
But as his wife? There was something about her which was too
cut and dry. Maybe her propensity to reduce everything to
monetary values. The more he thought about it, the less he
liked the idea.

Dom sat cross-legged on her bed staring vacantly across the
room at the painting. It was a painting made by a struggling
artist she had met in Montparnasse. Touched more by his
poverty and passion for painting than by artistic merit, she had
bought the painting. It was a painting of the Champs-Elysées
in the rain, the lights and colours glistening, smudged, blurred.

She opened the letter clutched in her hands and read it
again. Her employers had given her an option. She could either
come to Paris, where there was a vacancy in the cultural page
department, or go to New York, where they needed an extra
hand for a few months, as one of their employees had gone on
a longish leave. Dom had written to them about new openings
outside India and was surprised that they had replied so
promptly. She wanted to get away from it all, and the letter was
a godsend.

All her life, Dominique had known only one home—
Chennai. Paris was, for her, not a home—it was just the place
her parents had come from. Every time she went there, she

realized how much of a stranger to the city she was. She loved
Paris, no doubt. But she was not yet a part of it. She was more
than a tourist but less than a Parisian. And in Chennai, she was
as good as any Chennai*vasi* but still couldn't depend on the city
for her sustenance entirely. When it came to finding a spouse,
she had to find one in France. She didn't quite belong here.
Chennai was not ready for a French girl looking for a
bridegroom. It was frustrating to grow up somewhere only to
realize after a lifetime that one didn't belong there. Or at least
that one couldn't find everything there. Well, not a husband
anyway. Her mind was made up. Dominique would move to
Paris.

As she closed the letter, she thought about her outburst
with Paati several days ago. Even now, the thought made her
feel embarrassed. She buried her face into the pillow trying to
blot it out. But the thought remained. It had been so
uncharacteristic of her to say what she had to Paati. It had been
Paati who had asked her about the break-up. It was still painful
to think about it and when Paati had asked, she had broken
down and cried. She sobbed out that she was all the more upset
because Rajan was leaving. Even when he had left for the US
to study, he was always due to come back. He had never really
left Clive Avenue. This time, she could sense that his departure
was for good. She had come to realize why she had, all these
days, been so cheerless. She loved him.

And then she told Paati something she never thought she
would utter. 'Paati, I have always loved Rajan,' she had sobbed
on Paati's shoulder. 'The more I see him, the more I love him.
I know he is fond of me too. But my being French and he
being . . . I have never spoken about this to anyone. Not even
to him. In fact, even as I speak now, I'm sorry that I am
unburdening it on you today, Paati. But it's just that I was very
depressed about him leaving and I couldn't keep it within me
any longer. Sorry, Paati, if I have said anything out of turn.'
Paati had tried consoling her by telling her that she was too

good a girl to be worried or upset over a break-up. And being in love with Rajan was not such a bad thing. Dom had been embarrassed. She begged Paati not to tell anyone what she had just said. Paati had promised.

The noose was tightening around the Income Tax Man, Devanathan. Daulat Singh had acted quietly but surely. Devanathan had been rearrested. No gloating policemen came to Sabarmati since they knew that the orders had come from the top. They looked at Sundaram with new respect. What didn't come from being a good citizen of India came from giving ten lakhs to the minister—Sundaram had gained respect.

Just when Sundaram was about to tell Rajan how justice finally prevails, Rajan and Jayaraman informed him about the ten lakhs. Sundaram heard them out and felt resigned. Nothing surprised him any more.

'The only thing I am now bothered about is how you are going to break the news to your Paramesh thatha. He is going to butcher you two.'

'Don't worry. We have conveyed this in so many words to the minister. He will keep his lips sealed now that the money is with him.'

She had not seen Paati for nearly two weeks. Dom was too embarrassed. She just couldn't get around to going to Sabarmati and made all possible excuses not to visit. What if Paati had secretly mentioned this to Lakshmi? Dom cursed herself for the umpteenth time. But she was dying to talk to Paati. To beg her again not to reveal what she had said in a fit of emotion. And to give her the news about Paris. Gathering whatever courage she could, Dom went over to Sabarmati, when all but Paati were away. Even Revati had gone to give some clothes for ironing.

Paati was reading, as she always did. Dom went in, cleared her throat to attract Paati's attention and gave her a nervous smile when she looked up from the top of the book.

'Dom! Where have you been? I missed you.'

'Paati, how are you? I'm sorry I couldn't come last weekend. My job kept me away and busy,' she said defensively.

'It's your loss entirely, Dom, since you missed a lot of gossip,' Paati laughed coarsely.

'Gossip?'

'Yes, you must be knowing by now—Rajan's second girl-seeing episode.'

'Oh, I didn't know,' she lied. 'Rajan came across twice last week but I was out and couldn't meet him.' This time she didn't lie.

'Oh! So you don't know. He has finally decided . . .' Paati paused to clear her throat and pour some warm water from the flask directly into her mouth.

Dom's heart sank. Rajan had decided.

'. . . he decided to say no.'

The relief on Dom's face was visible and she smiled.

'I see you are smiling,' Paati's eyes twinkled.

Dom turned red. She groped for words and couldn't think of what to say. 'Paateeee . . .' she cried exasperated as Paati laughed loudly.

'Well, it does look like Rajan will have to leave for America without a wife,' observed Paati still smiling her cheeky smile.

'Paati, you promised not to tell anyone what I told you the other day. I hope that you did not—'

'Of course not Dom, I haven't heard anything and that's how it will remain,' Paati assured.

'Thanks, Paati. Thanks a lot.'

'You didn't come here just to thank me, did you?'

'Paati, actually I have something else to tell you. With all this happening, I had asked my employers for a change of venue. They got back to me a couple of days ago. They have asked me to choose between New York and Paris and I have chosen Paris. It's about time I left, had a change of scene and tried to put my own life together. I thought that Paris would be the best place to start over. It's easier. And it would suit my parents as well. I plan to leave in a month. What do you think?'

Paati thought. Her eyes were closed. She did that when she thought about something very deeply. When she opened her eyes, the twinkle had gone. Her eyes were serious. 'Dom, if I were you, I would choose New York.'

DECEMBER FLOWERS

Come December, Chennai changed gears. Music was in the air. It was the season for music. Music and dance. All the cultural *sabhas*—and there were several of them—vied with each other to organize festivals. The biggest, the newest, the oldest and the youngest *vidwans* were invited to perform. It was the most pleasant season of the year. The light drizzle kept the temperature low. And long before the music season actually began, the Chennai*vasis* started preparing for it.

The Music Academy on Cathedral Road was the focus. To perform at the Music Academy was the ambition of young and old alike. One never tired of performing there or aspiring for it. Like a medley, from early morning to late night, the music went on. And on, for a fortnight. Learned discussions and *sadas*, Dikshadar's Sanskrit compositions, Tyagaraja's Telugu medley, Swati Tirunal's multilingual *kritis* and Annamacharya's devotionals rent the air. A large canteen had come up in the precincts of the Music Academy compound and was soon the liveliest eating joint in Chennai. Forgotten were the fast-food joints, the hotel coffee shops and Bell Metal. Young and old came to the Music Academy canteen for breakfast, lunch and dinner. For all of two weeks. Hot dosas, vadas—with or without rasam—uttapams, idlis and hot coffee measured by the metre.

The other *sabhas* did brisk business as well. They aped the Music Academy without quite measuring up to it. The prime tickets were overpriced. But it was important to see and be seen. Members of the Music Academy gave their tickets to their relatives and friends as gifts for which they earned their eternal gratitude. Some members received curt letters reminding them that their dues had not been paid yet, jolting them out of their reverie. The scramble for paying dues began.

There was even a night of Hindustani music thrown in, which most Chennai*vasis* didn't understand or appreciate but respected nevertheless. After all, Hindustani music was Carnatic music's sister. In some way, Hindustani music was even more refined than Carnatic music, but to say that during the music season in Chennai would have been heretical.

Carnatic music was born out of poetry and devotion. Without devotion, it sounded like the croaking of a frog. Music gave utterance to devotional poetry and soon, music of all hues and colours enriched the Tamils—bhakti, Carnatic, film, folk, bhajans—there wasn't a Tamil soul untouched by music. And it was not an exclusive Brahmin preserve.

Devotional poetry came from everywhere, the lowest to the highest caste. Kannappa Nayanar had been a hunter and Tiruneelakantar a potter. And a range of poets had followed— Arunachala Kavi, Arunagirinathar, Pattinaththar, Thayumanavar. Music had become a leveller of Tamil society.

But Sabarmati was a distracted household. The music season didn't seem to have much effect on it. Sundaram and Lakshmi had given up, finally, any hopes of getting Rajan married. In any case, one couldn't do any girl-seeing after mid-December, not for a whole month. There was hardly anything they could do.

Even though they felt helpless, a lot remained to be done. The usual round of last-minute shopping. Ten shirts, three pairs of shoes, six pairs of pants—they were much cheaper in India and could be paid for in rupees. Rajan made an obligatory stop at the old shop near the temple to pick up a dozen undies and banians. Lakshmi packed instant food, ready-to-eat mixes. Rasam powder, idli mix, tamarind rice. Rajan vetoed tinned food. It would be carrying things too far.

Everyone suddenly remembered all that they had wanted Rajan to do earlier but had forgotten about. Sundaram insisted that Rajan visit Tirupati and then Kancheepuram to pay his respects to the Sage of Kanchi. You simply couldn't leave without making these two obligatory stops. Rajan's mind was elsewhere. His visa, his tickets, his accommodations. He had to go to Trichy to check out a group there from which they planned to outsource. His relatives and friends wanted him to dine with them before departure. It was physically impossible to do everything. Rajan felt that it just wasn't worth leaving Chennai—not with all the hassles which came with it.

With Rajan eating out every day and doing his farewell rounds, Sundaram and Lakshmi cribbed that Rajan was spending all his time with his friends and gallivanting when he should have been spending extra time with Paati and them. He had even found time to talk to Gayathri and bid her goodbye.

Events moved with breakneck speed. He was perpetually in and out of buildings, cars, offices and homes. He endured a sweaty ride to Kancheepuram in light rain and returned blessed by the Sage of Kanchi. Rajan had had to urgently get a new *poonal* for the trip when he realized—in the nick of time that too—that the sacred thread was no longer hanging around his neck. He would have been ostracized from the Brahmin community if he had been seen without it in front of the Kanchi Sage. The sage looked at him and then at his *poonal* and blessed them both.

Dom's change of heart had not come a moment too soon. She was heading for New York. She had discussed it with her parents. They had been a bit disappointed but had respected their daughter's wishes. 'The Americans are not the best in the world, ma cherie,' they had warned. 'The world doesn't revolve around them any more. And don't forget, the New York vacancy is temporary.' Dom heard all of this but knew that it was a decision she had to take. For her future. It was a leap of faith. Faith in Paati. Faith in herself.

It was a double blow for Clive Avenue. Two of their children were leaving, practically one after the other.

Dom's change in plans delighted Rajan. 'Dom, I can't get better news than this! I wish we were going to the same city but that's asking for too much. The US will take your mind off all the Blanchemaisons of the world,' he promised.

Sundaram and Lakshmi remembered Paati's words. Dom and Rajan were going to the US. Even if they were heading for different cities, was it too much of a coincidence? Paati merely shrugged off the issue when they pointed this out to her. So what, she asked. That didn't mean this was preplanned. After all, wasn't everyone in Chennai leaving for America? The fact that Rajan did not show any real inclination in Dom's direction confused them. Maybe the whole thing wasn't preplanned after all. We should just put it down to coincidence and not read too much into it, they concluded.

'In a way, I will be relieved if Rajan takes the decision on a life partner away from our hands,' Sundaram sighed, giving voice to what Lakshmi herself was thinking. 'At least we would have completed our duties as parents.'

'He will,' nodded Lakshmi with philosophical resignation. 'Whatever fate has in store for him is what is going to happen. You and I are hardly in a position to change it.'

It was surprising how Devanathan—who had almost assumed a *vishwaroopam* in Sabarmati—had been relegated so easily and so quickly to the background. It was almost as if he was a road peddler, a nuisance to be dispensed with. The news of his arrest, the rounding up of the goondas yet again and the ongoing trial didn't find a place in their conversation. Ten lakhs had erased Devanathan from their memory.

'Rajan, there is something you have to do before your departure. You know Karuppayee, the cow from which Balan had brought special milk when you were recuperating after the attack. Well . . . Karuppayee died a month back . . .'

'That's a pity. She was the apple of his eye. Poor Balan, it must have broken his heart.'

'Yes, very much so. Balan has now decided to set up a trust in Karuppayee's name to take care of his remaining cows—for regular healthcare and sanitation. I have decided to give him a startup donation of twenty-five thousand rupees.'

'That's very generous of you, Appa. It is indeed a wonderful gesture. Balan will be pleased.'

'You know something, Rajan. Balan has been with us for a long, long time. In fact, he has done more for us than we realize or care to admit. If for nothing else, I think he deserves something for being a faithful milkman.'

Balan had indeed made the transition from being Balan the Milk Diluter to Balan the Friend.

'Balan has just gone around to the back. When he comes back this way, give him this money with your own hands,' said Sundaram handing over a brown packet to Rajan. 'This has the twenty-five thousand. When you give him this, tell him these words: This money is real, not fake like the fake trip you made to meet a fake Nallamuthu in Madurai. Then, tell me what his reaction was.'

'What does it mean?'

'I will tell you after you tell me his reaction,' Sundaram smiled.

Rajan waited in the verandah with the brown envelope while Sundaram went in. It was strange how Balan and his father had this love–hate relationship. From the time they had stopped buying milk from Balan—the milk was too thin mixed as it was with water—to the time when his father bailed him out of a tight spot by loaning him money to build up his business again, it had been a love–hate relationship. One couldn't completely like one's milkman or completely dislike him.

As the portly Balan came around the house towards the verandah after emptying his quota of unadulterated milk from the long cylindrical steel vessels, Rajan was waiting. He called him over and gave him the brown packet.

'What is this, *thambi*?' Balan took it thinking it was *prasadam* from a temple.

'Twenty-five thousand rupees for the Karuppayee Trust. My father wanted to be the first to contribute.'

Balan stood there perplexed as if he had been hit on his head with a stone. He looked at the brown envelope again and looked up questioningly.

'What is this? And why?'

'I'm leaving tomorrow for America. I was keen to give you something before my departure . . .' Rajan tried to explain.

A range of emotions flooded Balan. He tried to speak but choked.

'By the way,' Rajan had almost forgotten, 'my father asked me to say, "This is real money, not fake like the visit you made to meet a fake Nallamuthu in Madurai."'

Balan looked up as if he had been hit with a whiplash. Then, he smiled, and broke into laughter. Loud, uninhibited laughter. Then, just as suddenly, the laughter gave way to sobs. He hugged Rajan and cried. He tried to speak again. And again, nothing intelligible came out. Balan gave up. He patted Rajan's cheek, and blessed him. 'May you live . . .' and left without looking back.

There had been a light drizzle that morning. By evening, Rajan was all packed. Two huge America-sized bags sat ready near the door. He had been to the Hanuman Temple in Luz to bid farewell. He had stopped briefly at the Pillayar Temple before heading back. He was finally ready to leave.

Sundaram and Lakshmi were ready to let him go. Practically everyone in Clive Avenue had wanted to see him off. The flight left late at night but that didn't deter anyone. They had brought along their respective cars and waited patiently for Rajan to come out. Rajan touched Paati's feet and sought her blessings. He stepped out onto the driveway. It was dark outside and the garden lights were on. As he got into the car, a shock of elongated blue shell-shaped flowers caught his eye.

The December flowers were in bloom again.